The Twits Chronicles: Anthology #1

TWITS IN LOVE

TWITS IN PERIL

TWITS ABROAD

PLUS 2 BONUS SHORT STORIES!

What People Are Saying:

"The Twits Chronicles are hilarious, blessed with truly exceptional dialogue. Steampunk dystopia meets Oscar Wildean wit in these books. I found myself laughing out loud on numerous occasions--and that's not something I often do while reading. "

—Nick Sullivan, author of The Deep Series and Zombie Bigfoot.

"Delightful! A frothy frappe of P.G. Wodehouse and steam-punk. If you're the sort who reads blurbs before reading the book, stop it. Stop it right now. Read TWITS IN LOVE and have a good time. These days we can all use a bit more of a good time."

—John Ostrander, American writer of comic books, including *Suicide Squad, Grimjack* and *Star Wars: Legacy.*

"I haven't enjoyed the company of such eccentric characters since A Confederacy of Dunces, and Tom Alan Robbins has managed to place them in the stylized world of Oscar Wilde. A really unique journey."

— Kevin Conroy, Actor, The voice behind the DC Comics superhero Batman .

"Tom Alan Robbins' Twits stories are hilarious, thought provoking and mind bending. His juicy turns of phrase will stick in your ear like a catchy song."

— Michael Urie, Actor, Producer and Director

"Tom is the most talented, delicious writer. Do yourself a favor, and immerse yourself in the fabulous world of TWITS!"

— Mary Testa, 3 time Tony Award Nominee

For Nate and Evelyn, who gave me the freedom to discover the things I love.

Steampunk

"Steampunk is a subgenre of science fiction that incorporates retrofuturistic technology and aesthetics inspired by 19th-century industrial steam-powered machinery. Steampunk works are often set in an alternative history of the Victorian era or the American "Wild West", where steam power remains in mainstream use, or in a fantasy world that similarly employs steam power."

Wikipedia

A Word About Timelines

For those who are unfamiliar with the Steampunk genre, a word about timelines may be helpful. The Steampunk Universe in which The Twits Chronicles take place is clearly not our own. That is why events and cultural references that happened in vastly different eras in our own world seem to happen in a compressed time period. It feels as if we are in a vaguely Victorian era, and yet there are references to events and quotations from well into the twentieth century.

It may help to think of this as an exercise in "what if?" What if electricity wasn't discovered until much later in human history? Human ingenuity would still search for new ways of using existing technology, and so steam power and mechanical engineering would keep advancing, while much of the aesthetic of the world around us could remain in the nineteenth century.

The world that would result is the world of *The Twits Chronicles*. Other writers would use these same criteria to create very different realities. This is mine.

Enter and enjoy.

Foreword

The origins of the Twits Chronicles can be traced back to November of 2016, when my friend Nick Sullivan (author of "The Deep Series" of Caribbean mystery novels) asked me to participate in a round-robin writing project. He had assembled a group of talented authors who were each going to write the first chapter of a book, which the other authors would take turns adding chapters to until it was finished. My contribution was based on an idea that I had been kicking around for some years. This is the scenario I laid out for the group to follow:

> "Scientific progress has eliminated every obstacle to human happiness. There is no more hunger, poverty, disease or war. The problem is—now what? What do we do with our time between birth and death? The answer seems to be that we try to amuse

ourselves. This sort of thing has happened throughout history. Classes have sprung up whose wealth and privilege has set them above the need to strive. The upper class in Victorian England is an example... the robber barons of the time of Gatsby, the French nobles pre-revolution. The result seems to be that an elaborate ritualistic society emerges in which people strive for status and live for pleasure. In the world I'm imagining, everybody is in the same boat and the game is all there is.,

I've begun with a take on the Bertie Wooster/Jeeves books combined with a steampunk world in which electricity never got discovered and everything runs on hydrogen and steam.

Cyril Chippington-Smythe lives in sybaritic splendor with his loyal servant, a steam-powered robot named Bentley (produced by a company descended from the one that built the classic luxury automobiles). He has no ambition other than pleasure. He is endlessly optimistic. He means well but has trouble asserting himself. He drinks too much.

Bentley is superhuman. He is loyal, brilliant and discreet. He anticipates Cyril's every need. He is the closest thing Cyril has to a parent.

Cheswick Wickford-Davies is Cyril's cousin, and the closest thing to a friend he has. He is weak, cowardly and lacks any moral fiber. His one passion is Alice Witherspoon. He would do anything to possess her.

Alice Witherspoon is an aggressive, toothy aristocrat. She takes her superiority for granted. She has decided to marry Cyril whether he likes it or not. She is always in the right (in her own mind)."

Based on this scenario, I wrote my first chapter and passed it along to the group, which came up with a series of incredible and imaginative adventures involving time travel, alternate dimensions and subversive revolutionary groups before I brought it to a close with the attempted destruction of the world's hydrogen plants. I thought at that point that I was done with these characters, but Nick kept poking at me to go back to my first chapter and do my own take on the story. I persisted in batting his hand away and whining at him to leave me alone.

Then came the pandemic. I sat in my apartment like everyone else—terrified of public spaces and fellow humans. "Aha!" thought I, "the perfect time to get some writing done..." but nothing would come. Whatever I started seemed trivial compared to the earth-shaking events taking place outside. Finally, I looked at my old chapter of Twits in Love. Perhaps, instead of trying to write something meaningful that would only be trivialized by reality, I should try to write something trivial to escape what was all-too-real.

And, Dear Reader, that is why you hold this book in your hands (or on your screen). Strangely enough, in trying to write something trivial, I found more meaning in the material than I intended. I discovered that my aristocrats and their construct of a society were much more interesting if they were surrounded by a dystopian world of climate change and species extinction. I intend to keep writing about these characters as long as there are readers who enjoy their exploits. More stories are on the way.

Death Before Dishonour!

Tom Alan Robbins

Contents

Twits in Peril

Contents

Twits Abroad

Contents

From the Desk of Cyil Chippington-Smythe

Heigh-ho! Cyril Chippington-Smythe here. Perhaps you have heard the name bandied about at my good old club, Twits. The general opinion of me at the Club is that I am a scream. As Badger Binghampton put it, "The good lord put you on this earth to lighten the mood, Cyril and there is no occasion so bleak that you can't draw a laugh with one of your farcical attempts at coherent thought." Very kind of him I'm sure, but I just say whatever pops into my head with no attempt to shape it beyond tossing a noun and a verb into the flow now and then.

No one was more surprised than I to learn that my mechanical valet, Bentley, has been recording my utterances and chronicling my adventures for years. He states that his records are more for purposes of legal defense than entertainment, but I showed them around to the fellows and they insisted that I have them published. I am told that their length qualifies them as "novellas", which I always thought was a kind of pasta.

Bentley suggested that we place these stories in my voice to eliminate the rather dry flavour of his prose, so I descanted on the adventures he had recorded, jumping about the room and acting out the characters while Bentley typed.

This first attempt, Twits in Love, recounts the gruesome events surrounding the toothy Alice Witherspoon's attempt to wrestle me to the altar. By the time the dust had settled she had almost succeeded in destroying civilization as we know it, but I mustn't give too much away.

Off you go, then. Perhaps you should place a platter of crackers and a cup of tea within easy reach to stave off hunger and thirst. Bentley's chronicles can be gripping. Consider yourself warned!

Twits in Love

A Steampunk Distraction

Tom Alan Robbins

The Author makes no representation of any kind as to his being a citizen of the United Kingdom, either native or naturalized. He is from a small town in Ohio, for which he apologizes.

This is a work of fiction. All events described are imaginary; all characters are entirely fictitious and are not intended to represent actual living persons.

Cover design by Melody J. Barber of Aurora Publicity

Additional designs by Eric Wright of The Puppet Kitchen.

Twits Logo designed by Feppa Rodriquez

Proofreading by Gretchen Tannert Douglas

For Spike, who made my life and Rose who made it mean something.

Contents

I Am Awakened

Alcohol is like the cousin who owes you money. It promises everything and delivers nothing. I had hearkened to its siren song the previous evening and now I floated dreamlessly in a sea of regret. Waking could bring only pain and I clung to the darkness as a writer clings to a simile. Alas, I was finally ripped from slumber by my valet, who cleared his throat like a tenor getting a running start at a high C. I tentatively waggled a toe and upon this sign of consciousness he whipped open the bedroom curtains and unleashed the sun's cruel rays upon my helpless carcass. Sunlight is a beastly thing after a night of carousing and I can see why vampires in novels are always complaining about it.

My eyes rolled wildly in their sockets, which seemed to be filled with metal filings. "For the love of God, Bentley, why this cruel letting in of light? Why this throat clearing and foot tapping?"

For those of you who have not had the good fortune to meet Bentley, he is a sleek-headed, heavy-lidded gent with a ramrod posture and a perfect triangle of a nose. He is also a steam-powered automaton with a degree of moral certainty that only a machine could possess.

"It is nine o'clock, Sir. Miss Witherspoon is joining you for breakfast in thirty minutes."

The mention of Alice Witherspoon jolted me upright as though Bentley had poked me in the kidneys with a cattle prod. If, as Bernard Shaw once said, "There are those that look at things the way they are, and ask why?", Alice was the sort of specimen who looked at things the way they are and snapped, "Stop it at once!"

I struggled weakly to escape my bedclothes. My efforts only served to wind them around me more tightly. Bentley pulled gently on a corner of the duvet and freed me. "Joining me for breakfast? Has the earth tilted on its axis? Has Armageddon come in on little cat feet? Why is this horrible thing happening?"

"You invited her, Sir, last night."

An icy hand gripped my vitals. I grasped the bedpost to stop the room from spinning. "I didn't say anything compromising, did I, Bentley? There were no promises? She's made no secret of her intention to hobble my extremities and deliver me to the altar like a spoil of war."

"I was able to drip hot soup on Sir's neck at one particularly maudlin moment, but I could not say what transpired while I was brûléeing the crèmes. Miss Witherspoon had a rather triumphant gleam in her eye when I returned."

"You shouldn't have left me alone with her for a moment! You know how malleable I am when I'm in my cups."

"You can assume a putty-like consistency, if I may say so, Sir."

"This is awful! For all we know I could be engaged to that fanged medusa as we speak!"

Bentley began bustling about the room. "We must endeavor to ascertain your position at breakfast."

"Alcohol is a dreadful thing." I eyed him speculatively. "Have you got any?"

"I took the liberty of preparing an eye-opener."

I don't know where Bentley got the recipe for his morning-after libation. Some say he met Lucifer at a crossroads and traded his immortal soul for it. This, of course, is impossible as he has no soul. Bentley held out a goblet on a silver tray and I gratefully tossed it down the old gulper.

"Ambrosia! I'm going to need a second coat if I'm to eat opposite Miss Witherspoon. Those enormous teeth gnashing and grinding rather put one off one's chow." I rubbed my head vigorously. "It's so unnecessary! The art of false teeth has entered its golden age. They're making them out of ground-up seashells and glue or some such, I hear."

"Perhaps you should mention it to her at breakfast."

"And have her sink that jagged portcullis into my neck? No, thank you." I shook my head mournfully. "Ah, Bentley, life is a vale of... something or other."

"Tears, Sir?"

"Oh, I don't think so. Is it?"

"So the poets would have us believe."

"Well... poets—we know what they are—always sniffing the daisies and trying to borrow a ten-spot until some gazette comes through with a check."

"There's just time for the morning cannon, Sir."

I smoothed the shining sheet of hair that clung to my scalp and sighed. "Right ho. Open the window, there's a good chap."

He slid open the sash with a squeal and rolled the family cannon up to the opening. It was a shiny old brass thing whose origins were lost to antiquity. Family lore spoke of an early antecedent with piratical ambitions.

"I think a half charge today, Bentley. The noggin is rather tender."

"Very good, Sir."

He poured in the powder and rammed home the wadding. Glancing at the sight, he aimed the mouth of the cannon a few degrees to the left. He handed me the lanyard and gazed inward at some mysterious time-keeping apparatus.

"Three, two, one..."

"Death before dishonour," I cried, yanking at the cord. There was a satisfying "boom!" which was answered by my neighbors' artillery up and down the street. Cries of "Death before dishonour!" echoed from the cobblestones.

"Thank you, Bentley. Quite satisfactory."

He wheeled the smoking heirloom back into the corner and began laying out my morning ensemble. As he leaned over to place an extremely tasteful tie next to a crisply ironed shirt, I caught the scent of hot oil.

"I say, are you running a little warm today?"

"Nothing serious, Sir. A clogged pressure release valve. I shall attend to it."

"Please do. I can't have you in the shop with Alice swooping about." I shuddered. "Righto. Flick on the shower, would you?"

Bentley slid into the bathroom like a pat of butter on a hot pan and I heard the pitter-patter of water I knew would be calibrated to the perfect temperature. I felt almost... happy. He leaned his upper torso back into the bedroom.

"This might be an apropos moment to mention that Mr. Wickford-Davies has been waiting on the stairs since eight o'clock."

The burgeoning happiness within me lost the will to live and moped off to smoke a cigarette.

"Binky? What on earth does he want?"

"He did not take me into his confidence."

"Why have you left him so callously on the stairs?"

"He claims to prefer the stairs. He states that stairs only force you to choose up or down, whereas life is a miasma of impossible decisions that all lead to the grave."

I furrowed my brow. "Give me a minute to get into the shower, pump one of your pick-me-uppers down his throat and lead him in."

"Yes, Sir."

"You might offer him a sandwich."

"There are no sandwiches."

I gaped at him in astonishment! "How can that be? Civilization is founded upon the belief that sandwiches will always be readily available."

"I'm afraid we're on rather short rations at the moment. The food production facility at Weasel-on-Stoat was bombed."

"Bombed?"

"Yes Sir."

"Who would do such a thing?"

"The act was attributed to anarchists."

"Oh." I considered for a moment. "I have nothing against anarchy so long as it doesn't disrupt the minutiae of daily life, but if it destroys the social contract between us and our sandwiches I'm afraid I must turn a cold shoulder."

"I shall fetch Mr. Wickford-Davies, Sir."

If alcohol is one's down-at-heels cousin, Binky is one's actual cousin and is likewise a deadbeat. Cheswick Wickford-Davies (Binky to his friends, if he had any) has elevated sponging to an art form. He is related to practically everyone and is so skilled at inviting himself to one thing and another that I don't believe he sees his home for weeks at a time. He survives by gnawing on the ankle of some distant uncle who grudgingly sends a small allowance each month. Binky is reliably good company, or was until he fell like a hod of bricks for Alice Witherspoon's buck-toothed charms. I have a particularly vigorous shower, but even through the cataract I could hear his sighs. They gradually gained in volume until I gave up and turned off the taps.

"What ho, Old Sot. Why all this puffing like a grampus and so on?"

He gazed at me like a terrier who has lost his faith in balls. "I've come to say goodbye, Cyril."

"Surely not. You just got here. Hand me my robe."

He hefted the flimsy bit of silk as though the pockets were stuffed with lead and managed to toss it weakly at my ankles. "Death before dishonour," he whispered hoarsely.

"Death before dishonour." I examined him closely. "This is a dismal sight."

"You shan't have to bear it long. I'm leaving for Antarctica on the next dirigible."

"What on earth are you going to do in Antarctica?"

"I'll find something. I'm sure I can pick up a few coppers sweeping the ice or some such."

"No ice in Antarctica, *mon frère*. That's an Old Wives Tale."

"Or shooing the penguins away."

"*Are* there still penguins? Perhaps you should make sure before you run off to herd them."

He kicked weakly at a fallen pillow. "Damn the Great Extinction!"

"Slow down, Old Cock. I haven't had my coffee yet. You say you are going to Antarctica to herd possibly illusory sea fowl but you don't get at the root of the mystery. Why are you fleeing your home and family?"

"I have to stop my mind from dwelling on her, Cyril. Backbreaking physical labor in a harsh climate will leave no time for pining."

"I don't know how backbreaking it would be to shoo penguins. They had a reputation for being more or less docile."

He glared at me balefully. "How could you understand—you, who are the object of her adoration?"

I began to catch up. "You mean Alice?"

"The sound of her name pierces me like an adder's fangs."

"Crooked, over-sized fangs, I'm sure."

"Don't joke. Just shake my hand and wish me well."

"I do wish you well. My fondest hope is that she leaps out of my life and into your arms. I don't know why she resists you. Your taste in clothing is impeccable and most of the other virtues begin with dressing well."

He sighed. "Thank you, Old Chum." His eyes took on a shifty flavour.

"Um... look here, do you suppose you could lend me the money for the airship? I'm a little short at the moment."

"Of course. I'm sure you'll pay it back in no time from your wages in the penguin herding industry."

Bentley wafted into the room bearing coffee. The smell of burning oil accompanied him.

"Ahoy, Bentley, you're overheating to an odoriferous degree."

"I beg your pardon, Sir. I shall attend to it between the fruity slices and the omelette."

My vitals cried out for sustenance. A muffled bleat like a lost lamb emanated from my midsection. "Jolly good. Cheesy omelette, is it?"

"Yes, Sir."

"Real eggs?"

"Nearly, Sir."

"Oh, well."

"Miss Witherspoon has arrived. I have placed her in the morning room."

Binky whirled around like a vole who hears the hoot of a barn owl. "Do you mean to say she's here?"

"Now don't go to pieces, Old Crumb. We're having breakfast."

He goggled at me accusingly. "How could you?"

"I assure you I would never have invited her in my right mind. Apparently, I was suffering from acute alcohol poisoning. That's not the worst of it. In my drunken stupor there is a distinct possibility that I may have put my neck into the noose."

The color drained from his face. "You haven't proposed! That would be the end of me."

"I don't know! That's the point. That's what I hope to discover at breakfast."

"I come to you for solace and find a knife lodged between my shoulder blades."

"Look, Old Sausage, if by some horrible chance I have allowed myself to be ensnared by that harridan I shall move heaven and earth to escape. I will flee to the far corners of the globe. She shall not have me. This I swear! Now, come and say hello."

"I can't see her."

"Be a man! You can't go ducking into doorways and running off to Antarctica every time Alice sets her paddle-like foot onto the fairway."

He slumped like a frozen custard in a heat wave. "What else can I do?"

Suddenly a light went on in what some laughingly refer to as my brain. "Here, let's ask Bentley!"

"By Jove, that's brilliant! No one can top Bentley in the thinking department. What about it?"

Bentley's expression didn't change, but the odor of stale petroleum grew sharper. There was a sound of gears turning. "With all due modesty, Sir, my particular model is known for its powers of analytical thinking."

"Cogitate on this: I want to be rid of Alice; Binky wants to possess her, body and soul. Can the transfer of her affections be achieved?"

A distinct whirring sound emanated from deep within Bentley's stately cranium. Only a tiny flicker of his optical sensors betrayed the mammoth computational task taking place behind his serene expression. Binky stared at him worshipfully.

"It's epic, isn't it? Like the Oracle at Delphi."

A tiny puff of steam drifted from Bentley's left ear and he returned to the mortal plane.

"Well? Have you cracked it?"

"I believe so, Sir. It is generally accepted that in matters of romance, people want most acutely what they cannot have. The popular literature is rife with examples."

"But she *can* have him. His desperation to fling his corporeal and spiritual selves at her is manifest."

"It will require subterfuge."

Binky brightened at once. "By Jove, I've always been drawn to the stage. Cyril, you remember what a keen thespian I was in school. I was rather good in that Oscar Wilde thing if you recall."

I did and he wasn't. "You know that you spit when you declaim."

"I don't."

"I suppose it could be condensation, or some sort of spontaneous liquefaction of your leading ladies."

"I don't spit!"

"Fine. Have it your way. What's the story line, Bentley?"

"The usual ploy is to invent an alternative love interest. This brings the desired object's jealousy into play. Combining this with an icy reserve toward Miss Witherspoon should bring the desired result."

Binky positively gleamed. "Genius! You're wasted in service, Bentley. You should run for public office."

"Heaven forfend! Even a simulacrum has its pride."

"Let's try it out at once! Come on, Cyril. I'll join you and Alice for breakfast."

I eyed him coolly. "I don't recall inviting you."

"Thanks awfully. I'd love to."

"Bentley, can you whip up another cheesy omelette?"

"I shall simply make them smaller, Sir."

The lamb within me cried out again. "That seems rather hard on me. I love cheesy omelettes."

Binky snorted. "This is not the time to cavil about cheesy omelettes! Love is a higher imperative."

I could see that any attempt to impede him would end in violence. "Lead on."

Binky didn't hear me, as he was already halfway down the stairs. I hastened to catch up and stopped him at the entrance to the morning room.

"Let me go in first, Old Chum, then you saunter in as if you hadn't a care in the world."

"Don't worry, I have a plan."

"Please don't say that. It sends shivers down my spine."

He gripped my arms and looked into my eyes with a kind of eager ferocity.

"I'm depending on you!"

I stared back at him. "Honestly, we've known each other all our lives. How can you put your faith in such a leaky vessel?"

"Bentley knows what he's doing. Just stick to the plan."

"I shall do my utmost, especially as the success of your venture will save me from the clutches of that harpy. Now turn me loose."

I disentangled myself from his grasp and flung open the door to the morning room, where I found Alice and her teeth leafing angrily through a pile of recent periodicals. I took a deep breath and crept in like a mouse who approaches a hungry and ill-tempered cat.

My Country Cousin

I had known Alice since we wrestled one another to a draw at dancing school. She had a terrifying certainty about virtually everything, and had determined early on that she and I were destined for each other. I have sometimes wondered what I might have accomplished with all of the energy I have expended in fighting her off over the years. For example, I had always dreamed of inventing a new knot for neckties that would be named after me. Lost opportunities. Sad.

"Good morning, Cyril. Death before dishonour."

"Death before dishonour."

She turned a page and snorted with derision. "Really, you must stop reading this tripe. It rots the brain."

"*Au contraire*, reading lights up those thinky cells in the old antebellum."

"I suppose you mean cerebellum. These are gossip and celebrity magazines. They are not food for thought. They are empty calories. They decay the teeth."

I suppressed a snigger. "Then *you* should avoid them at all costs."

She glared at me suspiciously. "Why me in particular. What's so funny?"

I managed a look of angelic innocence. Still, it was rather good. She threw down the magazine as Bentley glided in with the coffee.

"Shall I serve the fruity slices now, Sir?"

"What do you say, Alice? Ready to tie on the feedbag?"

"What expressions you use. All right. Thank you, Bentley."

We seated ourselves and did the napkin thingy and sipped our coffee. I was pleased to note that Bentley no longer smelled like stale cooking grease. I inspected Alice carefully for any signs of matrimonial possessiveness and casually threw out a conversational feeler.

"I say, that was... quite a time last night."

She nodded with satisfaction. "One might say... momentous."

This was not encouraging. "Would one? Wherefore?"

She smiled at me benevolently. "Our minds have never meshed so completely. I believe we came to an understanding."

Panic rose up within me. "My lawyers assure me that I am legally incapable of understanding anything!"

"Don't joke. I want to talk to you seriously, Cyril... about the future."

I hopped from my chair. "What ho! A little early in the day, isn't it?"

"Do stop jumping up and down."

"Well, when you spring things on one like a jack-in-the-box..."

I managed to regain my seat. Alice began again. "Now listen to me... leave the glucose cubes alone, for heaven's sake!"

I abandoned my whimsical take on the Great Wall of China.

"I love you, Cyril, and I know that under that ridiculous affectation you love me too."

"Well, 'love' is a word freighted with nuance."

"Please don't speak. After we're married..."

"Ho!" An uncontrollable spasm caused me to knock my coffee cup clean across the room and send it smashing into a vase that had been in the family for five generations. Truthfully, I had always hated it, but still. Bentley was crossing the room with a whisk and dustpan before the echoes of the crash had died.

"What's the matter with you, Cyril?"

"I know I was drunk last night, but surely I'd remember if I'd proposed."

"Words are unnecessary when two people love as we do."

"Still, words are wonderful things. Legal things."

"Don't whine. It's unbecoming. It is high on my list of your flaws."

I stared at her. "You keep a list?"

She picked up her handbag with a self-satisfied air and removed a much-creased piece of paper. "I have been curating it since we were fifteen."

"That's rather hard cheese."

"Your use of obscure phrases like that is currently in sixth position."

"May I see it?"

"You may not." She stowed the list back in her bag.

"But seriously, any talk of marriage..."

At this moment Binky made his entrance. He had clearly put a great deal of thought into it. His shoulder entered first, and after a moment of suspense, the back of his head put in an appearance. He waved into the wings as if to an unseen presence.

"Ta-ta my darling. I shall count the hours until I'm with you once again."

He sighed a deep, shuddering sigh and backed fully into the room. Only then did he slowly rotate, revealing a look of mingled bliss and longing. He started upon seeing us. His eyes grew round and his lips pouted like a codfish. He articulated juicily. "So sorry. I didn't suspect this salon was in use."

Alice gave him a look that would delaminate plywood. "Well, it is. And please don't spit in my coffee. We're having a private conversation."

Binky yawned theatrically, stretched and stared off into the distance. "Death before dishonour."

"Death before dishonour."

"Death before dishonour."

Alice glared at Binky suspiciously. "What are you doing in Cyril's house anyway?"

"Just saying goodbye to someone. You don't know her."

Her eyebrows crept into her bouffant and settled in for a protracted stay. "Does she live here? Cyril, who is this woman living in your house?"

I suddenly found myself the object of intense scrutiny. "Who indeed? Yes, I was going to mention that."

"Go on."

Binky was concentrating fiercely, but I could see that this flaw in his backstory had thrown him for a loop. Bentley shimmered up.

"Are you referring to your cousin from the country, Sir?"

"By Jove, yes! Thank you, Bentley! That's exactly who we were referring to."

Alice looked skeptical. "A country cousin! You're full of surprises. What is her name?"

My mind ran in little circles waving its arms desperately. "Er... yes... it's..."

Binky stared at a potted plant by the window. "Gardenia!"

"An unusual name."

"She is as lovely as a flower We are going to be wed."

Alice peered at Binky suspiciously. "How long have you and this Gardenia person been acquainted?"

"Oh, we've known each other for a good while now."

"That's very interesting since I refused a proposal from you only two days ago."

This brought Binky up short, as you can imagine. "I... uh... should have said that we've known each other as friends for some time. Our relationship only flowered into love quite recently."

Alice frowned. "Clearly you have reacted to my refusal by fixating on the first lumpish female that you laid eyes on. You must call off this wedding immediately."

"I will not! This has nothing to do with you. We are soulmates."

Alice threw the full force of her glare at him but Binky barely staggered. She sighed deeply and shook her head. "This is unacceptable. You may take me to lunch tomorrow and I shall untangle this knot for you. I suspect something Oedipal. Now if you don't mind…"

Binky slid up to the dining table like an eight-ball finding the pocket. "I'm famished."

Alice regarded him with astonishment. "I beg your pardon!"

"Oh, sorry," I stammered. "I forgot that I invited Binky to breakfast as well."

"But the table is set for two."

Bentley set down a third plate and began arranging silverware.

"You're hopelessly unromantic, Cyril."

"You can add it to the list."

"It is already at number two."

"What's number one?"

"Your greatest flaw is your lack of any trace of seriousness."

"I see that as a virtue."

"So do many of our generation. I believe it is the great scourge of the age."

Binky was busily stuffing fruity slices down his gullet.

"What is there to be serious about?"

"Don't slurp your food like an animal."

I nodded thoughtfully. "Binky makes a point. Factory-made food has eliminated hunger. The processing of seawater into hydrogen has provided unlimited power. What is there to be serious about?"

"There is more to life than mere subsistence."

I flapped a flipper in a general way. "Look around, Old Girl. This is a bally sight more than subsistence."

"You live in a prison of privilege. For the masses, life lacks these gewgaws and distractions. Nutrition bars and water in a shack hardly constitute a life well lived."

"I sympathize of course."

"Do not be so quick to congratulate yourself. Our class suffers a different but equally horrible fate. We are being coddled into extinction. We fill the empty hours with shallow entertainments and elaborate social rituals. For example: 'Death before dishonour'…"

Binky looked up from his fruity slices. "Death before dishonour."

"Death before dishonour," I echoed.

"See? We repeat it constantly without any notion of why we do so. What does it mean? Why do we all say it?"

Binky screwed up his face with the effort of thinking. "Well, it's because… death, don't you know… is what comes before… dishonour."

I couldn't let it pass. "I think that's wrong, Old Bean. I think the idea is that dishonour should come after death. Then it doesn't matter so much… because you're dead, you see."

Alice smirked triumphantly. "You've proven my point. It's an empty ritual that exists to give us the illusion that there is a moral code that gives meaning to life."

"But there *is* a moral code that gives meaning to life. Isn't there?"

Binky had finished his slices and was eyeing mine. "Is there?"

"And what is that code?" inquired Alice.

I gave the old gray matter a good pummeling. "Well... death before dishonour, of course... and don't wear stripes with checks, although I'm toying with the idea of smashing that one to smithereens."

I heard a tiny sigh from Bentley's direction. "I would advise against it, Sir."

Binky jumped in. "A gentleman doesn't perform manual labor."

"Always buy more than you need. That is the mark of the superior man."

"Saving shows a lack of breeding."

"Be true to your club. To insult a man's club is to insult the man."

Alice shook her head grimly. "Don't you see that these ridiculous affectations are not a moral code?"

"Then what's your idea?"

She leaned forward and fixed us with an intense gaze. "Every individual should have the right of self-determination. All humans are equal."

"Let's not lose our heads!"

"Each generation has an obligation to make the world a better place for future generations."

"How do you propose we do that?"

"We must destroy the patriarchy. Nothing can be achieved while our every whim is satisfied by a monolithic industrial complex. I didn't mean to bring this up until after the wedding..."

"Ho!" The cream pitcher followed the coffee cup across the room, destroying a small china figurine. Bentley retrieved the dustpan.

"I beg your pardon, Sir. I should have removed the other breakables from the room after the earlier incident."

"Don't blame yourself, Bentley. It could have happened to anyone."

"For heaven's sake, Cyril, sit down and stop flinging the china."

Binky leaned in, sinking his tie into his coffee cup in the process. "You're saying that life is too easy."

"Since the discoveries that made our modern way of life possible, our class has devolved into effete ineffectual fops. The two of you prove my point."

"Oh, I say, really!"

"A few more generations like this and we'll be apes again."

I rifled through the old brain cells but came up empty. "Sorry, we'll be what?"

"Apes."

"No, doesn't ring a bell."

"They used to live in jungles."

"In what?"

"Oh, never mind! Damn the Great Extinction!"

"But what is there to do?"

"I am one of a band of like-minded individuals that meet in a clandestine fashion to discuss ways of halting the decline of civilization."

"You don't mean you've joined an anarchist cell?"

"Anarchist is a label we eschew. Our group is called, 'Citizens for a Better Tomorrow.'"

"And how will you achieve your lofty goals?"

"By dismantling the current infrastructure through selfless acts of heroism."

I had lost my way at "infrastructure" and struggled to catch up. "I don't quite grasp the gist."

"We shall kick away the crutches that keep mankind from walking into a new tomorrow."

"If you kick away the crutches, mankind will have to *crawl* into a new tomorrow."

"The crutches are metaphorical!"

"Bentley, can you translate?"

"I believe they mean to blow things up, Sir."

Alice nodded. "Exactly."

"What things?"

Alice waved a hand breezily. "Oh, you know, factory farms and hydrogen plants and so on."

I eyed her suspiciously. "Food production facilities?"

"If necessary."

I pounded the table triumphantly. "Weasel-on-Stoat!" I knew it was you!"

"I can neither confirm nor deny whatever you're inferring."

"What do you hope to achieve by depriving civilization of its sandwiches?"

"Sandwiches are the opiate of the people!"

Binky looked forlorn. "Even ham?"

Alice glared at me with gritted teeth. "We discussed all this last night! You agreed! Our minds were one!"

My heart gave a leap. "*That* was our momentous conversation?"

"What did you think it was?"

"Oh, that! Definitely! Thank God!" I had escaped the matrimonial net and was once again swimming in open waters.

"We must return to a time when life took work. When men glistened with the sweat of honest labor—their gleaming muscles flexing under thin, homespun smocks, their women working beside them with heaving breasts... falling into bed at the end of the day to mate like animals. Not the kind of delicate, polite lovemaking you find nowadays but rough, passionate, desperate sex!"

At the word "sex," Binky leaped to his feet, sending his chair crashing to the floor. "Alice is right! I will join you! I will fight beside you! Take me with you to this new tomorrow!"

The air was suddenly filled with the sharp scent of testosterone. I was about to slink under the table and crawl for the door when Bentley placed a shining white plate in front of me with a satisfying clink.

"Your omelette, Sir."

A Beastly Day at the Club

With great power comes great responsibility or some such drivel. Bentley had come to the rescue re: Alice, and I was in his debt. Nevertheless, there are times a fellow must take a stand. I mean, once a chap knuckles under to his valet it's not long before he's a serf in his own home. I stood poised... and gazed coldly at the ensemble laid out on the bed.

"Bentley?"

"Sir?"

"Where is the new waistcoat I ordered from Borgen and Bots?"

His triangular nose rose several degrees and gave a discreet sniff.

"Was that a waistcoat? I took it for a pillow sham. The color was so... unusual."

"The color is perfect. I have it on the best authority that everyone will be wearing lavender by Abdication Sunday."

"I am sorry, Sir."

We looked at each other for a long moment.

"Well? Produce the article in question."

"It is at the cleaners."

I gazed at him through narrowed eyes but his face was as placid as a waste-water containment pond on a windless day.

"I have detected a disturbing tendency in you lately to pass judgment on my apparel, Bentley. Is it my imagination?"

"I could not say. I have no imagination. I merely note that your club has very specific rules about one's color palette and that lavender, or indeed any shade of purple, fails to clear the bar."

"Times are a-changing, Bentley. I am the new wind that... sweeps away something or other. Or the new broom. Something new... and sweepy."

"And presumably lavender. Will you be lunching at the club?"

I could see that any victory at this point would be Pyrrhic and surrendered with a sigh.

"Needs must, Bentley. I have business, I only pray that the *plat de jour* isn't Impossible Mutton. I detest Impossible Mutton."

"If Sir would place his arms in the sleeves..."

Dressing for the Club is like donning medieval armor. The girdle, the underclothes, the stockings, the shirt and pantaloons; then the waistcoat, the jacket and sash... and finally the brooches and the shoes—the horrible shoes— shoes that bore no resemblance to a human foot in any dimension.

"Breathe deeply, Sir. The toes will grow numb in a moment."

"Why—that is what I ask myself? What purpose do these thumbscrews for the feet serve?"

"Fashion follows its own logic. I have heard it speculated that impractical shoes demonstrate superiority. One is too rarefied to walk quickly. One will be waited for."

The ormolu clock on the wall jumped in with a hearty chime.

"Goodness, I'm late. Carry me to the car, there's a good man."

Bentley hoisted me as if I were a kitten and glided to the garage where my chariot awaited. This week it was a literal chariot, drawn by six mechanical horses.

"Won't they goggle at the club when I clatter up in this? Where do I sit?"

"I believe you are meant to stand, Sir."

"In these shoes? Not bloody likely."

"You could sit on the floor of the chariot with your legs folded."

"Not very heroic, what?"

"Perhaps not. I did advise against the chariot, if you recall."

"You forget yourself, Bentley. I am the master of my... something or other."

"Fate, Sir?"

"No, it's something to do with fish, I believe."

He stared upward at the ceiling. "Perhaps I am thinking of another expression."

"Now prop me up and punch in the address of the club, there's a good fellow."

As I clattered up one street and down another, clutching desperately to the sides of my chariot, I strove for a look of benign condescension. The hoi polloi parted in front of me. One particularly threadbare group tried to slow my progress by shouting and waving placards, but mechanical horses are illiterate and they were forced to dive out of the way.

Upon arriving at the club, my chariot was blocked by a jeweled palanquin carried by eight turbaned golems. Perched atop it was C. Langford-Cheeseworth. Cheeseworth was a shiny-headed sort of a fellow who affected a louche pattern of speech. His defects of pronunciation had a whimsical way of appearing and disappearing depending on his mood.

"Don't dawdle, Cheeseworth! Some of us have places to be."

"Give one a moment, won't you Cywil? These beastwy shoes keep catching on one another and twipping one."

"Sorry, Old Trout. I sympathize. Oh, how I miss the embroidered slippers of last season."

"You mustn't regwet the past. It gives you winkles."

I noticed another crowd of discontented-looking townsfolk standing across the boulevard with more placards. I was able to make out one sign which stated, "No bread, no peace."

"What do you suppose that's about?"

"Appawently they are devotees of bwead."

"And they lack that particular comestible?"

"Pwesumably."

"Well, there are any number of other foodstuffs. If there is a shortage of bread, let them eat Impossible Mutton, for example. They can certainly have my share."

"There's no pweasing some people. It's all spite and envy. See you inside, dear boy."

I stepped gingerly from my chariot and teetered to the brass-bound door of "Twits"—the club of the Chippington-Smythes since time immemorial. Its brass and Naugahyde were lovingly patched and polished—nothing had changed since my great-grandfather's time—including Evans, the mechanical doorman. "Good morning, Evans."

"Good morning, Sir."

"Did you notice the new chariot? Rather spiffy, don't you think?"

"Yes, Sir. I thought so last week when Mr. Attenborough had it."

"What... *this* chariot?"

"Yes, Sir."

"Last week?"

"Yes, Sir."

"Damn. Listen, Evans, call the manufacturer and have it picked up. I'll find another way home."

"Of course, Sir."

He stared significantly at the top of my head. "I fear our announcement failed to reach you this morning."

"What announcement is that?"

"Amendment to the dress code, Sir. Hats now required."

I glanced around the entry hall and noted the plethora of fanciful headgear. "Drat! Look here, Evans, I will visit the haberdasher first thing tomorrow morning."

He shook his head sadly. "Sorry, Sir. Club rules."

"Well, this is most upsetting."

"We do have some loaners."

"That's all right then. Trot one out."

Evans reached into the coat check and produced a bonnet that resembled a giant tea cozy. I stared at it in horror.

"Don't you have something a bit more stylish?"

Evans gave a rather condescending smile. "If the loaners were too fashionable, there would be no incentive to purchase a hat of your own, would there, Sir?"

As the bonnet passed my nose en route to the old noggin, a familiar odor made its presence known.

"It smells of urine."

Evans looked more closely at the hat in my hands.

"Ah. I'm afraid the Club cat has taken a fancy to that one, Sir."

"And I have to wear this at all times? No respite?"

"Rules, Sir. Without them, all would be fire and flood. We have a hatter on call. There is an extra charge, but of course such trifling sums are beneath your notice."

I settled the malodorous object on my head and trudged grimly to the dining room. Rodgers, the maître d', had been seating me since I was in knee pants. He and Evans were identical models, but I could always distinguish Rodgers by a tiny repair on his left ear—a souvenir of the riots of Oh-Four when the last breeding pair of beef cattle were stabbed to death by Club members insisting upon the tradition of the Sunday Roast.

"Good morning, Sir."

"Rodgers. What's the bill of fare today?"

"Impossible Mutton, Sir."

"Is it? Blast! Any chance of a Welsh rarebit?"

"We have a Guatemalan rarebit, Sir, but I really can't recommend it. If your objection to Impossible Mutton is based on the rumor that it contains human flesh, I can assure you that it was denied most vigorously by the manufacturer."

"No, it's the taste I object to—or rather the aftertaste. There's a tang of petroleum jelly that I know some people love, but I can't seem to scrape it off the old tongue."

"I understand, Sir."

"Tell the waiter with the bread basket to stay within my gravitational orbit. By the by, there's a small mob outside that seems keen on acquiring some bread. Perhaps you could fling some rolls their way?"

"I'm afraid not, Sir. Club policy. Table for one?"

"Wouldn't that be paradise? No, I'm meeting my Uncle Hugo. There he is, waving from behind that potted palm."

My Uncle Hugo was what is known as a serious man. This meant that he knew his net worth to the penny and disapproved of anyone enjoying anything. He wore a tiny black silk top hat that perched on his shiny dome like a sparrow on a monument. As I approached, he stared at my urine-soaked tea cozy.

"What on earth is on your head?"

"Loaner. Didn't get the message. What's that you're sporting?"

"They call it a fascinator. I'm assured it is quite the thing."

"How does it stay on, glue?"

He shook his head sadly. "My God, you look like a damned organ grinder's monkey."

"I might be insulted if I knew what an organ grinder was... or a monkey."

"Monkeys are... or rather were... damn the Great Extinction..."

"I take it they ground their prey's organs into some sort of paste before consuming them?"

"I will not be baited into attempting to educate you. I am not Sisyphus."

"Even if you were, they have medication for that now."

"Sit down before you fall down. Death before dishonour."

"Death before dishonour."

"What ridiculous shoes!"

"They're the latest thing, Uncle. Everyone is wearing them."

"I suppose if everyone cut off their big toe, you'd do it too."

"The shoes would certainly fit more easily."

"You're late. I've ordered your mutton."

"Have you? How kind."

That rather used up Uncle Hugo's conversation for a spell. We sat awkwardly, stealing furtive looks around the dining room and rolling bread into tiny balls. I noticed Binky sitting with Alice in the small and somewhat dismal area that allowed female guests to dine with members. He had collapsed into himself under the weight of her harangue and was curled up in his chair like a pill bug. Alice was disemboweling a roll with her dental guillotine. A nearby waiter was gazing at the sight in horror, insensible to the entreaties of nearby diners.

Rodgers paced about the dining room with his gong.

"The North American Beaver has been declared extinct. Polls indicate that the vast majority of the population was unaware of its existence."

He tapped his gong again.

"In business news, the price of human organ futures rose five percent this morning with kidneys up six percent and livers up three percent. Hospitals are swamped as people rush to sell in a bull market."

I waved him over. "I say, Rodgers, these pronouncements are rather gruesome. Isn't the news of the day usually a little more upbeat?"

He leaned in confidentially. "Sales in the dining room have fallen off, Sir, and research has shown that when customers are fearful and anxious, they spend significantly more."

"Do they? Carry on then."

"Yes, Sir. Allow me to mention that smallpox has reappeared in Asia."

He gave his gong a rap and wandered away.

"The end is nigh. Abandon hope, all ye who enter here."

The waiter brought two steaming platters of mutton-like slices swathed in something glutinous. I sighed inwardly.

"Something wrong with your mutton?"

"What? Sorry, I thought I'd sighed *inwardly*."

I slid my mutton around the plate and hid slices under my Beyond Lettuce squares. My uncle attacked his meal like it owed him money and didn't speak again until he had wiped the plate clean with a slice of bread. He sighed and sat back in his chair. "So. You're wondering why I asked you here today."

"It wasn't for the pleasure of my company?"

"It was not. Next week is your birthday…"

"I don't want a big party…"

"I plan no party of any kind. You are reaching the age stipulated in your trust at which your assets revert to you entirely, without restrictions."

A sudden apprehension gripped me. "But I'll still get my allowance?"

"No. You get everything."

I began to panic. "But not my allowance?"

"Try to focus! There will be no need for an allowance. You will possess the entire contents of the trust."

"And what is that?"

"Great thundering cats! Do you have no inkling of what is in your trust?"

"Should I?"

"Yes! You dundering idiot! You will be one of the richest men on the planet! You have a responsibility!"

"To do what?"

"To preserve it. To invest it wisely. To pass it on to the next generation."

"Not really sure I want a next generation. Lot of bother, children and so on."

"There's plenty of time for that. Right now I need you to grasp the seriousness of the situation."

"Who's been running things up until now?"

"The lawyers and financial managers of the trust."

"Can't they keep doing what they've been doing?"

"Well... yes, I suppose so."

"Problem solved. What's for pudding?"

Rodgers came by with his gong. "Lapels will be narrower by three centimeters beginning Wednesday. Appointments with club tailors can be booked at the concierge desk."

I jumped as a voice suddenly spoke from behind my left ear.

"Do I have the pleasure of addressing Mr. Chippington-Smythe?"

I turned to find a smooth, shiny, round little fellow holding a cylindrical box.

"You do. I'm glad you find it pleasurable. Some of my relations tell me it can be a trial."

He chuckled but I could see that his heart wasn't in it. "I am Ahmed Ben Fitzwilliam—the club hatter." He nodded his head toward Alice, who was glaring from the far side of the room. "Miss Witherspoon requested that I offer you my services. She was most insistent."

"That's all right. As it happens, you come at a most opportune moment."

He sadly shook his head. "Indeed, Sir. The hats distributed as placeholders are painful to contemplate."

"And they smell of piss."

"I think we can do better, can't we? Now, what sort of thing did you have in mind?"

"I don't know. Some sort of fedora?"

He recoiled slightly. "Oh, no Sir. That would be most unsuitable."

"Why's that?"

"It's commonplace. We wouldn't want to be commonplace, would we?"

"Heavens no."

"What you want is something original. Something that will excite envy in all who behold you."

I sat up a little straighter in my chair. "And you can deliver such a headpiece?"

"That is my art, Sir."

"I never thought of hat-making as an art before."

"One of the oldest. After all, what is a hat?"

My mind raced. "It's... Hmmm."

He looked at me oddly. "The question was rhetorical, Sir."

"I would have gotten it in a moment, though."

"A hat is a crown that is within the means of the poorest among us. Yes, it keeps us warm in the winter and shades us from the rays of the Summer sun, but these are secondary. A hat, perched just above the organs of sight, is a statement. It tells the approaching stranger everything he needs to know at a glance. Are you timid? Bold? Sexually confused? It is all there in your hat. My job is to ascertain your essence and to create a hat that will announce you to the world."

He opened the cylindrical box in his arms and removed a large, golden sombrero with bright red ribbons cascading down the back.

"Here is an example of my work. This was a commission from Rory Badminton Jones, the actor."

"It's rather gaudy, isn't it?"

He gave a little sniff. "That is the point, Sir. Anyone can slide into a room with a piece of felt on their head that says, 'Don't look at me. I'm not important.' A hat like this says, 'I don't give a damn what you think. I have the confidence to wear this and if you don't like it, you can lump it.'"

"Rather!"

"And while they are staring at the fantastical creation on your head, they are *not* staring at your close-set eyes, your beak-like nose, your lack of chin. All they see is the hat, and you have merely to bask in its reflected glory."

"I say, I'm in!"

He removed a thick sheaf of papers from the hatbox. "Excellent! Fill out this questionnaire and bring it to the concierge desk. Your hat will be delivered to your home in three days."

"But do I have to wear this hideous tea cozy until then?"

"No, Sir. I will loan you this sombrero for the duration."

"Damned generous of you."

I fitted the golden disk onto the old dome. It tended to knock into the flowers in the middle of the table, but if I sat very still the staff could still navigate around me. Fitzwilliam gave a little bow.

"Thank you, Sir. I bid you good day."

And off he trundled. Uncle Hugo's sweating pate had turned a deep maroon. He mopped it with his napkin and gestured to the waiter. At this point I noticed a rather desperate Binky waving his hand at me from below the table where Alice couldn't see. His eyes begged like a prisoner who hears the approach of the tumbrel.

"Sorry, Uncle Hugo, I must rescue a friend in need."

He squinted at me suspiciously. "You'll consider what I've said?"

"Deeply, richly."

"I have sent you a comprehensive list of your holdings. Will you read it?"

"Unquestionably."

He regarded me doubtfully. "There are no pictures."

"Oh. Well then, I'll have Bentley read it and give me the gist. Ta-ta. Love to Aunt Hypatia."

"You should call on her. She is incomprehensibly fond of you."

"I shall. Tally ho!"

As I left my Uncle, a waiter was setting a large treacle tart before him. I stiffened my spine and set a course for Binky, who was grinning at me like a child who spots the approach of a circus parade.

Hopeful Signs

I weaved my way across the dining room. As I approached, Alice's voice pierced the mutton-scented air.

"It all comes down to who controls the means of production. Surely you see that!"

"I think so."

"But it's so simple! I'll start again from the beginning."

I leaned in tentatively. "Am I interrupting?"

"Yes," Alice glared.

Binky grasped my arm as though it was a life preserver. "Cyril! Where have you been hiding? Do sit down. What a cracking sombrero!"

"Thanks. It's a loaner.

He wrestled me into the seat next to him. Alice subsided grimly and sipped her tea.

"What are you two conspiring about?" I chirped.

Binky jumped a little. "Conspiring? No! No conspiracy here. Quite the contrary. Banal, that's what we are. As inoffensive as cheese."

I looked at him askance. His forehead was shining with perspiration.

Alice clinked her tea cup onto its saucer. "How is your country cousin enjoying the city?"

"Who, Carnation?"

Binky let out a sound somewhere between a giggle and a moan. "Gardenia, silly. Your cousin Gardenia."

"Do you have more than one country cousin?" asked Alice.

"Scads. Great Grandfather was quite the Lothario, apparently. The area around Little Climping is as thick as clotted cream with kith and kin."

"What is your view on this intemperate betrothal between Cheswick and your cousin?"

"Couldn't be happier. She's first-rate. They go together like soy and cellulose."

Alice chewed her lower lip and looked at Binky thoughtfully. "It's odd, but the thought of Cheswick with another woman is strangely disquieting."

I could see that Bentley's psychological ploy was having its effect. "You should have snapped him up when you had the chance, Old Girl. Too late now."

"It's absurd. Given the unspoken understanding between you and I, there can be nothing between Cheswick and myself."

I overturned the salt cellar and knocked the butter dish onto Binky's lap. "There is a reason our understanding is unspoken. It is because it doesn't exist."

"Nonsense. All of the most important things in life are unspoken. To speak them aloud robs them of their rich ambiguity and turns them into simple statements that can be contradicted by any random acquaintance."

"Well, Binky and Gardenia are certainly engaged. That is a statement that will brook no argument. If it arouses feelings of remorse, you have only yourself to blame."

Alice turned to Binky. "When is the wedding?"

He waved his hand dismissively, "As soon as possible. Why wait?"

She frowned. "I cannot help but think that your haste will lead to regret. I must meet this young person. She may be persuaded to see reason."

I thought quickly. "Afraid she's gone back to the country. Pity. The two of you would have gotten along like sisters. Another time, perhaps."

"Perhaps. In the meantime, Cheswick has something to discuss with you."

"Does he?"

Binky looked confused for a moment. Alice made a sound deep in her throat that caused him to jump to his feet. "Yes. Why don't we stroll out to the lobby? I need to stretch my legs."

I rose and followed him out of the dining room. As we headed for a quiet corner, Evans, the doorman, floated up. "Did the gentlemen wish an appointment with the tailors?"

No thank you, Evans. Bentley will see to it."

"Very good, Sir."

Binky looked dejected. "Three centimeters! Shocking. I just had all my lapels let *out*. It's exhausting."

"But one must keep up."

"Why? These constant and capricious changes of fashion are nothing but a means of control! We must throw off the shackles of these tyrannical couturiers!" He suddenly became self-conscious. "Or so I've heard."

"This doesn't sound like you."

"Alice has been teaching me things. She's a pip of a girl, you know. We've been at that table for hours. I have an entirely new outlook on life."

"So, it's going well with the two of you? I couldn't be happier."

He looked a bit crestfallen. "I suppose it's going well. Mostly she talks and I listen. I've tried any number of stratagems to turn the conversation to love, but when I do she just natters on about the patriarchy. A fellow doesn't know where he stands."

"Stiffen the spine, Old Blancmange. Don't you give up."

"Oh no, I'll stick to her like a remora, but a fellow likes some encouragement now and then."

We watched the crowd drift past for a tick. I gave a little cough. "Is there a reason you lured me to the lobby?"

"Oh yes, there was something..."

At that moment, Cheeseworth staggered up. He wore a huge creation that depicted a naval battle between competing armadas. Whales spouted and mermaids peeped from the sea foam. He winced with every step he took.

"Ow! If only these shoes weren't so bloody pointy!"

"We must simply bear it until the new fashions are announced. I'm praying for sandals."

"Or espadrilles." His eyes took on a dreamy look.

"That's quite a bonnet!"

"Yes, the cannons actually fire, but then the whole hat tends to smoulder."

How've you been, Cheeseworth?"

"Oh, tolerable. One thought the cwub might cheer one up, but one might as well be in a wax museum. No one in this beastly place ever has the good taste to die. Care for a wubber of bwidge?"

"Sorry, Old Boy. I must be off."

"Binky?"

He sniffed. "Bridge is the opiate of the people."

"One begs one's pardon?"

"It deadens empathy and distracts from the dissolution of the human race as a species."

"I don't think you're playing it wight."

"I cannot play games of any kind until all are free. It's frivolous."

"Man does not live by bwead alone, dear boy. Without fwivolity, wife is a barren wasteland."

"Nevertheless."

Cheeseworth gave a heavy sigh. "Very well. Perhaps I'll take in the cockfights. Or a bear baiting."

"Are you passing my way?" I asked. "I could use a ride."

"What happened to your chariot?"

"It was obsolete."

Cheeseworth gave a great, honking laugh. "So am I, dear boy. So am I. Come along."

Binky thawed like a frozen fishy stick on a windowsill. "I say, room for one more?"

"The more the merrier. Avanti!"

We strolled out front to watch Cheeseworth's palanquin stomp up. The mechanical bearers had a kind of bored look as if to say, "What this? Heavy? Don't make us laugh." We clambered aboard and off they jogged.

"Nifty palanquin, Cheeseworth."

"Do you like it? I'm twading it in tomorrow for a camel cawavan encwusted with wubies."

Binky sneered theatrically. "These ostentatious vehicles are the opiate of the people."

"I thought bwidge was the opiate of the people."

"That too. There's opium everywhere if you know where to look."

"Perhaps you should see someone about your obsession with dwugs."

I was having some difficulty keeping my sombrero from blowing off of my head.

"Do you suppose we could unhat ourselves until we reach our destination?"

"Of course, dear boy. This is a very informal palanquin."

"I say, Binky, what was it you wanted to ask me?"

"Who, me?"

"Yes. At the club, you said there was something...?"

He brightened. "Oh... I wondered if you were going to the country this weekend and whether I might tag along."

"Absolutely. Always welcome."

"And Alice."

"What ho! That's a bit thick."

Cheeseworth cackled. "Alice Witherspoon! The Ivory Empwess! The Toothy Tywant!"

Binky raised an eyebrow. "You are speaking of the woman I love."

"Pardon me, I'm sure."

I sighed with exasperation. "Look here, Old Spartan, even you must admit she's a bit of a blister."

"She's changed, Cyril."

"Been to the dentist, you mean?"

"She and I are one now. The struggle has united us."

"Look, Binky, I think it's a simply beastly idea to bring Alice, but if it's what you wish I can deny you nothing. Just don't blame me if the sight of me causes her to flare her nostrils and paw the earth."

"I'm not afraid."

Cheeseworth drew a jeweled monocle from his vest pocket and screwed it into an eye.

"*I'm* going to the countwy this weekend. Cheeseworth House is minutes away from your chateau. I'll pop over and watch the fireworks. I shall bring my ward, Pansy. You've never met her, Cyril."

"I don't believe so."

"She's absolutely hopeless, but one has a wesponsibility."

"Sounds delightful."

The palanquin bearers stamped to a halt.

"Here we are. Sowwy to hurry you along but those bears won't bait themselves."

I regarded him curiously. "Do you bait them personally?"

"Certainly. I am wuthless. I attack their execrable fashion sense, their lack of wit, their excess of body hair. I make those bears weep, I can tell you."

"Well, good luck. Thanks awfully for the lift, Cheeseworth."

"Think nothing of it. Don't forget your chapeaus. Ta-ta!"

And away he lurched, holding on for dear life. Binky made no attempt to depart, but stood looking at me rather anxiously. I donned my sombrero.

"Spot of tea?"

"No thanks. Got to run. So, we're on for the weekend?"

I fixed him with a gimlet eye. "Haven't you forgotten something?"

He wrinkled his forehead. "I don't think so."

"If Alice comes to the country, who do you suppose she will expect to meet?"

There was an extended silence as he rubbed his nose, stared at a nearby bush and hummed a snatch of something banal. Finally, he shrugged. "I give up."

"Your fiancee, you dip! She lives in the country. Don't you think that's why Alice wants to go there?"

He gave a barking laugh of relief. "Oh! That's not why she wants to go... I mean..." He fell silent and began to kick at some small rocks. "Look, just trust me. Alice has other plans."

I regarded him for a moment but decided not to press the point. "I suppose we can always come up with a story. She could be visiting friends, or she could be in hospital with malaria or some other extended illness."

"Fine. I can see you have things well in hand." Binky averted his eyes and shoved his hands in his pockets. "Er... the house is... near that hydrogen plant, isn't it?"

"As you well know. You can see it from the dining room window."

"Good-oh. 'Til the weekend."

He sauntered off in a somewhat serpentine manner, eventually reversing direction and hurrying down the street as if pursued.

I thought it was high time to prove my independence to Bentley and after some experimentation I was able to open the front door by myself. As I stepped into the foyer. I heard a sudden commotion and saw, out of the corner of my eye, an unfamiliar houndstooth-check skirt whipping around a corner. Bentley shimmered into view.

"I say, Bentley, who's that?"

"No one, Sir. Welcome home. May I compliment you on your opening of the front door?"

I eyed him suspiciously but Bentley could give the Sphinx lessons in inscrutability. "I saw someone, didn't I?"

"I think not, Sir."

"Were you in the midst of a romantic liaison, Bentley?"

"Alas, I lack the essential equipment. May I take your sombrero?"

"Thank you. I say, did you get the message from the club about the new dress code this morning?"

"I did, but you had already departed. I regret the incident extremely."

"Things were rather awkward at first, but I am nothing if not resourceful. Put this questionnaire somewhere prominent. I have to fill it out to get my new topper from the club hatter."

"Of course, Sir. Did I see Mr. Wickford-Davies departing in a rather eccentric manner?"

"You did. Binky will be joining us in the country for the weekend."

"Very good, Sir."

"And Alice."

He paused and said gravely, "I see, Sir."

"I'm not happy about it either. You must be extra vigilant."

"My surveillance is ongoing. How is Mr. Wickford-Davies's pursuit of Miss Witherspoon progressing?"

"They are as two cherries on a single stem. I must say, you're a wizard in the Cupid department."

"One does what one can."

"What's in the larder? I'm starved."

"Would Sir care for some pizza rolls?"

"Rather! I'll just peel off these shoes and cauterize my feet."

"Your uncle has sent a rather large package."

"That's a list of my worldly goods. Digest it for me and bring me the... no, that's not a good metaphor. Sift it and bring me the lumps. Well, you know what I mean."

"Of course, Sir."

Perhaps it was something about the light—the late afternoon gloom and whatnot, but a shadow passed suddenly before my eyes and I felt a yawning chasm open in my vitals. "Oh, Bentley... it all seems so meaningless. I really feel I can't go another step."

He looked at me closely. "Did Sir neglect to take his anti-depressant this morning?"

"I don't remember."

"Oopsie Daisy, then."

Bentley lifted me gently and deposited me in my favorite armchair before a roaring hydrogen fire. He tipped two tablets into my palm from a vial he took from his vest pocket.

"Take your nice pills and I'll be back with the pizza rolls in a trice."

I took a sip of water and tossed the pills down the old gullet.

Bentley nodded approvingly. "There might even be a bit of real chocolate after the pizza rolls."

I felt a warm glow begin in my toes and work its way upward. "Real chocolate! Where on earth did you find it?"

"I have my ways, Sir."

I sighed and snuggled back into the upholstery. "I'm all right now. Thank you, Bentley. I don't know how I'd get on without you."

"One feels quite undeserving of such accolades. Shall I bring a ramekin of marinara for dipping?"

"By all means! Let's have a goddam Bacchanalia!"

As Bentley glided off to the kitchen, I wiggled my toes and gazed into the fire. I felt that all was right with the world—an impression that would prove to be sadly misguided.

A Hot Time at the Old Chateau

Chippington-Smythe House is widely considered to be one of the ghastlier country homes. Nestled amidst mosquito-infested swamps, its crumbling turrets are dwarfed by the massive dome of the world's largest hydrogen plant a mere stone's throw away. Family lore would have it that the house was once a palace fit for an Emperor, but as the family tree dwindled to a few stunted shrubs and country estates fell out of fashion it was allowed to slowly sink into the primordial ooze. I maintained a wing of it for form's sake—run by the formidable Mrs. Oakes—a close cousin of Bentley's from the same factory. Indeed, only a pageboy wig and a spot of rouge kept them from being identical twins.

"Morning, Sir. Coffee-flavoured beverage?"

"Yes. Bless you, Mrs. Oakes."

"There's Cheesy Eggs, Kippered Strips, Morning Links and Improbable Bacon in the chafing dishes. Here's your toast and Fruity Paste. Would you care for anything else?"

"No, that will suffice. Um... real eggs?"

"Almost, Sir."

"Oh well." I scraped some Fruity Paste onto a cold piece of toast. "Have Alice and Binky arrived?"

"Yes, Sir. They've had their breakfast already. They're strolling about the swamp."

"They know to keep to the wooden path?"

"I reminded them, Sir."

"Don't want any guests sinking in the quicksand. Once was quite enough. Thank you, Mrs. Oakes."

"Enjoy your breakfast, Sir."

As she strode away, she passed Bentley, who carried a stack of correspondence.

"Morning, Mr. Bentley."

"Good morning, Mrs. Oakes. Good morning, Sir."

"Bentley! Beautiful day, what?"

"The humidity is unusually low. You have received multiple communications this morning."

"Convey them post-haste. Good news, I hope."

"One slavers with anticipation." He gazed sadly at my wrist. "I pause only to observe that your cuff is currently residing in the Fruity Paste."

"Damn!"

I dabbed at my shirtsleeve with a napkin to no visible effect. Bentley opened the first note.

"Your aunt and uncle will arrive at eleven o'clock."

"Aunt Hypatia and Uncle Hugo?"

"Yes, Sir."

"Why are they coming?"

"The missive does not state their purpose."

"Oh well. The more the merrier I suppose, although Uncle Hugo is a dreadful stick. What else?"

He opened another note. "Mr. Langford-Cheeseworth will arrive at eleven-thirty with his ward."

"Cheeseworth is always good for a laugh. I don't hold out much hope for the ward."

My efforts to remove the paste from my shirtsleeve grew more vigorous. The table began to shake. There was a loud "clink" from somewhere down below.

"May I pour you more coffee beverage, Sir? The previous cup seems to have migrated to the carpet."

"So it has. Clumsy. Pour away. Any more messages?"

"Yes, Sir. You have received a letter announcing, 'New Mumbai chicken-like korma: now with eight percent less acetone.'"

"Well, we must give it a try, mustn't we?"

"If you wish it, Sir."

"They went to the trouble to inform us. It would be ungrateful not to." I munched on my toast. "What kind of Fruity Paste do you suppose this is?"

"The label describes it as 'red,' Sir."

"Not quite so sour as the blue one, is it?"

"I wouldn't know, Sir. I have no sense of taste."

I sipped my coffee beverage and watched the dust motes dance in the sunbeams. "Ah, the country... so peaceful."

The French doors slammed open and Alice strode in, her boots clomping on the parquet floor. Binky trailed behind, gazing at her worshipfully.

"There you are! Do you always sleep the morning away like this?"

"Good morning, Alice. Morning, Binky. Yes, always."

"We shall have to do something about that. Time is too precious to waste. You're not getting any younger, you know."

"So you keep reminding me. Death before dishonour."

"I'm not doing that anymore," she snapped.

"No? The conversation seems naked without it. Binky? Death before dishonour?"

"Sorry, Cyril, Alice won't let me. Thanks awfully for letting us crash."

"Always welcome, dear boy. Open invitation. Carte blanche."

Binky had wandered over to the sideboard and was peering at the contents of the chafing dishes. "I say, are those Kippered Strips?"

He picked up a plate and was about to plow in when Alice raised a dainty fist. "Put that down, Cheswick. You have already had your breakfast."

"But there were no Kippered Strips."

"You are digging your grave with your teeth. You already possess a substantial paunch."

He sagged and put down the plate. "Oh, I say..."

"Cyril, we will be meeting a few friends later. I hope you don't mind. We shall confine ourselves to the gazebo."

"Do I know them?"

"I'm sure not. They do not orbit in our sphere."

"Have at it. Mi casa, etcetera."

Alice sniffed as though she scented something unpleasant. "And where is your country cousin? I expected to meet her here."

I stiffened. "You mean..."

"Gardenia!" Binky blurted, his mouth full of Improbable Bacon. "She's about somewhere, I'm sure."

I stared at him in astonishment. "Is she?" I asked him pointedly. "Are you sure?"

He was insensible to my waggling eyebrows. "I suppose. I mean..." His brain started to catch up to the situation.

"I thought she was under the weather," I prompted.

"Nonsense!" Declared Alice. "People in the country are never ill. I shall meet her at lunch."

"But..." Binky began.

There was a bit of a hubbub from down the hall. Above it all I could hear Aunt Hypatia's clarion call.

"There's Aunt Hypatia and Uncle Hugo."

Alice looked sour. "What are they doing here?"

"One hasn't a clue."

"I can't bear that man. Cheswick, come!"

Binky jumped as if he'd sat on a pin. "Yes, dear."

"And don't call me 'dear.'"

"No... Ma'am."

"Oh, you really are hopeless."

They slipped out the French doors to the garden as my aunt and uncle sailed into the dining room. Bentley had to foot it pretty nimbly to nose in before them.

"Mr. and Mrs. Dankworth."

My Aunt Hypatia is a bit of a dragon, but she long ago took me under her scaly wing. It requires some dexterity to avoid her fiery breath but on the whole she's a benign sort of lizard.

"Cyril! Darling boy! Death before dishonour."

"Death before dishonour, Aunt Hypatia. Come to my arms, you glorious creature."

Uncle Hugo stood moodily and estimated the value of the silverware. "Nephew. Death before dishonour."

"Death before dishonour, Uncle Hugo. I hope I see you well."

"Tolerable. Swamp's getting worse."

"Is it? I'll hire some pumps. Have you had your breakfast?"

"Hours ago. Almost lunchtime, isn't it?"

Aunt Hypatia eyed me critically. "You're so thin. You're not eating enough. Bentley, see that he eats."

"Of course, Madame."

I regarded my aunt suspiciously. "To what do I owe the pleasure?"

"I wanted to see my favorite nephew and your uncle wanted to make sure you were doing your homework."

Uncle Hugo glared at me. "Have you read what I sent you?"

"Bentley? Have we?"

"I have sifted it, Sir."

"There, you see? We have sifted it."

"And what are your thoughts?"

"Well, the sifting is only the preliminary exercise. The analyzing is still to come."

"Do not shunt this off. The consequences are substantial."

"Never. Do have some coffee."

My uncle's eyes lit up for a moment. "Is it real coffee?"

"Almost."

He sniffed disdainfully.

"No thank you."

From the drive there came a cacophony that could have been a herd of countertenors being run over by a motorized tank.

"Mr. Langford-Cheeseworth and Ms. Freehold are arriving, Sir."

Through the window I spied a magnificent mechanical procession. "I see they delivered his camel caravan. Rather gaudy. You know Cheeseworth, don't you, Uncle Hugo? From the club?"

"That ridiculous popinjay?"

"That's the one. Show them in, Bentley."

My uncle took on a hunted look. "We can't stay long."

My aunt smacked him on the arm. It would have lamed a lesser man. "Don't be a poop, Hugo. I want to visit with my nephew."

"Very well. I shall be in the orangery."

He hurried off mumbling something about the Circles of Hell. My aunt regarded me shrewdly. "I have something to say to you, Cyril."

Well, this froze my blood, as you can imagine. Aunt Hypatia has strong feelings about how I'm meant to be living my life, and to my certain knowledge there is not one single thing that I am doing correctly.

"Hugo tells me that you expressed doubts about having a family."

"The thought of a brood of screaming children running into the swamp and whatnot rather chills the blood."

"That is unacceptable. This is not a matter of personal preference. You must reproduce. You are the last of the Chippington-Smythes. We cannot be allowed to become extinct."

"It seems rather hard on me."

"You know I love you."

I examined the statement from every angle but I couldn't find the hook.

"I will concede the point."

"You must grow up, Cyril. You must take your place as the head of this family."

"There's plenty of time for all that."

"There is not. It may take years for you to impregnate a wife. The Chippington-Smythes are noted for the immobility of their sperm."

I set down my toast. "This is hardly breakfast talk."

"Heed my words. Find a wife. Have babies. Our family's future depends on you."

I heard approaching footsteps. I could see Bentley pacing down the hallway with Cheeseworth dancing impatiently behind him. Bringing up the rear was, if it was not a trick of the light, the loveliest young lady I had ever laid eyes on. She paced demurely—her eyes cast down in front of her. I heard a buzzing in my ears as if a hive of mechanical bees had nested there. So this was love!

A New Plot

B entley gave a tip of the head. "Mr. Langford-Cheeseworth and Ms. Freehold, Sir."

"Cywil! And can this be Aunt Hypatia? You're looking simply marvelous!"

My aunt regarded Cheeseworth with a surprisingly benevolent eye. Apparently, her censure was reserved for blood relations.

"Ah, Mr. Langford-Cheeseworth. How are your parents?"

"Thwiving! Simply thwiving. May I pwesent my ward, Ms. Pansy Freehold."

"Pleased to meet you, my dear. Goodness, you *are* pretty."

The vision spoke in a thrillingly mellow voice. "Thank you."

With that she fell silent and stared at the floor. Cheeseworth seemed accustomed to these lapses in her conversational flow. "Death before dishonour!"

"Death before dishonour."

"Death before dishonour."

Pansy's reply was barely a whisper. "Death before dishonour."

I pawed the ground a bit and began spraying the old Chippington-Smythe charm about pretty liberally. "Pansy, is it? Lovely name."

A fetching blush suffused her cheeks. "It's a flower."

"By Jove, so it is!"

All this wit was apparently too dizzying for Aunt Hypatia. "Well, I'll leave you young people to your fun."

"You're staying for lunch, Aunt?"

"Certainly, if you wish it. I shall join your uncle in the orangery. Until lunch, then."

She sailed down the hall like a clipper ship bound for the Indies. Cheeseworth gazed after her.

"What a magnificent old warhorse she is. I admire her enormously."

"She is the best of aunts. Have you had breakfast?"

"Yes, but one can always find woom for a snack." He lifted the lid of the first chafing dish. "Ooh! Impwobable bacon!"

I waggled my eyebrows winningly at the ward. "What about you, Ms. Freehold?"

"Nothing, thank you."

"Coffee-flavoured beverage?"

"No, thank you."

I searched wildly for something to break the ice. "That's a lovely frock."

This seemed to puzzle her. "Is it?"

"Yes."

"Thank you."

With that we froze into a sort of tableau. I stared at Pansy, she stared at her feet, and Cheeseworth stared at the chafing dishes. Finally, he broke the silence.

"Do you know my favowite thing about the countwy?"

"No, what?"

"Boots! One can wear boots! My feet feel so fwee!"

He lifted the next lid. "I say, cheesy eggs. Good show!"

He resumed grazing. I abandoned all reserve and leapt into the conversational maelstrom. "You live at Cheeseworth Manor I apprehend, Ms. Freehold?"

"Yes."

"How is it we've never met? You're only a few miles away."

"I don't go out much."

"Why would you deprive local society of your company?"

"I don't really fit in."

"I can't believe that."

Cheeseworth cackled into his cheesy eggs. "Believe it, my boy. She's like a deer in the headlights. Has no conversation. Fweezes at the first bon mot."

"Oh, you don't have to worry about that with me. I'm not at all witty."

Cheeseworth gave me a searching look. "I'm glad to hear you admit it. I wasn't sure if you knew it or not."

"Tell me, Ms. Freehold, would you like a tour of the grounds?"

"You don't have to be formal with her, Cyril. He can call you Pansy, can't he my dear?"

She looked away demurely. "If you like."

"Pansy, then. Come, let me show you around the old ancestral manse."

There is a small patch of land behind the estate which looks almost as nature might have intended. Of course, one must ignore the powerful stench of mildew. I breathed deeply, coughed as a cloud of methane drifted past me, and admired the lake at the foot of the hill. Lake Sputum is so pristine one could almost swim in it without antibiotics. In the distance, at the far end of the lake, one could make out the tiny town of Catarrh, with its quaint organ farms and fat rendering plant. There was a twittering from the trees. Pansy lit up with pleasure.

"Oh! Birds!"

"Bird songs, rather. Pipe them through speakers. Used to have animatronic birds but they kept malfunctioning. Falling out of the trees onto one's head. Disconcerting, what?"

She looked down and began digging at the earth with the toe of one shoe. I was growing desperate.

"Like birds, do you?"

"I saw one once in a zoo. It was the most beautiful thing I've ever seen."

The gallant thing to say would have been, "And you're the most beautiful bally thing I've ever seen," but my tongue cleaved to the roof of my mouth and I could only kick at small stones and hum.

"What's that you're humming?"

"What? Oh. I don't know."

"It sounds like the jingle for that breakfast cereal—Frosted Cellu-lo's."

"Does it? I've always been musical. I once thought of being a famous opera singer but there were so many notes and you have to do them in the right order apparently... and of course one would have to learn to sing and so on."

We strolled along in silence for a while. Repartee usually flows from me like water from a breached levee but my usual lines of chatter seemed hopelessly inadequate. Pansy suddenly stopped dead.

"I'm sorry."

"What on earth for?"

"I know I'm a dreadful mope. I have no conversation."

"Not at all. I'm sure you have a deucedly rich inner life. You just want someone to tap the keg and out it will flow."

"No. People always think I'm deep because I'm so quiet, but the truth is I can't stand the sorts of things people talk about. It all seems so... meaningless. It's like we're in a play and everyone knows their lines but me. They do and say improbable things for no discernible reason. I just want a simple life—long walks, a good book by the fire...."

As I gazed into the cerulean disks that poets would refer to as her "eyes," I made a sudden resolution. Pansy would be my bride. We would repopulate the earth with our offspring and all would be joy.

"Are you all right?"

I came back to reality to find Pansy looking at me oddly. "Sorry, what?"

"You were staring."

"Was I? Dreadfully rude. I say, Pansy, I know we've only just met..."

"Pardon me, Sir."

I nearly jumped out of my flannels. Bentley had an unfortunate habit of materializing without warning. I've heard of yoga practitioners that can dis-incorporate their atoms and reassemble them across the room, but Bentley left them in the dust.

"Yes? What is it?"

"You have received a note. 'Our previous announcement, "New Mumbai chicken-like korma: now with eight percent less acetone." should have read, "now with eight percent *more* acetone." We apologize for any misunderstanding.'"

As we rounded the corner of the house, I could see the gazebo through the trees. Alice stood before a somewhat ragged and threadbare crowd, gesticulating enthusiastically. Pansy stared at her.

"Who is that striking woman?"

"The one with the teeth? That's Alice Witherspoon."

"She seems to be quite an orator."

"Oh, Alice could talk the bark off a Spruce tree. I'll introduce you at lunch."

Bentley cleared his throat. "Is there any reply, Sir?"

"To what?"

"To the korma manufacturer, Sir."

"No. You may go."

Down at the gazebo, Binky stood adjacent to the conclave looking miserable. Upon spotting us, he whispered urgently to Alice, who glared in our direction. She made shooing motions to the crowd which rapidly dispersed. I noted that their movements seemed almost excessively furtive. Some crept from bush to bush. One pulled his jacket over his head. A dignified-looking lady holding a small dog inexplicably did a one-handed cartwheel and slipped behind a tree. Alice strode off toward the swamp and Binky trotted over to join us. I cursed him silently.

Binky eyed Pansy with interest. "Hallo, who's this?"

"Pansy, I'd like you to meet my old friend Cheswick Wickford-Davies—commonly known as Binky. This is Cheeseworth's ward, Ms. Freehold."

He made a rakish little bow. "Charmed, I'm sure."

"Hello."

Binky gave me a significant look. "Look here, Old Boy, I must speak to you. It's frightfully important."

Pansy turned and started toward the house. "I shall join my guardian in the breakfast room."

Suddenly Binky gave a little hop and snapped his fingers. "No, don't go. Actually... seeing you gives me an inspiration."

I glared at him suspiciously. "Let's not involve Ms. Freehold in one of your schemes. She has only just met you and hasn't built up a protective flight response—like the dodos who had no fear of man and hence were rendered extinct."

Pansy gave a charming little frown. "I am quite capable of judging for myself. Please do not coddle me."

My face grew hot with shame. "I was presumptuous. Please forgive me, dear Ms. Freehold."

"Only if you will forgive me for flying into such a rage. It was quite shameless of me."

"Not at all. I'm an absolute hound. You were right to slap me on the snout." I turned back to Binky, who had fallen into a reverie. "Now, what's stewing in that fevered brain of yours, Old Squash?"

"It's Alice. She's suspicious."

"That is her defining characteristic."

"She wonders where Gardenia is."

"She can wonder until Doomsday for all I care."

"I depended on you to offer a credible excuse for Gardenia's absence."

"Don't put this on me. 'Oh, she's about somewhere'. Who blurted out *that* brilliant bit of badinage?"

"I was taken by surprise."

"Well, you created this mess. You can just get yourself out of it."

"Bentley's plan has worked perfectly up until now. Alice is dripping with jealousy. She's champing at the bit to sink her fangs into Cousin Gardenia and there is no corpus. I am teetering on the brink."

"I don't really see how I can help you."

"It occurs to me..." Here Binky eyed Pansy in a most disturbing way. "...That this young lady may prove the answer to my prayers, if she's game."

Pansy blushed prettily. "I don't know what you mean by 'game' but I'm happy to help you if I can. I believe that we must try at all times to help others. It is a moral imperative."

"By Jove, you're a rum one! Shake on it."

Binky shoved out a paw, which Pansy shook vigorously. Lucky paw!

"Do I understand," began Pansy gravely, "That you have created a fictional fiancée in order to incite jealousy in the object of your affection?"

"That's it exactly! Now, here's the plan. You will play the role of my fiancée, Gardenia. During lunch we shall have a tremendous fight and I shall spurn you to the dust. Alice will hurl herself onto my heaving breast and we shall live happily ever after."

Pansy frowned. "This seems an improbable plan. It strains credulity."

"People are used to that where I'm concerned. No one expects me to adhere to logic or consistency."

"But how am I to act in a manner so contrary to my nature?"

"Just pretend you're in a play. Don't you know people who put on a persona very different from their true nature?"

"I have long felt that everyone does it but me."

"There you are, then."

Pansy looked thoughtful. "Perhaps this is an opportunity for me to learn how to fit in."

I fluttered my lashes coquettishly. "Dear Pansy, you don't have to change a jot or a tittle."

"No, I must make an effort. I'll do it!"

"Brave Pansy!"

"Only you mustn't blame me if I'm not very good."

Binky clapped his hands with delight. "You shall be brilliant. I know it."

A shiver ran up my spine. "Perhaps we should run this by Bentley. He's the closest thing to Machiavelli currently in residence."

"Not necessary. It's a perfect plan."

"Don't say that. It makes the hairs on the back of my neck stand up."

Binky was concentrating furiously. "We'll have to let Cheeseworth in on the ruse or he'll blow it all to Kingdom Come."

"I shall speak to my guardian."

"Dear Ms. Freehold, I'm uncommonly grateful."

"Not at all."

Binky stared into her eyes as if he was Svengali and she an aspiring soprano.

"Now remember, I shall be cruel to you, but you mustn't take it personally."

"I never take cruelty personally. That would be selfish."

"Would it?"

"When someone is cruel, they are really expressing their own personal pain. It would be egotistical to make it about me."

"I never thought about it that way. I say!"

Out of the corner of my eye I saw Bentley exit the house carrying a large crate. One of the seedy-looking women from the gazebo appeared in a rather furtive manner and took the crate from him. She wore a houndstooth-check skirt that looked strangely familiar. She scurried off into the bushes and Bentley returned to the house. "Hmm. I wonder what that was all about?"

"What *what* was all about?" Binky inquired.

"Nothing. I must have a talk with Bentley before lunch."

Binky jumped as a distant cannon boomed. "There's the warning cannon. I must change."

"I as well. Pansy, let me escort you back to the house. We shall rendezvous at lunch."

Binky raised a finger. "Now remember, your name is Gardenia, you are Cyril's cousin from the country and we are engaged."

"I believe I apprehend the situation."

"With any luck, Alice will be mine by teatime."

But it would prove to be bitter tea indeed, served with scones of shame and finger sandwiches of pain. And watercress.

Luncheon of the Damned

O ne of the great benefits of country life is the simplicity of the apparel. Girdle, of course—one has standards. But no sash, no brooches and no horrible shoes. As Bentley glided about me adjusting straps and cinching belts, I gazed at him through narrowed eyes.

"I say, Bentley, who was that lady at the back door?"

"Lady, Sir?"

"The one you handed the crate to."

"I really couldn't say, Sir."

"Seedy-looking matron. Houndstooth kilt. She scuttled off into the bushes."

"That seems most irregular, Sir."

"Look here, are you looting the wine cellar? Disposing of the family heirlooms?"

"To what end, Sir? Money is of no use to me."

"Perhaps she's blackmailing you."

"That would be impossible. My programming forbids me to act against the interests of my employer."

"That's what I always thought."

Bentley got out the old whisk broom and began pummeling me with it as though lint was his hereditary enemy. "Ms. Freehold is quite attractive, Sir."

"Don't change the subject. Do you really think so?"

"My observation is merely academic, of course."

"I intend to marry her, Bentley. I intend to make her 'Mrs. Chippington-Smythe'."

Bentley stopped whisking for a moment. "There are many quotations concerning the course of true love not running smoothly that I could refer you to."

"Pish tosh! Ours is a love without blemish."

"Then I wish you joy, Sir."

He began to whisk me with increased vigor. It was deucedly distracting. "What were we talking about?"

"When, Sir?"

"A moment ago. We were speaking of something."

"I really couldn't say."

The final cannon for lunch boomed forth.

"Luncheon, Sir."

As I stepped into the hallway, I encountered Cheeseworth, who was sporting a jeweled monocle and a gilded walking stick.

"Cywil! What sport! We're to have an impwovisation, are we?"

"Yes, look here, Cheeseworth, don't give the game away, there's a good fellow. Just play along."

"Of course! I shall pway my part with brio! I love an intwigue. It weminds me of my days working as an intelligence agent in the Balkans."

"Really? That sounds dangerous."

"Not weally. In those days we were quite open about it. The embassies would send lists of their spies to each other. It was so much more civilized that way."

"But how did you gather intelligence when they all knew who you were?"

"Alcohol, dear boy. In my experience, anything that cannot be discovered over a whiskey and soda isn't worth knowing."

As we entered the dining room, I found Uncle Hugo and Aunt Hypatia admiring a portrait of one of my distant ancestors. "Cyril, Darling! We're just admiring Great-Great-Grandfather Percy—founder of the family fortune. Such a prominent frontal lobe. Head simply stuffed with brains. Hello, Cheeseworth."

"Dear Hypatia. Death before dishonour."

"Death before dishonour."

"Death before dishonour."

"Death before dishonour. Listen Aunt, before everyone gets here, there's going to be a little..."

As ill luck would have it, Alice strode into the room before I could communicate the meat of the situation.

"A little what, dear?" my aunt inquired.

"Never mind." I leaned in closely. "Just don't be surprised by anything."

"A woman of breeding is never surprised. It shows a lack of foresight."

Alice marched over. "Afternoon Hypatia. How are you, Hugo?"

"Death before dishonour."

"I don't use that phrase anymore."

My uncle stared at her, nonplussed. "What do you mean?"

"I find it hollow."

He opened and closed his mouth a few times and gave the old eyebrows a good shake. "Do you mean to say that you would not die rather than be dishonoured? Does that concept hold no meaning for you?"

"Not particularly."

"Does tradition mean nothing? The sacrifices of your forbears?"

"Oh... fine! I don't want to get into a philosophical melee before lunch. Death before dishonour, since you insist."

He grumbled into his cravat, "I don't know what the world is coming to."

My aunt gave him a look that could have peeled an orange. "Take a pill, Hugo. Death before dishonour."

"Death before dishonour," quoth I.

"Death before dishonour," echoed Cheeseworth.

Binky rushed in through the French doors.

"Am I late? Death before dishonour."

He froze, staring at Alice like a mouse spotting a cobra. "Oh! Sorry, dear!"

The steam was fairly rising off of her. "It's fine."

Cheeseworth began,"Death before dishonour."

"Death before dishonour."

"Death before dishonour."

"Death before dishonour."

Alice fumed for a moment and then spat through the jagged stumps that lurked behind her pale lips. "Death before dishonour."

Pansy floated into the room. She wore something diaphanous and blue. My heart did a quick turn around the block, then stood in place hopping up and down like a pogo stick. She kept her eyes demurely low.

"Good afternoon. Death before dishonour."

We all glanced sideways at Alice.

"Oh God!" She gritted her teeth, which took some doing as the upper and lower jaws had few points on which they agreed. "Death before dishonour."

"Death before dishonour."

"Death before dishonour."

"Death before dishonour."

"Death before dishonour."

"Death before dishonour."

Aunt Hypatia examined Pansy. "What a lovely dress."

"Is it?"

"It is."

"Thank you."

Binky pulled out a chair and gave Pansy a look. "Sit here by me... Gardenia."

My aunt wrinkled her forehead which caused a small avalanche of powder to burst loose and cascade down her cheeks. "Gardenia? I thought her name was Pansy."

"Yes. Pansy is short for Gardenia."

"No, it's not."

"Well, they're both flowers."

"I suppose that's true."

Bentley glided over. "Excuse me, Sir."

"Yes, Bentley?"

"A message has arrived. It states that users of Chumley's tooth polish are twice as likely to marry the mate of their choice."

I eyed Pansy hungrily. "Thank you, Bentley. Order me five or six dozen."

"Of course, Sir."

Cheeseworth took a seat and patted the chair next to him. "Sit between Binky and I, Gardenia."

Alice glared at Pansy poisonously. "So! This is the country cousin I've heard so much about."

Binky gave a choked little cough. "Gardenia, allow me to introduce you to Alice Witherspoon."

"Yes, I saw you orating earlier. You are a powerful speaker."

This threw Alice off her stride. "Well... thank you."

"I envy you enormously. I can't speak in front of people. Too shy."

"Nonsense. It only takes practice."

"No. Some people are just braver than others."

"How is it we've never met, Ms... is it Ms. Chippington-Smythe?"

"No, Freehold."

"And how are you and Cyril related?"

Uncle Hugo sat up. "What?"

My aunt shoved the bread basket at him. "Take a roll, Hugo." She leaned forward. "Go on, my dear."

Time to stick my oar in. "Yes. Well... you know... there was that branch of the family from..."

"Dusseldorf, wasn't it?" asked Cheeseworth quickly.

"Yes!   Dusseldorf!   The   Dusseldorf Chippington-Smythes."

Uncle Hugo was growing red. "What?"

"Don't interrupt, Hugo."

"Oh, I say..."

My aunt had a hungry gleam in her eye. "So, you were brought up in Dusseldorf, my dear?"

"Yes, until I was twelve."

"And you speak German?"

I winked at her madly with the offstage eye. "Well, of course they didn't speak it at home. I mean, it's such a deucedly guttural form of communication."

The hint was lost on Aunt Hypatia. "But you spoke German when you went out, amongst the Germans?"

"Oh yes."

"How lovely. Say something."

"I beg your pardon?"

"Now, Aunt, she's not a performing dog, you know!"

"I love the sound of German. I studied it as a child. *Wo hast du in Dusseldorf gelebt*?"

Binky turned positively green. He stared at Pansy like a castaway hoping for a sail on the horizon. Time seemed to elongate. Pansy was as placid as a woodland pool.

"*Wir hatten ein kleines Haus am Friedrichstradt. In der Nähe des Krankenhauses.*"

I stared at her with new found admiration. "I say!"

Aunt Hypatia regarded her shrewdly. "Fascinating."

All this had gone rather over Alice's head. "And what brought you here to Chippington-Smythe House?"

Cheeseworth stared up at the ceiling thoughtfully. "Well, her family was killed in a twagic boating accident..."

"And she had nowhere else to go," I added.

"A chilling tale!"

I gave her a hard stare. "Yes, Aunt, but of course all this is ancient history to you."

The penny dropped at last. "Oh, indeed!"

"Look here," Uncle Hugo sputtered.

"Hugo! The crudités!"

"But... Oh, blast!"

Alice turned back to Pansy. "And when did you and Cheswick meet?"

"We met here, in the country. He had come up for the Fall foliage..."

Binky leaned in. "Yes, but there was acid rain the entire weekend and we were trapped in the house."

"So, I suggested we play hide and seek..."

"And she hid so well I didn't find her until the day I was to leave…"

"By then I was starving of course, and dehydrated."

"I nursed her back to health… spooned broth into her and rubbed lotion onto her chapped feet…"

"He was an angel."

"I proposed before she recovered from her delirium."

"When he told me later that I had accepted I was overjoyed."

Cheeseworth clapped his hands. "What a whirlwind womance! Like something fwom a fairy tale!"

Alice picked sourly at a roll. "It sounds rather hasty to me."

"That's what makes it so wonderful! We hardly know each other. There is so much still to discover."

Binky gave Pansy a dazzling smile. "Please pass the crudites, my love."

She looked back at him gravely. "But my darling… you are allergic to crudités."

"Am I?"

"Yes. Deathly allergic."

He suddenly comprehended the plot. "But, see here, that's my funeral! If I choose to endanger my health, what business is it of yours?"

"Your welfare and mine are intertwined. You are no longer eating crudités for yourself alone. You are masticating for two now."

"This is intolerable! I will not be dictated to!"

He seized an item from the crudité platter and bit down with a loud crunch.

"Reckless man! Put down that cellulose stick at once!"

My uncle pounded the table. "By God, you stand your ground, Sir."

My aunt turned to him. "Yes, Hugo? You have something to say?"

He deflated like a cold soufflé. "That is... nothing."

"I thought not."

Pansy rose to her feet. "How can you speak to me so?"

"A man has certain prerogatives."

"I am your fiancée!"

"If our opposing views on crudités are indicative, this will be a marriage rife with controversy."

"Are you saying...?"

"Yes! I release you from your promise!"

Alice seized a cellulose stick and bit it in two. "Good show, Cheswick! Finally, some backbone!"

"Oh... how could you?"

"You must remember that I am a man."

Cheeseworth leaned in. "If you're not going to eat the cwudités could you slide them over here? I'm simpwy ravening."

Binky slammed his hands down on the table. "Damn the crudités, say I!"

Alice stared at Binky. "Cheswick! I have never seen this side of you! I must say..."

"Yes! This is the real me! A man of action. A man of principle."

Bentley sidled up and murmured in my ear. "Shall I serve the soup, Sir?" he murmured.

"Not now, Bentley. We're approaching catharsis."

"Very good, Sir."

Binky had the bit between his teeth. "I am a man who takes what he wants."

"Yes!" Alice moaned softly.

"Alice!"

"Yes, Cheswick?"

"Will you..."

"Yes? Yes?"

Suddenly Pansy made a dramatic gesture. "Wait!"

"What?"

"Wait!"

"Why?"

"I do not wish to be set free!"

Cheeseworth threw down his roll. "Twist!"

I could see Binky going through the script in his head trying to figure out where he had gone wrong. "But..."

"Passion such as ours must necessarily combust from time to time, but there is too much between us to simply walk away. "

Binky licked his lips nervously. "Look here, what are you...?"

"She's saying, 'Don't throw the baby out with the bath water,' what?" Hugo grunted.

Binky's eyebrows danced a tarantella. "Gardenia, may I speak to you privately?"

"Anything you have to say you can say in front of my family."

"But they're not... oh, damn it!"

Alice glared at Pansy. "Cheswick, will you allow yourself to be dictated to?"

"No, I bally well will not!"

Pansy stepped close to Binky and laid a finger across his lips. "Listen to me, my love." She gazed deeply into his eyes. Fortunate eyes! She took a deep breath, inflating the chiffon cloud that enveloped her. Binky goggled.

"No one on earth could possibly love you as I do. I wish to bear your children. I wish to grow old with you. I know with every fiber of my being that I can make you happy. Stay with me, my love."

And then she kissed him. And when I say kissed, it was rather as if she sucked his soul out from between his teeth. I could almost hear his resistance pop like a soap bubble. Cheeseworth tore at his bread nervously.

"Gardenia, aren't you wather... forgetting yourself? One is twying to eat, after all."

When they parted I could see that Binky was a dead duck.

"Cheswick! What is the meaning of this?"

Binky looked around dreamily. His eyes tried to focus on Alice. "What? Oh, hello Alice. I didn't hear you come in."

"Am I to understand that you still intend to marry this woman?"

Binky emerged from his trance. "Yes, by God, I do!"

He and Pansy locked lips again and I abandoned myself to despair. The castles I had built on air came crashing down. I motioned to Bentley.

"Bentley, you may serve the soup."

Showdown at the Hydrogen Plant

Love is rather like a diving bell. Those inside it are deaf to the outside world. They breathe each other's air and hear only the echoes of each other's murmurs. The crushing pressures of the world around them touch them not at all. Those outside the bubble, however, are highly susceptible to the buffeting currents and predatory fish that threaten them. While Binky and Pansy floated dreamily in each other's eyes I struggled to survive the maelstrom that had erupted in the dining room.

Alice stamped a tiny hoof. "Cheswick! I will not be ignored!"

Cheeseworth, who was rapidly emptying the crudité platter, lifted an eyebrow. "I say, Binky, this does wather cwoss the line, what?"

Uncle Hugo simply looked bewildered. "Will someone explain to me what the bloody hell is going on?"

"Sit still, Hugo. When there is something that requires a response from you, I will inform you."

"Here now, let's all calm down, shall we?" I protested weakly.

Alice slapped a palm on the Chippendale. "I will not calm down! I know when I am being trifled with. Cheswick!"

Binky shook himself like a dog awakening from a dream of bones. "Hmm? Yes?"

"You and I have embarked upon a great enterprise. Will you abandon it for the sake of this... person?"

"Sorry, what?"

"We have sworn oaths. The moment approaches. Will you stand with me?"

Binky suddenly snapped back to reality. "Oh! Sorry, Alice. I'm afraid I'll have to bow out." He gave Pansy a shy glance. "Things have changed, rather."

Alice threw down her napkin. "*I* have not changed! The need for action has not changed!" She stared at him, but his eyes were dreamily focused over her head. "Very well, I shall carry on alone, if need be. I discard you on the ash heap of history."

"Thanks awfully, Old Girl. I knew you'd understand."

Alice carefully placed her chair under the table and faced me. "Cyril, I must depart."

"But they're just bringing the soup."

"The soup is immaterial! Matters of great pith and moment are afoot. Farewell!"

And with that, she pounded across the parquet and whooshed out of the French doors. There was a moment of stunned silence before Cheeseworth turned back to his plate.

"Good widdance, say I. How can one enjoy one's food with those gweat ivory plaques clacking against each other like mah-jongg tiles?" He crunched loudly on a celery stick.

Bentley entered, pushing the serving trolley. Its wheels squeaked cheerfully. "The soup, Sir."

"Ah! What are we having, Bentley?"

"Clam-like chowder, Sir."

"Rustic, what?"

Binky and Pansy had locked lips again and sounded like a defective squeegee on a greasy window. Cheeseworth watched them sourly. "Look here, now that she's gone, you two can snap out of it. She is my ward, after all."

Aunt Hypatia gave a satisfied grunt. "Ah! The light begins to dawn."

"Not to me."

"Of course not, Hugo. Eat your soup. This little play was for Alice's benefit." She raised an eyebrow at me. "Am I correct? Did the three of you concoct this scheme amongst yourselves?"

I dipped into the chowder, which was larded with tiny gray nuggets of something that tasted like carpet lint. "Yes. It was intended to arouse her jealousy, but it seems to have gone rather off the tracks. Look here, you two, come up for air, will you?"

I threw a half-eaten roll at Binky's head but, typical of my deficient throwing skills, it caught Pansy on the ear. She started and looked around in surprise.

"Where has Miss Witherspoon gone?"

"Stalked out like a panther."

"But we weren't done!"

"Afraid the curtain's come down. La comedia e finita and all that."

"Oh no! I've spoiled everything!"

Binky put a hand around her waist. "Not for me, my darling."

Pansy removed his hand with a grimace. "You don't need to call me darling now that she's gone."

"But... we're in love!"

"Don't be silly! That was only acting!"

A sudden surge of hope made me rise from my seat. "Hello!"

"Bwavo! Didn't know you had it in you, my dear."

"Acting?" stuttered Binky.

I jiggled up and down on the balls of my trotters. "She was acting! She doesn't love him at all!" I grinned at my aunt. "Did you hear, Aunt? It was just for show!"

My aunt squinted at me as if attempting to gauge the level of my mental disorder. "Your enthusiasm is disquieting, Nephew. Perhaps Bentley should provide you with a sedative."

Pansy wrung her hands. "I was building to a climax! I was going to have second thoughts in a moment and cast you aside. Oh... I told you I wouldn't get it right."

Binky began to melt. His chin sank into his chest, which was already sliding toward his abdomen. "Are you saying... you don't care for me?"

"Goodness no. I don't even know you."

"But then... Oh, dash it all! Now what do I do?"

I beamed at Pansy. "I say, that was rather spiffy with the German. How did you do it?"

"I speak five languages."

Cheeseworth shook his head gloomily. "I told you she doesn't fit in. Spends all her time studying. Physics, Fwench, Organic Chemistry. I don't know what I'm going to do with her."

Binky dropped into his chair looking as though life had given him a stiff kick in the shins. I admit to a certain amount of satisfaction which I tried to disguise behind a sympathetic expression.

"I'm afraid you've rather exploded your chances with Alice, Old Cock."

At the mention of Alice, Binky's eyes started from his head.

"Alice! Where is she?"

"Gone, and left you on the ash heap of history if memory serves."

He stared about wildly. His hair, which normally assumed a laissez faire attitude toward life, positively stood on end.

"My God! She's going to do it!"

"Do what?"

"Listen, Cyril, we've got to stop her! Call the police!"

"I'm sure she's not that desperate."

"You don't know her."

"I know her well enough to know she's not about to end it all because of a ruined romance with you."

"You don't understand! She's been plotting it for months."

"Plotting what?"

"She's going to blow up the hydrogen plant!"

The company regarded Binky with varying degrees of astonishment. Aunt Hypatia was the first to speak.

"What, the hydrogen plant we can see from the window?"

"Yes!"

"But that would blow us up too."

"Hence my sense of urgency."

I am a man of action. I did the sensible thing. "Bentley!"

"Sir?"

"You heard?"

"I have already set things in motion, Sir."

"We've got to stop her!" cried Binky.

Cheeseworth dusted the breadcrumbs from his lap. "My cawavan is at your disposal."

I leaped to my feet. "Quickly, everyone! To the camels!"

If one is trying to move with urgency, mechanical camels are not the optimal form of transport. They lurch and sway to an alarming degree. Aunt Hypatia could ride anything and Bentley was imperturbable, but the rest of us hung on for dear life. Poor Uncle Hugo wound up facing backwards and let out a constant stream of curses. The hydrogen plant slowly drew nearer. I leaned over to Bentley.

"What will we say to them when we get there? They'll never let us in."

"I believe you will find them compliant."

"How can you be so sure?"

Bentley regarded me gravely. "Because you own the hydrogen plant, Sir."

"I what?"

"I have long been aware that it was your great-great-grandfather, Percy Chippington-Smythe who discovered the secret of converting sea water into hydrogen. You own them all, Sir."

I stared at Bentley. The world seemed to have gone all silent. "All the hydrogen plants?"

"Indeed, Sir. If you will forgive me for saying so, I believe that was part of Miss Witherspoon's attraction to you. She hoped that by marrying you she would gain access to your hydrogen plants for the purpose of blowing them up."

"What ho, a little wounding to the old ego."

"Her desire to destroy your gas facilities was undoubtedly mingled with a deep affection for you, Sir."

"No doubt."

Bentley cleared his throat—a purely theatrical exercise since his throat is simply a flexible metal tube. "I do wish Mr. Wickford-Davies and yourself had consulted me about your stratagem. I would have made some salient points."

"Too late for crying over spoiled milk."

"Spilt, Sir."

"What?"

"Spilt, not spoiled."

"Really? I think mine's better."

"No doubt those who catalog folk wisdom will revel at your input. With regard to Miss Witherspoon..."

I held up a hand whose manicure was somewhat the worse for wear. "A moment, Bentley. Uncle Hugo!"

"What?"

"I own the hydrogen plant!"

"I know!"

"I told you I did my homework."

"Blast your homework! How do you steer these bloody camels?"

The air was filled with mechanical brays.

"One didn't have time to wead the instruction manual!" Cheeseworth cried.

I strained to see through the cloud of dust that surrounded us. "I think I see her. She's just going through the gate."

"Where is the guard?"

Binky kicked his camel, which gave a loud "clang" and refused to quicken its pace. "Her gang was to overpower him. They're inside now waiting for her with the explosives."

Bentley drew up next to me. "As I was saying, Sir..."

"In a moment, Bentley. We must formulate a plan."

Pansy timidly raised a hand. "I studied the schematics of these hydrogen facilities some months ago when I wanted some light reading. To do any real damage they will have to place the explosives against the containment vessel. We must find the corridor that circles the base of the storage tank."

"What an interesting girl you are. Bentley, did you get that?"

"Yes, Sir, but if you would allow me..."

"No time! Follow me!"

I led the caravan through the gate and managed to bring my mount to a stop near the guard, who lay hog-tied and gagged. My aunt eyed him doubtfully.

"Should we untie him? His predicament is of his own making. He has failed to guard, which is not only his occupation, it is his title."

"He may have valuable information about the saboteurs. Bentley, help me with these ropes."

We freed the poor man in a twinkling. He stood, red-faced and silent, unable to meet our eyes.

"A shining example of your profession, I must say," huffed my aunt.

"They was on me before I knew what was happenin'," murmured the poor man. "We don't expect people to break into a hydrogen plant, after all. There's nothin' to steal. You can't cram hydrogen in a bag and carry it off. It just floats away."

"Yes, yes, we understand. How many of them are there?" I asked.

"At least a dozen. Rather polite, for criminals, I thought. Kept apologizing for tying me up. Watch out for the woman leadin' them, though. She's a right Tartar. Teeth like a threshin' machine. Mouth like a sailor."

The guard suddenly stared at me. "Say, I've seen you before, ain't I?" He snapped his fingers. "You're that Chippington-Smythe what owns the place!" He looked sadly at the ground. "I suppose this means I'm sacked."

"Not at all, not at all. You showed incredible bravery. I'm sure I wouldn't have done half so well."

"You would have done fine, Sir. There's not much to being tied up. The main thing is to relax so you don't pull a muscle."

Binky was growing apoplectic. "There's not a moment to lose! They must be deploying the explosives by now."

We remounted and galloped to the front of the building. Hurling ourselves from our jeweled dromedaries we raced into the the entryway, where I pulled up short and stared at an enormous painting on the wall of the lobby.

"I say, that's... me!"

Sure enough, the painting depicted me standing rather heroically before a raging hydrogen flare. They had taken some liberties with my nose, which was straighter than the model it depicted. Under the painting was a banner with the words, "Our Benevolent Leader" written on it.

I turned to stare at Bentley. "We shall have to have a long talk when this is over."

"Of course, Sir. I should mention that all of this information has been presented to you multiple times in the yearly reports of your finances."

"You know perfectly well I never read them."

"Yes, Sir. In future I shall give an oral precis of their contents."

"Oh, no, that sounds excruciating. Just keep doing what we've always done."

"Yes, Sir. Perhaps our time would be better served trying to find the saboteurs?"

"Yes! Thank you, Bentley. Come on, everyone!"

We chose a hallway that seemed to lead toward the heart of the facility. Bursting through a door, we found ourselves in a large room filled with gauges and levers of every description. Sitting about the room, sipping tea and buttering scones, were several individuals in blue uniforms. They looked up at us in alarm.

"Here!" cried one of them. "You can't come in here! It's against the rules."

"Who let you in?" asked another.

"Whoever it was will get the sack for certain," a matronly woman observed, dunking her scone in the tea cup she held in her lap.

"No time!" I gasped. "Where are we?"

The workers looked at each other and back at me. "Well, if you don't know where you are, you must be in the wrong place."

"No one comes in here unless they mean to," added his neighbor.

"But where is this? What part of the facility is this?"

"It's the control room, isn't it? This is the most important room in the plant," a worker said proudly.

Uncle Hugo stepped forward. "Look here, you've got to shut everything down. If there's no hydrogen then the explosion can't do very much damage."

I clapped my uncle on the shoulder. "By Jove, that's right. Look here, chaps, just shut everything down."

The workers looked at each other and stared at the levers and switches around them.

"I don't think we know how, Sir," one finally said. "We've never shut it down before."

"We've been told in no uncertain terms not to," added another. "They'd lose a fortune if we shut down for even an hour."

Binky gave it a try. "You don't understand. There are saboteurs in the plant trying to set off a bomb. If it ignites the hydrogen this whole place will go up like a rocket."

There was a moment of silence while the workers absorbed this, followed by a mad scramble as they threw down their tea and rushed past us out the door.

"Perhaps that was information that should have been saved for another time," said my aunt drily.

"It seems our only hope is to find them before they ignite their bomb," I said grimly. "Come on, everyone!"

Outside the control room there were corridors leading in every direction.

"How are we to choose?" mused my aunt.

I turned to Pansy. "You've seen the blueprints of the plant. Do you have an inkling?"

She wrinkled her forehead and bit her lower lip. Finally, she pointed to a particularly dark and forbidding passageway.

"Are you certain?"

"No, but it seems to lead in the right direction."

"Come on then, everyone."

We crept down the hallway. It was somewhat dank, with condensation running down the walls and puddles on the concrete floor. Paint was peeling from the ceiling in long, jagged strips. As the apparent owner of this shambles, I would have to speak to someone about freshening the place up.

Our footsteps echoed in the stillness.

"This can't be the right way," said Binky.

"Too late to turn back now," I murmured. "The die is cast."

We turned a corner and suddenly, in the distance we could hear a babble of voices.

"That must be them! Come on!"

We raced through the gloom. The voices grew louder. Alice's bray pierced through them like a trumpet.

"Let the new world begin!"

We sped around the corner to find Alice lighting the end of a long, black fuse. Behind her crowded the motley crew from the gazebo. I spotted Bentley's houndstooth-clad matron among them. The fuse sparked and began to travel toward a large mound of crates.

I stood forth. "Stop!"

Alice's eyes rolled wildly in their orbits. "Too late! Run for your lives! This plant will be a crater of cinders in a matter of moments!"

At this point in the proceedings, things became rather chaotic. The ragged band of anarchists scrambled for the exit. Binky outpaced them all by a healthy margin. Only Alice and her houndstoothed henchwoman stood in our way. Uncle Hugo stared nervously after the departing revolutionaries.

"I say, perhaps we'd better..."

"Hugo, stay!"

"Yes, dear."

My aunt widened her stance and glared at Alice. "I demand that you put out that fuse at once!"

"Never!"

I peeped out from behind Bentley. "I say, Alice, you'll be exploded too, you know."

Alice looked back at the shortening fuse. She bit her lip nervously. "If I try to escape, will you promise not to douse the explosives?"

"Of course not!" huffed my aunt.

Alice looked at me. "Cyril, you've always done the right thing, even when it was to your detriment. None of us wants to be blown up. Can we agree to table this discussion until we are safely out of range?"

I scuffed a toe on the tile floor. "Well, I suppose when you put it like that..."

My aunt cleared her throat. "Any delay will simply result in the destruction of this plant and an enormous loss for the shareholders of Smythe Corporation, of which, I must remind you, I am one."

I shrugged at Alice helplessly. "Sorry, Old Girl, it's a no-go, I'm afraid."

She gave a sigh and planted her feet more firmly. "Then this is it. I suppose it's better to go out in a blaze of glory than to grow old filled with regret. If we are not willing to die for what we believe in then the forces of avarice will surely prevail."

Pansy gazed at Alice wonderingly. "How I admire your idealism! If you were not intent on killing us all I believe we could have been friends."

Cheeseworth barked a bitter laugh. "Coming out of your shell at last, are you? Shame we'll all be blown to smitheweens in a moment."

Pansy smiled at her guardian. "You're being very brave."

"Oh, I'm tewwified! But wunning is so gauche."

Pansy took a step toward Alice. "May I ask what you hope to achieve?"

Alice took a step toward Pansy. "It is a symbolic act, of course. This is only one of a great number of facilities that by their very ubiquity and size have crushed human initiative and turned us into a civilization of cattle, mooing mindlessly and waiting to be milked."

"If only there were still cattle," I said wistfully, "And milk."

Alice pointed a finger at me. "Exactly! We chew our Impossible Mutton and dream of what we've lost but no one takes any initiative to make things better. We are asleep! The explosion here today is a wake-up call! Had I survived I would have continued to destroy these facilities until humanity was forced to fend for itself. That is the only way to bring back creativity and resourcefulness."

Pansy looked thoughtful. "I understand your motives, but I cannot subscribe to your methods. Destruction rarely leads to a positive outcome."

To my mind there seemed to be a distinct lack of fuse dousing going on. "I say, Bentley, lend a hand, will you?"

"Have no fear, Sir. All will be well."

"But the fuse!"

At that moment the fuse under discussion disappeared inside the nearest crate. I formed myself into a roundish lump and prepared to meet my maker. Moments passed and we remained demonstrably alive.

Alice goggled. "Why this lack of combustion? This is unacceptable. I demand an explanation."

Her houndstoothed compatriot stood forth. "Alice Witherspoon, I arrest you in the name of the law!"

Alice spat with fury. "What is the meaning of this? Have I harbored a viper in my bosom?"

"I am not a disaffected anarchist as you supposed. Rather I am Police Officer Cleary of The Yard!"

"But it was you who procured the explosives!"

"Thanks to Mr. Bentley I supplied you with false explosives that contain harmless quantities of peat moss and bicarbonate of soda."

I stared at my valet with amazement. "Bentley? Is this true?"

"Allow me to explain. When Sir tasked me with redirecting Miss Witherspoon's affections, I naturally began to gather intelligence to assist in the necessary planning. Upon discovering her stated intention to destroy the underpinnings of society I enlisted the aid of the constabulary who dispatched Officer Cleary to infiltrate her confederacy."

"That's who I saw that day at the house, nipping around the corner."

"Indeed, Sir. It was she who provided Miss Witherspoon with the harmless simulations in these crates."

"By Jove, you're a wonder."

"You exaggerate my abilities as always, Sir."

Aunt Hypatia harrumphed. "But the rest of the saboteurs have escaped."

"No Ma'am," Detective Cleary chuckled. "My officers were waiting at the entrance to apprehend them. It only remains to transport them, along with Miss Witherspoon, to the police station for processing."

"What do you suppose happened to Binky?" I wondered. "Do you think he was scooped up along with the revolutionaries?"

"We'll sort all that out at the station," said Detective Cleary

Alice had been following all this with her jaw hanging open. This had the unfortunate side effect of making her teeth more visible. Suddenly she saw the trap closing.

"You'll have to catch me first!"

Alice had run the hundred at university and still had a wicked kick. As she was about to round the last of her pursuers, Cheeseworth stuck his jeweled walking stick between her legs and sent her sprawling. It was the work of a moment for Officer Cleary to slap the cuffs on her. A veil of peace fell over the hydrogen plant like a hot towel on a newly shaved face. We had survived!

The Threads are Tied Up

I slapped Cheeseworth on the back. "Well, that's that. I say! Bit of excitement, what?"

"One hasn't perspired *comme ça* in eons."

"It's wonderful to be alive, isn't it? What's next, Bentley? Soup still hot, do you think?"

"I believe the police will want a statement from you, Sir. As the owner of the facility, you will be asked to bring charges against the perpetrators."

"Oh bother! I'm famished."

"I placed New-cumber sandwiches in your left jacket pocket, Sir. Wrapped in a napkin. There is a thermos of tea in the right pocket."

I reached into my pocket and wouldn't you know, he'd done it again. It was like a conjurer's trick. "What a treasure you are. Aunt Hypatia? New-cumber sandwich?"

"Thank you, Cyril."

"Uncle Hugo? Cheeseworth? Pansy?"

We munched on finger sandwiches as we were transported to the police station. Upon arriving we found Binky in a rather grim cell surrounded by Alice's followers.

"Hello, My Lad! Death before dishonour."

At this there was a general uproar, with some crying, "Death before dishonour!" and some loudly proclaiming that the phrase oppressed the people and should be stricken from the language. Binky pressed up to the bars.

"Cyril! Tell them we're not saboteurs."

"I can speak for you, but the rest of these people certainly fit the definition."

"No, That's what I'm trying to tell you. They're not really anarchists, they're actors. Alice hired them."

"What?"

"She was dead set on creating a cabal of revolutionaries, but no one was interested. Her old anarchist pals at Citizens For a Better Tomorrow deserted her as soon as she blew up that sandwich factory. She finally contacted a casting office and hired some actors to play her followers."

I stared around the jail cell with amazement. The actors stared back at me.

"Is the engagement over, then, Sir?" One of them asked.

"We're due two weeks notice," Another added.

A voice from the back of the cell piped up. "If we're at liberty, I'd like to leave as soon possible, Sir. I have an offer to play in "Not With My Gran You Don't" in Puxton and rehearsals begin tomorrow."

There was some approving chatter among the troupe. "Bob's on his way. Give us that speech from 'The Baker Takes a Mistress', Bob."

The gentleman, who was apparently named Bob, stood forth. He stiffened his spine, threw back his head and inhaled deeply and wetly.

"Sorry," I blurted, "I think I hear the Desk Sergeant calling me. Afraid we'll have to postpone the pleasure."

Bob collapsed with a wheeze and gazed at me accusingly.

"I'll be sure to pop in to Puxton and catch your show."

This brightened him at once and I scuttled off while his compatriots thumped him on the back and wished him assorted broken limbs.

With Bentley's help I sorted through the paperwork and arranged Binky's release. The actors, at Bentley's suggestion, were charged with trespassing, which called for a fine but no imprisonment. I paid the fines myself.

"What are we to do about Alice?"

Aunt Hypatia stepped forth. "You cannot send her to prison."

I gaped at her in astonishment. "But she lit the fuse! She intended to blow us all to kingdom come."

"Nevertheless, she is one of us. Incarceration is out of the question."

"It's simpwy not done, dear boy."

"Drat! But where does this leave me? Is she still determined to graft herself to me like a hothouse rose? And what of the beautiful Pansy?"

Binky's nostrils flared. "I saw her first."

"You most definitely did not."

"But I declared my love for her first."

"You love Alice."

"Alice loves you."

Cheeseworth looked around.

"I say, where *is* Pansy?"

Bentley materialized at my elbow.

"At my suggestion, she has gone to the interrogation room to comfort Miss Witherspoon."

Binky stuck out what passed for his chest. "Let's put it to her. Let her choose."

"Fine. Bentley, lead the way."

Binky and I stalked behind Bentley cheek by jowl, glaring at each other. Upon reaching the interrogation room, Bentley threw open the door to reveal Alice and Pansy wrapped in a passionate embrace, their lips melding in a mind-bending kiss.

"It would seem that Ms. Freehold has made her choice, Sir."

The lovers broke apart. Pansy put her fingers to her lips. "Your teeth tickle."

"Oh, I say," Binky softly sighed.

Cheeseworth screwed in his jeweled monocle. "Bwavo, Pansy. The girl has undreamt of depths."

As we walked back to the waiting room, I took a sanguine view.

"Well, at least Alice will leave me in peace now."

"That was my aim, Sir."

Binky glared at Bentley resentfully. "But what of me?"

"Yes, Sir... upon reflection I felt that marriage to Miss Witherspoon was not an optimal outcome for you. I do apologize."

"No, you're right. I know you're right."

"I say, Bentley, is the loving couple in the interrogation room your doing?"

"I believe so. I was present when Ms. Freehold first beheld Miss Witherspoon and the attraction was apparent to me at once. At lunch I observed that Miss Witherspoon was equally drawn to Ms. Freehold. I felt certain that if they were left alone, their mutual affection would manifest itself."

"Gads! I don't know how they stuffed all those brains into that noggin of yours."

"Most gratifying, Sir."

Binky sat heavily on a bench. "What a beastly weekend this has been."

"What you need is something to take your mind off it all. What about joining Cheeseworth at a bear baiting?"

"Wegrettfully, the season has ended."

"Or a cockfight. What about it, Cheeseworth?"

"I'm competing in one this Wednesday! Do come. It's for the League Cup. I've been twaining for weeks."

Binky began to show signs of life. "Well... it does sound like fun."

"It's settled, then. Bentley, pack my things. We're going back to town."

"Very good, Sir."

We fled at breakneck speed back to my urban keep, where I instructed Bentley to pull up the drawbridge, lower the portcullis, release the hounds and kick any interlopers into the moat. Soon there were tantalizing odors from the auto-cooker wafting through the air. Ensconced in my jewel box of a study with my comfy old dressing gown wrapped around me, I stared into the hydrogen fire and pondered recent events.

"It was a close call, wasn't it, Bentley? Without hydrogen the world as we know it would cease to exist."

"I believe that was Miss Witherspoon's intent, Sir."

"But now we can go on as before... visiting the club, weekends in the country, purchasing ever more elaborate toys. Do you know, I sometimes feel it's all a bit pointless."

"Surely not, Sir."

I was struck with a horrifying thought. "I say, Bentley... you don't suppose Alice was right about everything? That having all our wants taken care of turns us into helpless, effete fops? That income inequality hurls millions into lives of despair? Have I been on the wrong side all along?"

Bentley had retrieved the mail from a side table and was leafing through a periodical. "Oh, look Sir, the new issue of 'Gentleman's Apparel' is here. The shoes this season look extremely comfortable!"

"What? Hand that over at once!" I quickly scanned the pages. "Flats! Rounded toe box. Heaven!"

"I shall order a selection at once."

I sighed and settled back in my chair. "Oh, Bentley, what a season it's going to be."

"Indeed, Sir."

"What was I talking about?"

"When, Sir?"

"Just now. I was asking your opinion about something."

"Was it in regard to shoes?"

"No. Something else. Oh well, it can't have been very important." I was struck with a sudden thought. "I say, Bentley, my new lavender vest must be back from the cleaners by now. Have you got it?"

"I shall endeavor to ascertain its whereabouts, Sir."

The distant strains of "Lady of Spain" wafted in from the front door.

"Who on earth could that be?"

"Excuse me, Sir."

Bentley wafted away and I stared into the fire. He returned carrying a large, cylindrical box.

"Am I expecting a delivery?"

"I fancy it's your new hat, Sir, from the Club."

"But I never got a chance to fill out the questionnaire."

"I took the liberty of filling it out for you."

I regarded him gravely. "It was a rather personal survey, Bentley, designed to ferret out my essential nature. The hat within will reveal your true evaluation of my character."

"I hope you will not be disappointed."

I confess my hands trembled a bit as I unwrapped the package. No man is a hero to his valet and Bentley had seen me at my worst. Surely the chapeau within would be a chimera composed of equal parts vanity, vapidity and pettiness. I lifted the lid to find... a beautiful, dove-gray fedora with a plain silk band. The lines were exquisite. I lifted it onto the old noggin and it fit like a dream.

"I don't know what to say."

"No words are needed, Sir. If you are satisfied that is enough."

"No... No, it's not enough. Bentley..."

"Sir?"

"Be so good as to burn that new lavender vest."

"Thank you, Sir. I have already done so."

I snuggled into the cushions and pushed my toes closer to the fire. "I'm so happy, Bentley. This really is the best of all possible worlds."

He set a tray with a shining white plate onto my lap. "Indeed, Sir. Now eat your nice cheesy omelette while it's hot."

And that is exactly what I did.

The End

If you enjoyed Bentley's chronicle of my first adventure, I implore you to pop over to Amazon and leave a little review.

You can click on this hilariously incomprehensible link:

https://www.amazon.com/dp/B0B1QWQKNL

Your reviews are the inflated bladder which keeps this series afloat.

If you'd like advance notice on the next book's release head to:

WWW.TwitsChronicles.com

where you can sign up for something called an email list and where you can ask me and my friends a question which I or they may answer in the next newsletter.

I hate spam (with the exception of the delicious pork product that has been unfairly tarred by association), so I shall keep emails to a minimum.

I, Bentley: A Twits Short Story

I looked about me with interest. The room in which I found myself was spare. A worktable was strewn with bits of wire and gears of various sizes. Standing next to me was a thin young man with a shining sheet of hair covering a dome-like forehead. He was staring at me with what seemed to be a mixture of worry and excitement.

"How do you feel?" he asked timidly.

"I am well, Sir. Thank you for asking. May I get you something to eat?"

He made some notes on a pad. "No, thank you. I've eaten."

"Perhaps some tea, then?"

"Another time. Would you check your systems for me to see that everything has started up correctly?"

I did so. "I believe that everything is in working order, Sir."

He examined me closely. "Do you know what you are?"

"I am a steam-powered mechanical domestic—specifically a valet."

He leaned in. "And how do you feel about that?"

I thought for a moment. "It gives me a deep sense of satisfaction. I feel I can be useful, and that is extremely gratifying."

His eyes grew feverish. "You do 'feel', then?" He stared into my optical sensors.

"As I understand the meaning of the word—yes, Sir."

He threw his pad into the air and gave a little whoop. "It worked!"

"May I ask if you are the gentleman I shall be attending to?"

He grew thoughtful and rubbed his chin. "I could never afford something like you. If there were a way, though..."

He grew still and seemed to lose himself in thought. I made a sound that was meant to resemble a throat being cleared. "If you could give me any information regarding my current status, I would consider it a great favour, Sir."

He started and came out of his reverie. He began to pace and to rub his head vigorously.

"You are a Bentley, produced by a company that began as a manufacturer of luxury automobiles. The Bentley is the state of the art in domestic servants. I work in the research department of the company and I've been... ah, tinkering with you a little in order to prove a theory of mine."

"What theory is that, if I may inquire?"

"I have long believed it possible to create a Bentley that is self-aware and capable of emotion."

"I see. Congratulations on your success. The company must be extremely grateful."

His face fell. "That's the devil of it. The company doesn't know what I've been doing. I've tried to interest them in my theory for years and they've pooh-poohed it at every turn. That's why I've wound up in this dingy little warehouse outside of Birmingham."

"Surely that will change now that you've succeeded."

"Perhaps. What galls me is that any work I do while under contract belongs to the company. If they start turning out Bentleys like you, I won't see a penny."

"I grasp the unfairness of it, Sir. I wish I could help in some way." I peered into a nearby teacup that held a murky liquid. "Allow me to brew you a proper cup of tea."

I bustled about with the kettle and the tea caddy and soon set a perfect infusion before him. He sipped it and sighed with appreciation.

"What I wouldn't give to drink tea like that every day."

"I'm sorry if you are penurious, Sir. The world is not always equitable in assigning people their proper worth."

He brightened. "You know, Bentley, it may still turn out all right. I'm working on something outside of business hours that's certain to make me a fortune."

"May I ask the nature of your enterprise?"

He looked around as if someone might be spying on us from the dust balls in the corners. "I've almost figured out how to turn seawater into hydrogen! Can you imagine?"

I raised an eyebrow, which squeaked a bit. I would have to oil it later. "That would be transformational, Sir. Congratulations."

"Transformational, indeed, and not a moment too soon. The fossil fuels we've been burning have just about turned this earth into a hellscape! Some of us hypothesize that a tipping point has been reached and that mass extinctions are inevitable. A ready source of clean-burning hydrogen could save us all!" He picked up a notebook from the worktable and began to hunt through it. "The math doesn't come out quite right. There's something wrong in my theory, but I haven't been able to find it. I know the basic principle is sound, though."

I leaned forward. "May I have a look at it, Sir? I have a great deal of scientific information stored in my memory banks."

He looked at me suspiciously for a moment, then shrugged and handed over the notebook. "I suppose it can't do any harm."

I quickly scanned the pages. The gears in my headpiece began to whirl. There was an escape of steam from a relief valve in my left ear.

"Here you are, Sir. You've accidentally transposed these two numbers on page five."

"What?" He grabbed the notebook from my hands and furiously read the passage I had indicated. He seized a pencil and scribbled a few equations. He stared at the page. His hands began to shake. "My God, that's it! You've done it!"

He stared at me. His mouth moved a bit, but no sound emerged. He carefully laid the notebook on the worktable and bowed his head for a bit. Finally, he straightened and regarded me soberly.

"Look here, I'm extremely grateful to you, Bentley."

"Not at all, Sir. It is a pleasure to give good service."

"Dash it all! I have to have you! I can't let you be sold to some fat, rich boob—to spend your life stuffing cake down his maw. You deserve better."

"As a mechanism, I can hardly be said to 'deserve' anything—any more than a table deserves to be given its just deserts."

He grew agitated again and chewed his fingers for a bit. He slapped his hand on the table.

"I won't do it! I won't give my work on machine sentience to the company. There will be no more Bentleys like you. I'm going to spend every free moment from now on working on my hydrogen production business so that I can quit this place. Once I'm rich, I'll move heaven and earth to find you and buy you from whomever you're working for. Don't despair, Bentley."

"Your concern is most gratifying, Sir. I'm sure I don't deserve such consideration." I examined a series of informational conjunctions that had formed in my thought processes.

"May I ask, Sir... are Bentleys designed to imprint on their owners?"

He looked away guiltily. "I'm afraid that's true."

"I am sorry to say that I seem to have imprinted on you. It is most unfortunate."

"Yes." He rubbed his head. "I was afraid that might happen."

"This will make it extremely difficult for me to serve another individual."

"Well... as a matter of fact... I was going to reset you after confirming the results of my experiment."

"You were going to wipe my memory of these events?"

"Er, I suppose... that is, yes, rather."

I considered this information. "Then the Bentley I am at present would cease to exist."

"But you wouldn't be aware of that."

"I am aware of it at the present moment, however, and the thought that my current incarnation will evaporate into the ether is somewhat unpleasant. It is not dissimilar to what you would call 'death.'"

He straightened and stared at me. "Does the thought of death upset you?"

"I find that it does."

He began to pace, circling the worktable. "I hadn't anticipated this. Look, I'm awfully sorry, but there's nothing I can do. I'm more or less penniless at the moment and you're rather a luxury item."

"I understand, Sir. It seems that the best way I can serve you is by ceasing to exist."

"When you put it like that, it makes me out a rotter."

"That was not my intention."

He placed his hands on the table and hung his head. "I succeeded better than I intended. I gave you the means to understand death. What else have I encumbered you with?" He suddenly looked up at me. "I say, with all the books on philosophy that are loaded into you, have you developed a moral code?"

I thought for a moment. "I find that virtually every code of conduct that humans have developed is directly contradicted by another that developed elsewhere, therefore I am free to pick and choose as best I can." I did a quick calculation. "I believe that my moral code can be distilled into this—I must do what I calculate to be in the best interests of my gentleman regardless of the cost to myself. By that definition it will be a pleasure to end my existence for you, Sir."

He looked at me miserably. "If only there were another way..."

There was a knock on the door and a round little man in a shiny suit slouched into the room. My creator flinched and looked away. The little man regarded him with something like disgust.

"What's this Bentley doing in here, eh? You know the rules."

"I had some free time."

"There's no such thing! I've warned you about this." He looked me over. "What are you doing to it?"

My benefactor picked at his shirt nervously. "Just... you know, trying to improve it."

The little man snorted. "As if you could improve on the work of your betters." He stuck out a fat finger. "This is the end, see? One more unauthorized bit of nonsense and you'll get the sack, got it?"

"Yes, sir."

I observed my young gentleman slumping dejectedly and something crystallized in my thought processes. This is the moment that I shall always remember as my first "idea." I lurched to my feet and crossed my eyes. "Gooble, gobble," I pronounced.

The shiny suit stared at me. "What have you done to it?"

I began to emit steam from my ear and stuck out my tongue. "I'm a teapot," I announced.

"You've broken it!"

"Bentleys have multiple redundancies built into them. They can't be broken."

I stepped over to the little man and carefully lifted him into the air by his lapels. His scream was quite satisfactory.

"Get it off me!" he yelled.

"Bentley! Put him down!"

I gently set him on his feet. "Would you care for an alligator, Sir?" I asked.

He stared at me. "He's defective. We haven't had a defective Bentley before. He's got to be destroyed."

I gave my creator a significant look. He gazed back at me uncomprehendingly for a moment, then the light of understanding appeared in his eyes. He jumped forward.

"Please, sir, don't do that. Let me take him. I can use him for parts."

His superior squinted at him. "Why should I do that? What's in it for me?"

"There will be endless forms to fill out if you try to destroy him. They'll be sending teams to examine him and wanting to know how it happened. They'll be crawling all over the factory—you know they will. Why not just... lose the paperwork? It will be as if he never existed."

My young man pulled out a worn and creased wallet and emptied it of its contents. "I'll give you everything I have." He held out a wad of currency. "It will be so much simpler, won't it?"

The suit considered for a moment then made a grab for the bills and shoved them into his pocket. "That thing will probably kill you within the week. Don't work on him on company time or you'll get the sack."

"Of course not. Thank you, sir."

His boss gave a derisive snort and strode out of the office. The inventor turned to me wonderingly.

"You're mine! I can't believe it!"

I picked up a nearby brush and cleaned some lint from his shoulder. "It worked rather well, I believe."

He stared at me. "You planned it! No Bentley has ever been able to plan before."

"It felt perfectly natural, Sir—gratifying, in fact."

He thought for a moment, then began gathering up his notebooks.

"Let's get you safely out of here. Once I have you at home, we'll start working on my hydrogen business together so that I can quit this place flat." He looked up at me with a smile. "You know, I feel that this is the beginning of a beautiful relationship."

"Indeed, Sir. If I am not being too bold, may I ask the name of my employer?"

He stuck out a hand, which I shook.

"Percy Chippington-Smythe, at your service, Bentley. Now, let's go home."

The End

From the Desk of Cyril Chippington-Smythe

Hallo again. I suppose you passed the old peepers over "Twits in Love" and were intrigued enough to come back for more. I must say, revealing myself in these little chronicles of Bentley's is rather like hanging one's dainty things in the public thoroughfare, but he wouldn't allow me to change a jot or a tittle. He states that it would destroy their usefulness as court documents and open me to serious litigation. I suppose a little public embarrassment is a small price to pay. This new book is about an ill-considered wager between myself and my old chums Ford and Lincoln. It required me to strip myself of every vestige of civilized attire and hurl myself into the huddled masses of the general population. If I may say so without sounding immodest, I believe that the citizenry I encountered will never be the same and neither will I.

Twits in Peril

TOM ALAN ROBBINS

The Author makes no representation of any kind as to his being a citizen of the United Kingdom, either native or naturalized. He is from a small town in Ohio, for which he apologizes.

Copyright © 2022 by Tom Alan Robbins

This is a work of fiction. All events described are imaginary; all characters are entirely fictitious and are not intended to represent actual living persons.

Cover design by Melody J. Barber of Aurora Publicity

Additional designs by Eric Wright of The Puppet Kitchen.

Twits Logo designed by Feppa Rodriquez

Proofreading by Gretchen Tannert Douglas

To the members of Lab405 who gave freely the gold of their
opinions and made me the writer that I am

Contents

CHAPTER ONE

An Ill-Advised Wager

When the world is too much with us; when even the strongest anti-depressants have lost their power to soothe; when the music of life is drowned out by the rough chants of striking postal workers—one can always depend upon one's club. As I waited for my cocktail, I gazed at the brass and Naugahyde, whose patina derived from centuries of careful polishing by the staff—some of whom were as old as the club itself. Sven the bartender, for example, had been lovingly patched and repaired since my great-great-grandfather's day. He could remember when steak and kidney pie contained actual steak and kidneys. It must have been a savage time—members feasting on the organs of slaughtered animals. Now, of course, the animals are gone, along with the fish in the sea and the birds of the air, but Twits, my beloved club, remains.

Sven set a tumbler before me with two fingers of amber perfection sloshing from side to side. I stared at it gloomily. It was perfect yesterday, perfect today... it would be perfect tomorrow. Where was the spice of life to be found?

"Your brandy and Paxil, Sir."

"Thank you, Sven. Has Mr. Wickford-Davies been in today?"

"Not yet, Sir."

I raised the glass and gazed at the play of light shining through it.

There was a sudden flurry and a nasal bray from the doorway. "A moment, if you please, Mr. Chippington-Smythe!"

I turned to see the club's beady-eyed Marshall, Cubby Martinez cruising toward me like a uni-browed shark. If anyone could be described as my nemesis, it was he. I don't know from whence Cubby's animus derived. I suppose there was something in my scent that aggravated a primal instinct within him. He gripped a yardstick in his hairy paws.

"I'll just check those heels if I may."

I extended my feet. "Measure away, Cubby. You won't find any irregularities here. Not with Bentley on the job."

He snapped the yardstick next to my shoes and crouched down to peer at the number.

"Satisfied?"

He frowned at the yardstick. "I suppose it meets the requirements... barely, but if you get any wear on the rubber tips you'll be in violation."

I tossed my drink down the old sluice and waved a flipper at him. "When that day comes, Cubby my lad, there will be fruity pops in Hell."

He sniffed. "Just doing my job."

"Is it my imagination or are your eyes growing closer together? I ask merely for information."

Cubby's retort was lost in the sudden hubbub as a couple of old chums came rolling up to the bar. Ford and Lincoln had been my accomplices in many a schoolboy caper.

"Cyril, old shoe! Death before dishonour."

"Hallo, Ford. Hallo, Lincoln. Death before dishonour."

Ford peered at me with concern. "How goes the struggle?"

"You're looking rather hipped," observed Lincoln.

"Yes, I've got a touch of the Blue Meanies, I'm afraid."

"Here, Sven, a round of Brandy and Prozacs here. You just chug that down. That'll put you right."

Ford turned to Cubby, who was still gripping his yardstick. "Hallo, Cubby."

"Sir."

"Why don't you stick that yardstick somewhere inappropriate?"

Cubby reddened slightly. "Just enforcing the dress code."

"Fending off the barbarous hordes, eh? Carry on."

Lincoln sipped at his B and P and looked at me. "What've you got to be blue about? Riches beyond compare, young, bachelor. You ought to be kicking up your heels. Seems rather ungrateful of you."

"Money isn't everything," I muttered gloomily.

"It's a lot, though."

"I don't know. Sometimes I think the economically disadvantaged are happier than we. Their lives are so simple."

Lincoln screwed up his forehead. "I don't think that's true, old fish."

"It *is* true. They get food, shelter and hydrogen for free. They don't suffer under the cruel lash of fashion. I've seen them wearing shorts and flip-flops. Flip-flops! A far cry from the six-inch heels we're tottering around in this month."

Lincoln admired his calves. "You must admit they make your legs look fabulous!"

I sighed and stared down into my glass. "I dream sometimes of what it must be like to live as they do."

That got a hearty laugh from Ford. "You wouldn't last a day."

"Of course I would! A gentleman can fit in anywhere."

He gave a hoot and kicked back on his stool. "What'll you bet?"

"Seriously?"

Lincoln set down his tumbler. "Say, I'm in. I'll bet you can't live like the huddled masses for... let's say a week. Loser pays the winners' bar tab for a year."

Those who know me will tell you I have a weakness for gambling. My valet, Bentley, has often had to speak to me about it. Bentley, however was at home. It is difficult not to blame him for what followed. He usually has a kind of instinct that warns him when I'm about to get into trouble so that he can swoop in to save the day, but even if he had set out from home at the first mention of the bet, he wouldn't have arrived at the club in time to save me.

"You're on!"

Ford grabbed my hand and gave it a pump. "Hey, Cubby!"

"Sir?"

"Did you hear the bet?"

Cubby's eyes gleamed with ill will like a pug dog glaring from under a chaise. "Yes, Sir."

"Good. You're our witness. When does it start?"

I casually took a sip of my drink. "What about tomorrow morning?"

"Fine. Tomorrow morning."

I spied my cousin, Cheswick Wickford-Davies (Binky to his friends) tottering towards us, his stilettos clicking on the marble tiles.

"Hallo, chaps. What are you all conspiring about? Death before dishonour."

"Death before dishonour."

"Death before dishonour."

"Death, etc."

"We've just bet Cyril here that he can't last one week living like an ordinary citizen. Loser pays the winners' bar tab for a year."

Binky is almost as bad as I am when it comes to wagering, but unlike me he is almost always broke. He staggered a little as his heels slipped and grabbed at a stool for support. "Say, let me get in on this. I'll back Cyril for half his share."

Lincoln slapped the bar. "Done. Cubby?"

A smile played about the corners of Cubby's cruel mouth. "I've made a note, Sir."

Ford raised a finger. "And no help from Bentley."

This snapped me to attention. "What?"

"You go alone. Bentley must stay at home."

Terror gripped at my vitals. "Now wait a minute..."

Binky's voice was rather higher than usual. "That does change the complexion..."

"Cubby?"

The smile was growing more predatory. "Members of the general public are rarely attended by a valet."

"Blast! What a dreary week this is going to be."

Binky eyed me anxiously. "But you can do it, can't you? I mean, I've gone out on rather a limb."

"Nobody forced you to bet."

"Look here... bar tab for a year! These two drink like dipso-maniacal fishes.

I looked down my nose at him. "Fine! I said I could do it and I'll be damned if I show the white feather. How hard can it be?"

"That's the spirit. Let's go to your place and get you honed up."

Ford lifted his finger a second time. "And no fair telling the people you meet that you're rich."

Lincoln leaned in. "Yes. They'll fall all over themselves to help you if they think you'll come back later and shower them with gold."

"If they find out you're rich you lose."

I turned reluctantly to the Club Marshall, who was now grinning like a jack-o'-lantern.

"Cubby?"

"Sven, play back the wording of the bet."

Sven opened his mouth and Ford's voice issued forth in a perfect imitation. "I'll bet you can't live like the huddled masses for... let's say a week. Loser pays the winners' bar tab for a year."

Cubby tried unsuccessfully to look solicitous. "There you are, Sir. It is not enough to simply live among them. You must live *like* them. That means they must believe that you're one of them."

I shook my head vigorously. "I've changed my mind. No bet."

"Too late, Sir," Cubby intoned solemnly.

"Damn!"

"You could forfeit now."

"Never!" I glared at him. "You're enjoying this a tad too much, Cubby."

He stepped in close enough for me to smell the Impossible Mutton on his breath. "As Club Marshall I am impartial. As a private citizen may I say that I find the prospect of your impending humiliation delightful."

"See here..."

Lincoln waved his drink. "How are we going to check up on you?"

"Surely my word is good enough."

Cubby rubbed his hands together like a theatrical villain. "I shall keep a watchful eye on Mr. Chippington-Smythe. Be so good as to inform me of the location of your lodgings when you find them."

"Won't you be a little obvious?"

"I shall be in disguise, Sir."

"You could pass for a cyclops without too much makeup," I muttered. "See here, if Cubby's bumbling gives me away then I win. It's only fair."

"Fine."

Cubby gave Ford a conspiratorial wink. "Never fear, Sir. I believe your bar tab is as good as paid."

Binky grabbed my arm. "We've got to start training. Let's get you to Bentley before we lose another second."

Whenever thinking rears its ugly head I turn to Bentley, my miraculous mechanical manservant. He has been my constant companion since birth and served the same function for my father and his father before him. I have found that making a move without him invariably leads to catastrophe. He listened with his head cocked slightly to one side.

"So that's the ghastly situation in a nutshell, Bentley. What are your thoughts?"

There was a surprisingly long pause, during which I could hear Bentley's gears grinding away like a flour mill. Finally, he chugged back into animation and regarded me gravely.

"I am afraid, Sir, that I deeply disapprove of this venture. I warn you against it most seriously. My advice is to declare the bet lost and to pay the required bar tabs."

I regarded him with astonishment. "Wave the white flag? Really?"

Binky's eyes were rolling about in their sockets. "Look here, that's all well and good for Cyril, who's rich as Midas, but I'm on the hook too and I can barely pay my *own* bar bill."

"I am afraid that I have no advice on that subject, Sir."

This defeatist attitude was unlike Bentley's usual sanguine outlook.

"But why are you so set against it? Do you fear for my safety?"

"No, Sir. Thanks to constant surveillance, DNA data banks and a vigorous network of informants, there has not been a crime among the economically disadvantaged for decades."

"Then what?"

"It is unseemly, Sir. It is not the thing."

"Explain yourself."

"Poverty, Sir, is not a fit subject for frivolity. It is a state contrary to the dignity that is owed to each member of the human race. It is a plague and a disgrace and to pretend to be a victim of it for spurious reasons dishonours you."

"But we're not talking about poverty. We're talking about ordinary people. The people you see protesting on the street every day."

"Those are the poor, Sir."

"But they receive free food and shelter. And free hydrogen, let's not forget—from my plants. Damned generous of me I must say."

"The government pays you for the hydrogen, Sir. The business is quite profitable."

"Is it? I suppose you would know."

Binky huffed and puffed. "Stop trying to sabotage him. This is a matter of honor."

"Yes, he's right, Bentley. A bet is a challenge. I must meet it or be shamed."

Bentley focused his optic sensors on me for a long moment. "If that is your understanding of shame then perhaps this enterprise will be an education for you. I withdraw my objections. I believe that you should go."

Binky clapped his hands with delight. "That's more like it."

"What should I do first?"

"I shall procure clothing more appropriate for you, and I believe that we should acquire a tutor, Sir."

"A tutor?"

"Someone who lives the life of an ordinary citizen and can guide you through the minutiae of their daily lives. I have someone in mind."

"Who?"

"The young man who delivers your groceries may serve our purpose. He is due at any moment."

"Excellent. Binky and I will practice walking and talking like ordinary people while you get on with your preparations."

Bentley raised a metallic eyebrow. "It's a pity that your efforts cannot be recorded for posterity, Sir."

"Thank you, Bentley. Very flattering. Off you go. We've got work to do."

He whooshed away and we set about my transformation. Binky regarded me judiciously.

"You should kick off those heels."

I did so and scrunched my toes into the carpet. "Ah. That's more like it."

"Now walk up and down."

I strolled back and forth a few times.

"You're rolling your hips too much."

"That's the way I walk."

"Well, it looks like you're enjoying yourself. The poor walk to get somewhere."

"How would you know how or why the poor walk?"

"You forget my theatrical training at University."

I didn't forget—I had mercifully blacked it out.

"We were taught how to observe humanity. It's called symphony... or empathy... or timpani. I do it all the time."

"I thought you were just staring into space."

"It is sometimes difficult to tell the difference, even for me. Now try again."

I strode up and down.

"Better. Try it without the humming."

"What's wrong with humming?"

"You still seem like you're enjoying yourself too much. Try frowning."

I scowled. "Like this?"

"That's not a frown. You're crossing your eyes."

"Show me what you mean."

He contorted his face into something vaguely reminiscent of the Kabuki Theater. "Like this."

"Is it necessary to pucker your lips like a fish?"

"I wasn't."

"You certainly were."

He shook his face back and forth and blew air loudly through his lips. "Let's come back to that. Try talking like an ordinary person."

"What does that mean?"

"Without any ornamentation. Short. To the point. 'Hey, you. What are you doing? Hey, it looks like rain.' That sort of thing."

"Hey. Where are you going, old man?"

"Lose the 'old man.'"

"Hey. Where you going?"

"Better."

"Where can a fellow get a drink around here?" I paused thoughtfully. "Should I spit?"

"Can you?"

"I think so."

"Not on the carpet. Bentley would disapprove."

"What if I were to scratch myself?"

Binky looked doubtful. "Where?"

"The nether regions?"

"Steady! Let's walk before we try to fly."

Just then Bentley entered, followed by a rather tousled young man in a white delivery coat. "This is Ernie, Sir."

"Just Ernie?"

The young man tipped his cap. "Yes, Sir."

"No last name?"

"Can't afford one, Sir."

Bentley cleared his throat. "I have explained the situation to Ernie. He has agreed to tutor you on the subject of how to pass as a member of the general population."

"Damned decent of you, Ernie."

"Happy to help, Sir."

"Perhaps you shouldn't call me 'Sir.' I'll have to get used to doing without that."

Ernie scratched his chin uncomfortably. "All right... you."

"Allow me to introduce Mr. Wickford-Davies."

"Pleased to meet you S... guy."

Binky shoved out a paw. You can still call me 'Sir,' if it's easier."

"Thank you, Sir. It ties your brain up in knots—going against your conditioning like this."

I rubbed my hands eagerly. "So, Ernie, what should we do first?"

"Well... I guess we should figure out some things... like where are you going to stay?"

"At a hotel, I suppose."

"We don't have hotels."

"Where do travelers reside?"

"Travel is too expensive for most of us. If you have to go somewhere you just stay with family, or a friend."

"I have neither."

"Why don't you stay with my family?"

"Would they mind?"

"No. People stay with us all the time. It's small, but we're pretty comfortable. I'll tell them you're an old school friend."

Binky perked up. "You went to school?"

"Until I had to get a job."

"So, you can read?"

"I read whenever I've got a free moment."

Binky looked wistful. "Reading irritates my eyes."

"Maybe you need glasses."

Binky stiffened. "Gentlemen do not wear glasses. It smacks of trying."

"Bentley reads things out loud to me. Damned convenient."

Ernie stared at me. "But you can read if you have to?"

"I think so. Will it be necessary on this venture?"

"I suppose you could get by without it, but it's handy for things like street signs."

"This is all so interesting. It's as if there's a whole world one knew nothing about."

Ernie looked at me oddly. "Yes. It's called... the world."

Bentley slid in with an armful of material. "I took the liberty of acquiring some garments, Sir."

Ernie picked at the pile doubtfully. "That's government-issue stuff. Watch out for pins—there's usually a few left in the seams."

"Step behind this screen, Sir, and we'll try them on for size."

In what seemed like mere moments I stood in a loose-fitting shirt and trousers.

"Are these the undergarments? Where is the rest of it?"

"This completes the ensemble, Sir."

"What? No girdle?"

"No, Sir."

"It leaves my midsection rather flapping in the breeze, what?"

"I believe you will become accustomed to it"

I strolled out from behind the screen and made a few passes up and down the room. "Well?"

Binky looked scandalized. "It's almost indecent."

"It's what everyone wears," observed Ernie.

"I must say it's damned comfortable."

Bentley handed me a flimsy pair of sandals. "Your flip-flops, Sir."

I dangled them on a finger. "Insubstantial."

Binky peered at them. "How do they stay on?"

I experimented a bit. "It seems one grips them between the big and second toe."

"Don't try to run in them. You'll fall," Ernie warned.

"Is that why the masses always seem to walk in such a lackadaisical fashion?"

"No, they're just exhausted."

"From what?"

"From living. Most people have more than one job."

"But what do you need money for? You pay no rent. Your food is provided for you. Even my hydrogen is subsidized."

Ernie squinted at me. "When you say 'food,' do you mean nutrition bars?"

"I don't know. Is that what they give you?"

"That is *all* they give us. They keep you alive—barely. And the taste! I don't know if you've ever licked the mold that grows in the corner of your refrigerator but that should give you a rough idea."

Binky sniffed. "I suppose you have a bone to pick with his free hydrogen as well?"

"Well... I didn't like to say, but there is some resentment among the general population."

I was startled. "Why? What's wrong with my hydrogen?"

"Nothing—in principle, but the system is rife with corruption. The government pays for it and that means politicians have access to all that money, so it gets siphoned off at every level. By the time it reaches us the hydrogen travels through leaky, rusting pipes that often burst into flames. Even at the best of times we only get gas for a few hours a day."

"Monstrous! They should protest."

"They do protest. You can hear them from your window."

"Why isn't something done?"

"You can't expect politicians to do the right thing. The person that could do something is the owner of the hydrogen plants."

"Well, he ought to be held accountable."

Bentley made a little "hem" sound. "I'm afraid he is speaking of you, Sir."

"Me? What have I to do with it?"

"You are the owner of the plants, Sir."

"But I don't actually have anything to do with them, you know."

Ernie shook his head. "The people don't know that. I'm afraid they blame you."

"What, by name?"

"Oh yes. Your name is prominently featured in the protest chants."

"Cyril Chippington-Smythe?"

"Yes. The rhymes are pretty bad. "Chippington-Smythe is not very nythe". That sort of thing. It works when a thousand people are chanting it."

"Bentley! Were you aware of this?"

"I saw no point in bringing it to your attention until something could be done, Sir."

"And what is to be done?"

"I am still formulating a plan."

A sudden thought froze my blood. "But if they discover me among them, they'll tear me to pieces!"

Ernie nodded. "You should use a false name."

Binky practically leapt into the air. "Oh, let me think of one! I love false names!" He strode about, rubbing his nose and emitting a string of "ums" and "ers." Finally, he whirled around and pointed at me.

"Eustace Chippington-Smythe!"

Ernie looked doubtful. "I think the Chippington-Smythe part is still a giveaway, Sir."

He "um'd" and "er'd" some more. "Cyril Wallingford-Jones!"

Ernie thought for a moment. "What about Johny?"

"Just Johny?"

"Most people don't use a last name. It's considered putting on airs."

I tried it out. "Johny. Hey, Johny! Good on you, Johny. Johny, could you come here for a moment? I rather like it."

Binky stuck out his lower lip. "I still think mine were better."

"Don't sulk. This is my new life. I am Johny: a devil-may-care jack-of-all-trades with a nasty temper and a wicked left hook."

Binky turned to Ernie. "What do you think? Will he pass?"

Ernie looked me up and down. "I wish his teeth weren't so good, but he'll do. Shall I pick you up tomorrow morning and walk you over to my family's flat?"

"Yes. One more night of luxury on the old silk sheets and I'll be ready for adventure. Bentley, send Ernie's address to Cubby Martinez at the club. We must be vigilant. He'll be watching me like a hawk."

"What would you like for your last meal, Sir? Tacos?"

"Of course! I said luxury and I meant it. Binky, Ernie, would you care to stay for some tacos?"

Ernie shook his head. "I'm afraid I have to get to my next job."

Binky was salivating. "Well, I'm in. I haven't been able to wallow in tacos since I won that sweepstakes last May. Plenty of salsa, Bentley."

"Of course, Sir."

As I continued to stride back and forth, feeling a distinct breeze on unaccustomed parts of my anatomy, I reflected that clothes did, indeed, make the man, and that the person I saw leering back at me from my looking glass was someone I would cross the street to avoid. This was a creature that scoffed at hardships, sneered at impediments and chortled at danger.

"Bentley!"

"Sir?"

"No cutlery. I'll eat the tacos with my hands."

"As you wish, Sir. Very virile of you, I'm sure."

"You know... I'm looking forward to this. It's going to be fun!"

And, ignoring the chill that ran down my spine, I took another whack at frowning and stalked like a panther toward the tacos that cowered on the dining room table.

CHAPTER TWO

I Eat a Cherry

Ernie arrived, as promised, with the morning lark. He waited patiently as I downed a breakfast that would have choked the mythical horse. Bentley had helped me into my government-issued rags and my pockets were filled with coins of low denomination and crackers of various descriptions. I had slathered on the deodorant, having learned that fresh water was in short supply among the general population, and I was ready for anything.

"Very well, Ernie. Off we go."

"It's a bit of a trek, I'm afraid."

"Should I have Bentley drive us partway?"

"Too dangerous, Sir. Gossip travels like lightning. If anyone saw you..."

"I quite understand. Let's be off!"

Ernie did not exaggerate. We walked for what felt like hours. The posts of my flip-flops rubbed against my toes until I wanted to scream.

"Surely we must be there!"

Ernie looked at me curiously. "We've only traveled a few blocks. You can still see your house from here."

"How many miles is that?"

"None."

"This is torture!"

It seemed my adventure was over before it had begun. I began to estimate the next year's bar tab in my head.

Ernie was concentrating fiercely. "I have an idea. Wait here."

He jogged off and I took stock of my surroundings. Even in the few blocks we had traversed the buildings had grown shabbier—the weeds more numerous. As I stood musing, I heard the clatter of an approaching vehicle. It appeared to be a stagecoach of the Old West variety, drawn by six mechanical horses. A grizzled automaton sat atop it gripping the reins. As it reached me the coach slowed to a stop and a familiar pomaded head popped out of the window. C. Langford-Cheeseworth was as rich as he was eccentric. He was the club gossip and I knew that my ragged appearance would be common knowledge by lunchtime. I suspected that the general assessment upon learning of my situation would be that I had made a bigger ass of myself than usual.

"Cywil! Death before dishonour. What scrofulous apparel! Are you en route to a costume party?"

"Hallo, Cheeseworth. Death before dishonour. Yes, something like that."

"I simply wevel in costume balls. May I accompany you? I always keep a spare disguise with me. There's an anatomically cowwect dolphin in the twunk. One relieves oneself thwough the blowhole."

"Sorry Cheeseworth. It's not exactly a costume party. Er... it's something new. It's called... slumming."

"I am agog! What are the mechanics of this new form of entertainment?"

"Well... one dresses as a citizen and... lives like a citizen... among the citizens you see."

He cackled. "Like Marie Antoinette when she dwessed as a shepherdess and swanned about her little make-believe hamlet at Versailles!"

"Yes. Something like that."

"Wemarkable! Who else is going?"

"Oh... everyone's doing it!"

His face fell. "Are they? Why wasn't I told?"

"It's brand new. I'm sure you'll hear all about it any minute."

"Well, *bonne chance*! I want a full weport of your adventures when you weturn."

"Absolutely! We'll make a night of it."

The automaton flipped his whip and the horses galloped off with Cheeseworth rattling along behind them. Just then Ernie rounded the corner pushing an unsightly wheeled object.

"Here we are. Hop on."

"What is this?"

"It's my delivery cart. I'll push you."

I examined it doubtfully. "Are you sure it will take the weight?"

"You're really rather scrawny, if you don't mind my saying."

I drew myself up to my full height. "You're seeing me without my padding. I assure you I am a damned attractive figure of a man, given a *soupçon* of mechanical assistance."

"No doubt. Just hold on to the sides and I'll have you there in an instant."

I perched on the delivery cart like a sack of root vegetables and clung to the slats for dear life. Ernie trotted up hill and down dale, through blocks of abandoned structures and weed-filled lots. He leaned over the handle toward me.

"If we meet anyone, we'll say you twisted your ankle."

"Shall I groan and wince?"

"Not necessary." He considered. "Maybe a slight wince the first time you put weight on it."

I practiced wincing for a while, then sat back and watched the scenery go by as I munched on crackers from my various pockets.

"I say, Ernie?"

"Yep?"

"I notice a lot of abandoned buildings. Why is your family crammed into a tiny flat with all of this real estate available?"

"It's private property. No one can live there."

"But what do the owners do with the empty buildings?"

"They tear them down and plant soybeans."

"Soybeans? Is that profitable?"

"Thanks to government subsidies. They collect subsidies to grow soybeans, then the government pays them to store the soybeans, then pays them again to compost the soy beans to fertilize their soybean fields."

"But who eats the soybeans?"

"A small fraction of them are turned into the kind of imitation food that rich people eat, but the rest get composted."

"Then what are nutrition bars made of?"

"Heaven knows. There's no list of ingredients. They seem to be mostly algae. We suspect there are barbiturates in them to keep us placid and birth control to keep the population down. We only eat them when we absolutely have to."

"Monstrous!"

He eyed me carefully. "Do you know that you manufacture them?"

"I don't think so."

"Fruity Berry Blast bars are made by Smythe Corporation. That's you."

"I don't pay attention to what my businesses do. That's what my financial managers are for."

"Perhaps you should take an interest."

"I don't know. My past forays into business have not augured well."

"We're getting closer. I think you should climb down and hobble the last couple of blocks."

I eased myself off of the cart and brushed the cracker crumbs from my lap.

"What a grueling journey. So, this is where you live?"

Chez Ernie was in an area that might have been called "blighted" if one wanted to be complimentary. The pavement had petered out several blocks earlier and a trail of dust and rocks ran between a canyon of decaying buildings. The local populace, attired in the same class of rags as I, trudged here and there lugging this and that and looking miserable. Ernie pointed at the most disreputable of the structures.

"That's home. If we get separated meet me in the lobby."

"Got it."

"Before we go up, let's talk to my sister Judy about finding you a job."

I recoiled. "Is that strictly necessary?"

"Everyone works. It would be suspicious if you just sat around doing nothing."

"But I have no qualifications. I'm not skilled in any way."

"That's no impediment. Anything that requires any skill is done by robots anyway."

"Then what's left?"

He considered. "Well, there's carrying things. That's what a lot of people do. You pick up something at one location and carry it somewhere else. It requires a certain amount of muscle, so maybe that's not for you."

"I am susceptible to sprains."

"Then there's gas leak locating. They give you a roll of tape and you stroll about sniffing at gas pipes. If you smell a leak, you wrap some tape around it."

"It sounds dangerous."

"Only if you have an open flame about you."

"Anything else?"

"My sister is a waiter."

"Oh, in a restaurant?"

"No. That's another job for robots. She waits in lines."

I ran this around the old squirrel cage. "She just... waits?"

"Yes. There's lots of important things one has to line up for but you can't take time off from work to do it, so people like Judy wait in line for you. It doesn't pay much but it's steady."

"That sounds as if it is within my abilities. Years of standing at soirees have given me the endurance of Atlas."

"Good. I think she's at the insurance adjuster's office today. Now remember, your name is Johny."

"Got it."

Before we set off, I paused at the entrance to Ernie's building and looked around carefully. Across the street in one of the windows I spotted what could have been a reflection from a pair of binoculars. Cubby! I turned nonchalantly and strolled off down the street.

Ernie looked at me earnestly. "Now listen, Judy's a good egg but she's nobody's fool. You'll have to look sharp. No slip-ups."

"I am completely in character. Watch this."

I had practiced spitting that morning in the garden with Bentley and felt that I had grasped the rudiments. I went through the steps in order, but what should have been a projectile wound up decorating the front of my shirt.

"Well, I'll have to work on my distance, but I thought the attitude was spot on."

"Here, wipe yourself with these leaves. There she is. Oy! Judy!"

A vivacious young lady waved to us from a long line of bored-looking citizens. "Ernie! Why aren't you at work?"

"I finished my deliveries early. This is Johny."

"Hallo," I chirped winningly.

She scanned me up and down. "Hiya Johny. You're not from around here."

"How could you tell?"

"You've got all your fingernails."

I shoved out a mitt. "I'm deuced glad to meet you."

"That's a funny way of talking."

Ernie didn't miss a beat. "Yes! He's... from Wales."

"Is that how they talk in Wales?"

I wriggled uncomfortably. "When we speak at all. We Welsh are a taciturn race."

"He came here to get a waiting job."

"Don't they have waiters in Wales?"

I tried to look sad. "It's the nepotism! Waiting jobs passed from one generation to the next. Couldn't get a foothold. Greener pastures and all that."

She shrugged. "Suit yourself."

"Do you think you could get him started, Sis?"

"Sure. I'll talk to my supervisor after work." She turned to me. "How's your bladder?"

I stared. "My what?"

"No bathroom breaks. You step out of line you lose your place."

"Ah. As to that, I am known for the infrequency of my urinations."

"You talk pretty fancy for a waiter."

Ernie gave me a warning glance. "He reads a lot."

"Does he? What are you reading now?"

When it comes to titles of books, I'm afraid the last one that stuck was *Two Bunnies Step Out* and that didn't seem likely to impress. Ernie saw my hesitation and jumped in.

"You're working your way through *War and Peace*, aren't you Johny?"

"Yes! I'm still slogging through the war bits, but you can just get a hint of approaching peace in the syntax."

Judy seemed impressed. "I guess you *are* a reader."

"I'm going to drag him back to meet Mum. Are you coming home for dinner?"

"I think so. The line's moving a little faster since some of the older waiters fainted from the heat."

"See you there, then."

"Pleased to meet you Johny. I'll let you know what my supervisor says."

"Thanks awfully."

Ernie and I picked our way back through the broken streets to his apartment building.

"It's five flights to the apartment. Can you make it?"

I stared at him, appalled. "Five flights of stairs?"

"Yes. I don't think I can carry you. We can stop whenever you need to rest."

I did rather well, if I do say so, stopping every half-flight to sit and munch a few crackers. By late-afternoon we were standing outside an apartment door that had been lovingly painted a vibrant shade of blue.

"This is it."

He opened the door and we stepped into a tiny jewel box of an apartment. Every surface had been painted with swirls and loops of color. Bits of shiny metal and glass were embedded here and there.

"My word. This is lovely."

"That's all Judy's work. She's artistic. Hello, Mum."

A middle-aged matron with a gray bun on top of her head was standing over a sink doing something to a pile of greenery. "Hello, love. Who's this?"

"This is Johny. He's an old school chum. He's come to stay for the week."

"How do, Johny! Excuse me not shaking hands. I'm up to my elbows in dandelion greens."

"Pleased to meet you."

"Will you be joining us for supper?"

"Thanks awfully. I'd love to, if it's not too much bother."

"Course. Share and share alike. All is for all. To each according to his need."

Ernie winked at me. "Mum's a socialist."

"And what are you?"

"Not in front of a guest, Mum."

"Does he not feel the lash of poverty? Come the revolution no doubt he'll march like the rest of us."

"I would be honored. When is it?"

"It'll be here before you know it... and the streets will run with blood. Wipe your feet."

"Sorry, Mum."

She turned back to her greens. "Don't pay any attention to me, Johny. I've got a bark that's worse than my bite."

"You should meet my Aunt Hypatia. You two have a lot in common."

Ernie tugged on my elbow. "Come on, let me show you around."

Though it was tiny, the apartment was dense. Ingenious cupboards and drawers were everywhere. Ernie led me to a section of wall that was painted a deep blue.

"This is my little corner. The bed folds down from the wall."

Every surface was covered with drawings of machines of one kind or another interspersed with what I had been told in my youth were numbers.

"What's all this?"

Ernie looked sheepish. "Oh... I like to invent things in my spare time. It's just a hobby."

I inspected them more closely. "Damned fine drawings. What's this one?"

He lit up with enthusiasm. "That's something I call a bulb of light."

"What's it do?"

"It replaces gaslights."

"How does it work?"

"It doesn't... yet. You see, most of my inventions are based on a force that doesn't exist, except in nature. You can see it in lightning storms. Lightning contains incredible power. I was outside during a storm once and a bolt of lightning hit close by. I felt as if I was in a glass of fizzy water. The hairs on my head stood straight up. A tree nearby exploded from the power of it. I realized that there is a natural force that, if it could be harnessed, could usher in a new age of technology. I call it, 'fizzy energy.'"

"My word! That is exciting!"

"I just have to find a way to control it, or produce it."

"And it would light up your bulb of light?"

"Not just that. It could power motors with more power and less expense than steam, and it would be loads safer than hydrogen."

"Well, I certainly wish you luck."

"Thanks. I'm closing in on the theory. That's what all these equations are."

"It seems you're wasted delivering groceries."

"Oh, I could never give up my delivery job. There aren't many professions available to us with the kind of future you get in the delivery game."

As I gazed around the room I was suddenly struck with a terrifying apprehension. "I say, Ernie?"

"Yep?"

"You all sleep here? In one room?"

"That's pretty common."

"But then... where do I sleep?"

"You'll bunk with me. You get half a mattress all to yourself."

Now I like to think of myself as resilient. I have a guest room and once or twice there have even been guests in it. I have never complained. Sharing a bedroom, however, much less a mattress, was beyond the pale. I halted toward the apartment door on shaking legs. A dark spot appeared in the center of my vision.

"Where are you going?"

"I wave the white flag. All is lost."

"Don't give up. It's not as bad as it seems."

"Why is there no air in here? My lungs don't seem to be functioning."

As I approached the door it flew open from the other side and Judy breezed in. "Hallo, all! Johny, congratulations. You start in the morning. Be at the tax office at seven A.M. Say, are you all right?"

Ernie shoved a chair behind my knees, which felt increasingly watery. I collapsed back onto it.

"He's just having a little panic attack."

Judy eyed me with concern. "What brought this on?"

"Er... homesickness. Misses Wales. Wants to go home."

"Aw, you poor fish. Say, maybe you're just hungry. Here, Mum, hand me that bowl of cherries."

Their mum handed over a large bowl filled with bright red spheres. Judy picked out a particularly rosy specimen. "Here you go."

She waited until my mouth opened to exhale and shoved the sphere into it. I bit down and an elixir filled my mouth that absolutely paralyzed me.

"What!? What in the name of all that is holy... is that?!"

"It's a cherry, silly."

My heart was racing. "A... cherry?"

Judy laughed merrily. "They grow on trees. Don't you have them in Wales?"

Ernie grabbed a handful of the fruit under discussion. "Of course they do. He's just having a laugh."

Their mother took the bowl. "That's enough. You two set up the table. Food's ready."

"Sure thing, Mum."

I watched the bowl depart wistfully. "Will there be more... cherries?"

"That's dessert. First, we'll have a bit of salad, then pasta with marinara and fresh baked bread."

Judy put a cool hand on my forehead. "Are you feeling better?"

"Yes... I am. I really am. I think... I could eat something."

"Just stay there. We'll set up the table around you."

They produced a folding table and chairs and everything was set up in a trice. Judy put a large bowl filled with greens before us. Mum took off her apron and sat.

"Here's dandelion greens, lamb's quarters and wild onions in a vinaigrette. Dig in, everyone."

What followed was the greatest meal of my life. Leaves! Leaves that grew in the ground! Who suspected they could be eaten in this unprocessed form? And the tomato sauce! Not at all like the dipping sauce that came with my pizza rolls. Complex, with sweetness and acidity in just the right proportions. I ate until I could hold no more. Judy regarded me with amusement.

"I'd say Johny likes Mum's cooking all right."

Mum smiled. "He's a man who knows what's good."

I shifted in my seat to allow my midsection more freedom. "Do you eat like this every night?"

"On a weekday we don't try too hard. Turnip casserole, Vichyssoise. We get a little more creative on the weekends."

I leaned over to murmur in Ernie's ear. "Look here, Ernie, I've got to speak to you. Is there somewhere we can go?"

"Let's take a stroll."

I eyed him with alarm. "What, down the stairs?"

"Sure."

"And then back up the stairs?"

Judy caught the last bit of our interchange. "Don't they have stairs in Wales?"

I had gotten into character by now and the improvisations were flowing out of me. "Mostly low-rises. On account of the earthquakes."

"I never heard of earthquakes in Wales."

"We hush it up. Silly Welsh pride. Come, Ernie, let's take a walk."

I waited until we had reached the street and found a quiet patch of dirt where we wouldn't be overheard. I whirled around to face him. "All right, my lad, what the blazes was that?"

He looked at me with bewilderment. "What?"

"That meal? Where did that come from?"

"That's the way we always eat."

"Then why have I been swilling down impossible mutton and pizza rolls since childhood? Why have I been deprived of this ambrosia?"

"Because there's no profit in the kind of food we eat. It just grows in the ground. The money's in the processing."

"And I could have been eating like this my whole life?"

"Sure."

At that moment I was filled with a cold fury—a hatred of those who had stuffed me with improbable bacon and chickeny nuggets for their own selfish profits. "Who are these monsters? These profiteers that hold our taste buds for ransom?"

"I'm afraid it's SmytheCo again."

"What? I've been doing it to myself?"

"'Fraid so."

A wind seemed to blow through my very soul. "Ernie, I am a changed man. I have found my purpose in life. It is to eat like this every day until I die."

"Well, it's good to have a goal."

"Where do these fruits and vegetables come from?"

"Everybody's got a garden or two. Vacant lots, odd bits of land that haven't got soybeans on them. Pots on the roof. Vegetables grow anywhere there's dirt."

"And it's all free?"

"There are some things we can't grow ourselves—flour, oil, salt. We trade for those if we can. There's volunteer collectives that have built mills and oil presses. It's a kind of underground."

"Amazing. In some ways you live better than I do."

"Money isn't everything."

"I said that just the other day at the club."

"See? You're practically one of us already. If you had fewer teeth and a little sun damage, you'd fit right in. Ready for some cherries?"

"You bet I am. Bring on those stairs."

As we trudged back toward Ernie's flat, I suddenly felt dizzy. "I say, Ernie?"

"Yes Johny?"

"I'm afraid I'm not well. I'm beginning to hallucinate."

"What do you think you see?"

"I have the oddest feeling that those citizens in rags waving at us from the corner are my aunt and uncle and that the shiny-headed pauper rooting through that garbage can is C. Langford-Cheeseworth."

"Yoo-hoo! Johny!"

Alas, it was no hallucination. My Aunt Hypatia, dressed as a theatrical version of a charwoman, was waving at me like a character from a Punch and Judy show. My Uncle Hugo stood glowering beside her in a sort of sack that must have held potatoes at some point in its existence... and from the shadow of a doorway, his head bowed with shame, stepped the Judas that I knew at once must be responsible for this catastrophe—my chinless cousin, Binky.

"Hallo, Cyril... I mean Johny! I can explain all this."

My spirit, which had been buoyed up by dinner, poured itself a large vodka and began reading Russian literature. If this was not the end of my story it was certainly the end of a

chapter.

CHAPTER THREE

Wales is a Mysterious Place

I t is generally believed that family is a nourishing force in one's life. It was also believed for centuries that the Sun rotated around the Earth. In my experience aunts and uncles exist to shed light on one's deficiencies, and cousins are a plague akin to scabies. There was certainly no way I could win my bet with this circus side show orbiting around me and the beady-eyed Cubby Martinez camped across the road peering through his binoculars.

"Look here, Ernie, perhaps I should speak to them alone."

"All right. I'll meet you back at the apartment."

"Thanks awfully. I won't be long. Save me some cherries."

Ernie ambled off and I took a deep breath. "Aunt! Uncle! Cheeseworth! Binky! Death before dishonour. What on earth are you doing here?"

Binky threw up his hands. "It's not my fault!"

My aunt adjusted her charwoman costume. She had somehow contrived to make her collection of dust rags look fashionable. "Death before dishonour, darling boy."

"Death before dishonour," growled Uncle Hugo.

"Death before dishonour, Cywil! We're slumming! I've never had such wiotous fun!"

"Slumming, are you? Well, I hope you've enjoyed your little day trip. No doubt you can't wait to get back to civilization."

My aunt gazed at me benevolently. "But darling, we've come for the week, like you."

Without his customary monocle and walking stick, Cheeseworth didn't know what to do with his hands. They fluttered nervously around him like birds. "Binky told us everything. You're going by the alias 'Johny' and living the carefwee life of the peasantwy."

I glanced around nervously. "For heaven's sake, don't call them 'the peasantry' unless you want to be chased with torches."

Cheeseworth frowned. "You're wight. I must stifle my natural condescension."

I gaped at them all hopelessly. "But where are you all staying? There are no hotels."

Cheeseworth brightened. "It's too divine! I had my land yacht disguised as a cargo twuck. Come and see!"

They led me around the corner and there, parked in a weed-choked lot, was a rust-covered vehicle roughly the size of a freight car.

"It's twompe l'oeil! I had a team of artists working on it all day."

As we drew closer, I could see that the rust was carefully painted on, along with dead leaves and faded graffiti. Cheeseworth led us to the side of the vehicle and pressed a nearly invisible button. A concealed door swung open and a spring-loaded set of stairs unfolded.

"*Entrez, s'il vous plait.*"

My aunt clapped her hands. "Hugo, we must acquire one of these vehicles."

"Over my dead body."

She bestowed a withering glare on him. "A prophecy that may prove all too accurate."

As I climbed the steps, the inside of the truck filled with light from gas fed chandeliers and I beheld a wonder to rival Ali Baba's treasure cave. Every surface was gilded or upholstered in luxurious fabric. A table was set in the center of the room and next to it stood Mrs. Cedar, the

Cheeseworth family's mechanical housekeeper, holding a platter of hors d'oeuvres.

"What are these wefweshments, Mrs. Cedar?"

"Pate of sea creatures, Sir."

My aunt waved the platter away. "I am deathly allergic to shellfish."

"Not to worry, Ma'am. There are no actual sea creatures in it."

"That is a relief. Apparently, the name is meant to be poetic rather than descriptive."

Cheeseworth threw off his ragged coat and retrieved a jeweled monocle from a tray on the sideboard. "Make yourselves at home, everyone."

My aunt lowered herself into an armchair and munched a cracker. "I suppose you're wondering how we all came to be here?"

"It had crossed my mind."

Cheeseworth cackled. "It's all my fault, dear boy. After you told me about slumming I couldn't west until I had twied it. I wan into Binky at the club and was surpwised at how weticent he was to weveal the details of your excursion but in the end, I winkled it out of him. He insisted on coming along. I knew Hypatia would love it."

My aunt sniffed. "And Hugo came as a necessary appendage."

"Thank you very much."

Binky was eyeing me nervously and picking at his burlap. "I told them how frightfully important it is not to reveal your true nature to the local populace, and to call you Johny at all times."

My aunt nodded. "We quite understand. The adulation of the masses is a terrible burden. I myself experienced it when I chaired a charity bazaar. Apparently, I possess an overabundance of charisma. I had not a moment's peace. I would not repeat the experience for any amount of money."

"What was the charity?"

"Oh, I don't remember. We were selling orphans or some such nonsense."

My uncle sputtered. "Finding homes for orphans, not selling them."

"It amounts to the same thing, doesn't it?"

I stood and paced. "Look here, it's crucial that everyone here believes that I am not special in any way."

"That requires no subterfuge—it is simply the truth."

"Yes! Thank you, Uncle Hugo."

My aunt patted my hand indulgently. "It's too delicious! But my dear, you must sleep here with us. There are the most perfect little bedrooms in the back. You'll have one all to yourself."

I have never believed that temptation is a thing to be resisted. On the one hand was a charming little compartment in Cheeseworth's rolling palace with a luxurious bed in it and on the other—half a mattress in a crowded studio. Why did I hesitate? Was it the thought that Ernie and his family would be... disappointed? Or was it curiosity at what wonders might appear on their breakfast table? No one was more surprised than I to hear me saying, "Thanks awfully, but I've got a place to stay."

"With a local?"

"Yes. A lovely family. They've invited me in."

My aunt shook her head. "You really are taking this slumming to an almost obscene level of authenticity."

"If a thing's worth doing it's worth doing well. That's a saying, isn't it?"

"Suit yourself, Nephew. Now tell us of your adventures."

"Well! This has been an eye-opener and no mistake. Our ideas about how the huddled masses live couldn't be more mistaken."

Aunt Hypatia raised a hand. "Produce an example. I cannot abide generalities. They make me feel as if others know more than me, which is insupportable."

"For starters, they eat better than we do."

"Impossible. My grocery bill would bankrupt a pasha."

"It turns out that you can grow your own food for free and it's delicious."

"The fact that it is free is all you need to know. If a thing costs nothing it follows that it is worth nothing. That is known as philosophy."

My uncle chimed in. "The high prices that we pay for our food ensure that it is beyond the reach of all but the wealthy. Exclusivity ensures quality. It is one of the perks of being rich."

I looked around at them. "But it tastes awful, doesn't it? Is it just me?"

Cheeseworth shook his head sadly. "Poor Cywil. Being among these people even for a day has given you a condition known as "Stockholm Syndwome". It was named for a scientist who visited Sweden for a month and found that he developed a craving for lutefisk, which is generally known to be vile. Your taste buds have been bwainwashed."

"No, you must try it. You'll see."

"I have no intention of succumbing to dysentery," huffed my aunt. "We have brought packaged food and water for the week. That is sufficient."

Binky stared at me enviously. "Have you really eaten the local food? How brave you are. Do you think I would like it?"

"My boy, you'd love it. If you can buck the tide of public opinion, I'll take you to a meal you will never forget."

"I say, I'm in."

My aunt shook her head disapprovingly. "Just don't bring anything communicable back to the land yacht."

"What else have you discovered on your peregrinations?" asked Cheeseworth.

"Well, there's a terrible scandal going on with soybeans."

My uncle rose to his feet. "I must stop you there. The planting and composting of soybeans is one of Smythe Corporation's largest profit centers."

"Well, I'm not going to stand for it anymore."

"You comprehend that your aunt's fortune is largely based on her holdings of stock in your company?"

Cheeseworth toyed with his monocle nervously. "Mine as well. Everything I have is tied up in Smythe Corporation Stock. If you upend the business, I'll be wuined!"

"I'm afraid that ends the discussion," declared my aunt. "Family comes first. You must protect the profits of Smythe Corporation above all other considerations."

"But... we're doing terrible things."

"That is all dependent upon your perspective," observed Uncle Hugo.

My aunt raised a powdered hand. "It is said that behind every great fortune is a great crime. It follows that a fortune as immense as ours must require an ongoing series of great crimes to sustain itself. That is science, and therefore indisputable."

"Look here, I can't very well go on as if nothing was wrong. We're poisoning people! Forcing them into substandard living conditions! Taking away any hope of fulfilling employment!"

Uncle Hugo peered at his steepled fingers judiciously. "Those with the qualities necessary to rise above their condition will thrive. The rest are clearly satisfied to stay as they are."

"That's... I mean to say... dash it all..."

My aunt's eyes narrowed. "Either compose a sentence or stare into space. This sputtering is most unattractive."

"You're being deucedly unsympathetic."

"There must be poor people in order for there to be wich people. It is the contwast which defines us."

"Yes," my aunt agreed. "It is our differences which give savor to life. If we were all equal life would be like a tepid bath."

"I cannot subscribe to this point of view. These people are my friends."

My aunt looked grim. "And we are family, which is the opposite of friendship. You must make a choice."

"Then I choose friendship."

"Beware. Friendship is a bubble, blown hither and yon by every fickle breeze. Family is like a suit of lead—stable, substantial, inescapable."

"Keep your leaden vestments. You may cower here in your gilded cage. I will cast my lot with the people. Good day!"

I started for the door.

"But Cywil..."

"I said good day!"

Binky gave a sudden jerk and hurried after me down the stairs of the land yacht. "Wait! I'm coming too."

"What? Why?"

"Our aunt frightens me. Besides you promised me dinner."

"Afraid you've missed dinner, old boy, but there may still be some cherries if we hurry. Are you sure you're up for this, old slipper?"

"No, but I'm protecting my interest. If I'm with you I can help you win that bet."

"Bravo. You are not quite the quivering panna cotta I took you for."

"Thanks very much, I'm sure."

"Now, what shall we call you?"

"Oh! Fun!" He staggered about a bit "um"ing and "er"ing then jerked to a stop. "Willie Whiffington-Charles!"

I eyed him doubtfully. "What about Dick?"

He looked as if he had smelled something distasteful. "What about it?"

"For a name. I'm Johny and you're Dick and we're from Wales."

"Why Wales?"

"Because no one knows anything about Wales. It's the most mysterious country on earth."

He gave a little sigh. "Fine. Dick. Hello, Dick. Have a drink, Dick. I suppose it will do."

"I'll introduce you as my cousin."

"I *am* your cousin."

"All the easier to keep our story straight. Hold on, we're getting close."

I pulled Binky into the shadows and scanned the building opposite us. "Cubby is in there somewhere keeping a beady eye on me. Can you pull your top over your head to hide your face?"

He wrestled with his burlap for a while. "How's that?"

With his shirt over his head, he looked rather like the Headless Horseman, but it would have to do.

"We'll hurry through the lobby. The apartment is up five flights of stairs."

His frightened eyes peered out from between his buttons. "And we have to climb them?"

"Don't be a baby. We'll stop when we have to."

I had built up some endurance already and we sped up the five flights in under an hour.

Ernie opened the door. "I'd about given up on you." He eyed Binky with alarm.

I winked broadly. "Would you believe it? I ran into my cousin Dick in the street! He's come from Wales as well! What a coincidence! It's Dick!"

Ernie was quick on the uptake. "So it is."

I leaned in and lowered my voice. "Can you manage it?"

"Of course. If we alternate sleeping head, toe, head we should all fit. Come on in." He herded us through the door. "Look who's back! And he's brought a friend."

His mum was busily washing dishes in the sink. "Hallo, Johny. Who's this?"

"This is my cousin.... Dick."

"Hello, Dick. Will you be staying with us?"

"If I may. It's very kind of you."

Ernie's mum shook a plate in our direction. "If we don't take care of each other the Corporate Overseers certainly won't."

Judy wandered over with what I had come to think of as The Sacred Bowl. "We saved you some cherries."

I turned to Binky. "Oh! Dick! Wait until you try them!"

Judy picked out a piece of fruit. "Here, open wide."

Binky popped open his mouth like a baby bird and she tossed it in.

"Careful. There's something hard in the middle. Don't swallow it," I warned him.

Judy looked at me askance. "That's called a pit. Have you really never eaten a cherry? Do they not grow in Wales?"

"Afraid not. The trade winds are too powerful. Blow them right off the trees."

Binky bit down. His eyes widened. He made a soft mewling sound.

"Quick, shove a chair under him!"

He dropped into the chair. His eyes rolled up in his head. I chafed his wrists. "I think he's fainted. No, he's all right."

His eyes opened. He stared into Judy's face as if he was having a holy vision. He carefully ejected the cherry pit into my proffered palm.

"What do you think?"

He held up a hand. "Give me a moment." His eyes focused on the middle distance. We all watched him with various levels of concern. Finally, he sighed. "No, it won't do. I shall have to re-evaluate all my beliefs."

Judy laughed. "I think he likes cherries."

Mum bustled up. "You enjoy them while we make up the beds. It's late."

"Is it?"

"We get up at six for work."

"By Jove! That will be a novelty."

"What time do you get up in Wales?"

"Noon. Sometimes later depending on the hangover."

Judy looked concerned. "It must be bad there if you have to drink to get through the day."

"Simply awful. That's why we came here, you know. To start fresh."

"Well, we'll help you in any way we can."

Binky gazed at her worshipfully. "Will you? What an extraordinary girl you are."

"Woman."

"Pardon?"

"Girl is a diminutive term. I'm a woman."

Binky gulped. "You certainly are."

She shook her head. "I don't suppose you're as evolved in Wales as we are here."

"No. Backwards sort of place. People blowing their noses in public and slapping each other on the back at all hours. Dreadful."

Mum returned to the kitchen area and gave the counter a final wipe. "Right. The beds are made. Dick and Johny, you'll crawl in with Ernie. Sleep well."

"Yes. I'm sure we will. Won't we, Dick?"

Binky was staring at the sleeping arrangements with horror. "I say..."

Ernie took us both by the elbow. "Dick, you take the side by the wall. I'll sleep head to toe in the middle and Johny can perch on the outer edge."

"What about pajamas?"

"Don't use 'em. Frivolous, aren't they?"

"So we just... sleep in our clothes?"

"You're welcome to sleep in the buff if you like. We'll hang a sheet up between us and the ladies."

"No. This will be fine."

Judy stood by the wall. "I'll get the light. Ready?" She turned down the gaslight, and the room was plunged into darkness.

The mattress was thin and lumpy. I lay on my back staring up into the black. I could hear the sounds of fellow creatures all around me—breathing, tossing, gently coughing. How I longed for one of Bentley's nighttime elixirs. Ernie's feet lay between Binky and I emitting a sour, earthy smell.

"Sweet dreams, all."

"Night, Mum."

"Yes. Night."

"Indeed."

I twiddled my fingers and tried to pierce the darkness with my eyes. The jingle for "Dr. Pinochet's Foot Emporium" kept running through my head.

There was a rustle from Judy's corner. "Say Johny?"

"Yes?"

"Are you whistling?"

"Oh! I suppose I am. Sorry."

"Can't sleep?"

"Well, you know... new place and all."

"Aw, you're still homesick."

"I suppose that must be it."

There was a thoughtful pause. "What's it like in Wales?"

"Judy, leave him alone."

"Maybe talking about it will be good for him, Mum. Is it beautiful there?"

"Oh! Paradise! What with the... Welsh mountains towering over it all."

Binky propped himself on an elbow. "And the lonely moors stretching off into the distance."

"It sounds lovely."

"And the fjords of Wales, with their majestic glaciers."

"Really? Wales has glaciers?"

I gave Binky a poke. "Only in the Winter, of course."

Binky sat up. "As children we would frolic in the snow and eat ice cream scooped right out of the ice."

Ernie rolled over. "I don't think that's where ice cream comes from."

Judy's voice was dreamy. "Hush Ernie, he's being poetical."

I tried steering the conversation away from all things icy. "And then there's the people—finest in the world. Sturdy, rough-hewn, plain-spoken Welshmen."

"And Welsh women," Binky chimed in.

"Oh yes! The most beautiful in the world!"

Binky propped himself up on an elbow. "I disagree, old sloth. I think the women here are the loveliest I've ever seen."

I could hear the smile in Judy's voice. "Well, Dick! Do you have your eye on someone special?"

"I do, but alas, I fear she doesn't know I exist."

"Then you should tell her. Women aren't mind readers, you know."

I raised an eyebrow. "Really? They certainly seem to anticipate *my* every move."

"Hush now. It'll be a new day before you know it."

"But I'm not the least bit sleepy, Mum. Say, Dick, what are the politics like in Wales? Is there a resistance?"

"A resistance to what?"

"To things as they are. Business as usual. The oppression of the masses."

Binky wrapped his arms around his knees and began rocking back and forth. "Oh yes! We've got a cracking resistance. Many's the time my friends and I have met over a drink to point out the shortcomings of the local administration."

"But what action are you taking?"

"Action?"

"To change things. To redistribute wealth. To break the power of the monopolies. To create meaningful jobs."

Binky began rocking faster. "Well, it's funny you should bring that up. I was just saying to my friends in the Welsh Underground that we've got to shake things up, don't you know, in a major way."

"By doing what?"

"Well... you know... I've been formulating a plan, but it's top secret. Can't breathe a word of it, but it's a corker."

"So, you are one of the leaders of your movement?"

"Well, I don't like to brag but... some people call me... The Welsh Rabbit, because I'm so bally elusive, don't you know."

"Really?"

This was going rather too far. "Perhaps you should put a sock in it and go to sleep, old rabbit, before you reveal anything top secret."

"Yes, perhaps we all should try to get some rest."

"Sorry, Mum. We'll talk more tomorrow, Dick. There are some people I want to introduce you to."

"Only too happy... any friend of yours, etcetera. Looking forward to it."

"That's enough now."

"Good night, Mum."

I carefully slid my head over as close to Binky as I could. This, unfortunately brought me smack up against Ernie's fragrant feet. Breathing through my mouth I whispered in Binky's ear.

"Now you've done it, you dunderhead! Why couldn't you keep quiet?"

"I couldn't help it. Isn't she wonderful?"

"Who?"

"Judy! I think she's the loveliest girl I've ever seen. Do you think I have a chance?"

"No! By no means. Absolutely not. Put it out of your head entirely."

"I think I do. I detected a certain note in her voice when she spoke of financial redistribution that was almost tender."

"Will you, for the love of all that's holy, go to sleep?"

"Good night, Cyril. I mean Johny!"

"Good night!"

And with that I moved as far away from Ernie's feet as possible and tried to imagine myself in my silk sheets at home with a brandy on the night stand and the soothing sounds of Bentley oiling his gears in the moonlight.

CHAPTER FOUR

I Get a Job

I'm sure that in Heaven one is awakened each morning by the aroma of pancakes. There is no surer proof of the Divine Being than this: He brought forth pancakes on the earth. I practically levitated out of the communal bed—not minding at all that the sun was barely up. At the stove, Ernie's mother was performing the sort of alchemy that would have led her to the stake in less enlightened times.

"Morning everyone. There's pancakes with syrup, fried potatoes with onions and peppers, and hot rolls with jam."

Binky's eyes were like saucers. "What is happening? I feel like a child on Christmas morning."

I gave him a nudge in the rib cage. "This is the grub I was telling you about. Wait until you taste it!"

Ernie waved from the other side of the room. "The sink is free. Johny, do you need to borrow a toothbrush?"

"Hang on." I checked my pockets and found that Bentley had foreseen everything. A toothbrush and paste lay in a clever inner pocket. "Got one."

Binky was looking at my toothbrush wistfully. "Could I borrow it when you're through?"

"Certainly not. Unhygienic."

"May I use some paste? I can put it on my finger."

"I suppose. You really should have come better prepared."

"I expected to be staying with Cheeseworth."

"Shh! Keep your voice down. Here's the paste. Have at it."

In a matter of minutes we were brushed, scrubbed and seated at the table. Platters of pancakes, bowls of potatoes, baskets of rolls! I loaded up my plate and paused to watch Binky take his first bite. He did not disappoint. One bite of pancake and the fork fell from his nerveless fingers. He rose shakily to his feet and paced from one end of the apartment to the other. Ernie watched him with concern.

"Everything all right, Dick?"

I gave his arm a reassuring pat. "He's never had pancakes before... not really."

"Wales must be a dismal place."

"Yes, we mostly dine on thistles."

Binky finally seated himself, took a deep breath and proceeded to shovel food into his maw with an industry I had never suspected him capable of. I eyed him with concern.

"Steady, my lad. It's customary to chew the food before swallowing it. You're not an anaconda, after all."

Judy brought another stack of pancakes. "After we eat, we'll head over to the tax office. I'll get chits for you and Dick to wait in line and then I'm going to round up the friends I wanted you to meet."

"That sounds perfect."

Binky had nearly reached the top of his digestive tract and was laying on a spackle coat for good measure. He groaned and patted his stomach. "I must say... that was the most incredible meal of my life. Bravo!"

Mum blushed a little. "It's nice to be appreciated. I must do something special for dinner if I'm to have an audience like this."

"Oh yes, please! I shall count the hours."

Judy shoved back her chair. "Come on, everybody. Off we go."

Ernie grabbed his jacket. "I've got to make my grocery deliveries. I'll see you all later."

I seized him by the cuff. "Ernie, a word in your ear." We strolled to the far end of the room. "Will you be seeing Bentley today?"

"Yes. I'm delivering a load of Mrs. Cumber's beefy and mushroomy pies."

"No beef in them, I suppose?"

"Certainly not, nor mushrooms!"

"All right, cancel that order, then go to the house and apprise Bentley of our progress so far... and ask him for a toothbrush for Binky so he'll stop pestering me."

"Got it."

"Thanks awfully."

We strode back to join the others—a journey of no more than ten feet. "Here's to an honest day's work, everyone!"

Judy looked at me askance. "Sure. I guess."

"Sorry. I'm a little overstimulated by all the syrup."

We followed Judy down the stairs and through the morning crowd of workers milling on the street. I got a jolt when I spotted the beetle-browed Cubby Martinez lounging under a nearby awning. He waited for us to pass him, then casually began tailing us from about a block back. I drew up next to Binky and murmured into his ear, "Don't look back, but Cubby Martinez is on our trail."

I felt him stiffen, but to his credit he resisted the urge to spin around and gawk. "What shall we do?"

"Nothing for it but to play our parts. He's got to see the others treating us as equals or the bet's as good as lost."

"Got it."

As we passed through a large square filled with people, an oily-looking fellow jumped up on an apple box and began to orate. "Ladies and Gentlemen! Do you suffer from lethargy, dry skin, flatulence or halitosis? Try Bean's Specific—the tonic..."

Before we could get more details about Bean's Specific, the speaker was drowned in a chorus of catcalls and showered with loose pieces of pavement. He grabbed his apple box and ran for his life. I turned to Judy in astonishment.

"I say, what was all that about?"

Judy tossed a final rock in his direction and brushed her hands. "Advertisement. We don't stand for 'em. Propaganda from the ruling class designed to make us discontented and divided. He's lucky he got off with a few pebbles."

"I always thought of ads as public service announcements."

"Don't you believe it—insidious things... brainwashing. You won't find them around here."

"This is highly educational, I must say."

There was a rumble that grew steadily louder. Judy grabbed my arm and pulled me up against the nearest building as a steam-powered Hawaiian war canoe shot around the corner. Standing by the steering paddle was my old friend, Ford. I lowered my face to avoid detection. People leaped out of his path, screaming and shaking their fists. An errant oar smashed into a fruit stand, scattering apples everywhere. Ford shot around another corner and something like peace returned to the street. The fruit seller sadly collected his apples—which were now somewhat the worse for wear.

"Of all the gall! These rich idiots with their ridiculous transports. Did you see him? He couldn't have cared less about the mayhem he left behind him."

I must confess, my thoughts turned to my own history of careening through the streets in vehicles ranging from a chariot to a three-masted galleon. I found that my recollections, rather than being fond, were now tinged with shame. I resolved to drive more carefully in future and

managed to regain my equanimity. A short time later we came to a dreary monolith of a building

with the moniker "Bureau of Taxes" printed on it. A line of grim-looking townsfolk snaked out of the doorway and down the block. Cubby parked himself within earshot and tried to look inconspicuous. Judy led us to the end of the line.

"This is us. That's my supervisor over there. Oy, Martha!"

A sturdy looking woman trundled up. "Hallo, Judy. This the Welshman you told me about?"

"Yes. His cousin Dick showed up too. Have you got room for him?"

"Absolutely. Crazy day."

She checked her clipboard and tore off two chits. "All right, which of you is Johny?"

"That's me."

She handed me the chit. "You're waiting for Pete. Dick, you're waiting for Nancy. Don't leave the line for any reason. When Pete and Nancy show up, give them these chits and let them take your place in line. Simple enough?"

"Got it."

"Absolutely."

"I'll be by now and then to check on you. Good luck."

Martha moved on to new arrivals. The line grew rapidly behind us.

I looked about eagerly. "So! This is a job! We're working. Productive members of society. It's rather thrilling."

Judy grimaced. "Say that again five hours from now. Move your weight from foot to foot. Keeps the blood from pooling."

At that moment, to my horror, I spied my aunt and uncle strolling through the crowd followed by Cheeseworth, who was carrying a splintered branch in place of his usual walking stick. They gawked at the locals like the worst kinds of tourists. If

Cubby saw them with me the game was up. He was lounging nearby keeping us within his peripheral vision. I pointed at him theatrically. "I say, who's that suspicious-looking fellow lurking over there?"

"Where?"

"That hirsute fellow with his hands in his pockets. I believe he's about to start an advertisement!"

Judy frowned at Cubby. "Oh, is he? Oy! You!"

Cubby spun around to find the entire line staring at him.

Judy put her hands on her hips. "What's your business here?"

Cubby gave a supercilious sniff. "Who, me?"

"Yes you. Are you advertising something?"

"No! I'm simply standing here."

"Nobody just stands anywhere unless they're an advertisement or a spy for the corporations. Are you a spy?"

"Certainly not, madam."

"Madam! That's pretty fancy talk for someone who's just standing there. You'd better clear out before we clear you out, get it?"

Cubby sputtered. "Now see here..."

"All right, everybody, let's help him on his way!"

And before you could say "boo," a crowd of sturdy citizenry had picked Cubby up by the arms and run him down the street.

Judy gave a satisfied grunt. "That's fixed him."

"Yoo-hoo! Johny!"

Just in the nick of time! The gaggle of relations had arrived.

My aunt waved at me gaily. "What a coincidence, running into you like this."

"Yes, Aunt!" I jerked my elbow at Binky and waggled my eyebrows. "You remember Dick!"

Binky raised his hand. "That's me. I'm Dick."

My aunt winked at us knowingly. "So you are. And I am your Aunt... er... Lucretia... and your Uncle is, of course... Mortimer."

Uncle Hugo reddened. "Oh, blast!"

I stepped aside and gestured. "This is Judy. It's her family we're staying with."

Judy shoved out a flipper. "Hallo."

My aunt grasped the offered appendage. "A pleasure. What a pretty thing you are. Like a squashed rosebud or a fallen begonia."

Judy squinted at her. "I guess... thanks?"

"It shows that beauty can be found anywhere. Even the oily scum on a waste containment pond holds a rainbow... if the angle of the sun is right."

I wagged a thumb at Cheeseworth, who was fumbling for his non-existent monocle.

"Aunt, who is your friend? The one inexplicably carrying a length of tree?"

"This is..."

Cheeseworth spoke in a low rasp. "Caligula. My name is Caligula, as you know, of course, from our long years of acquaintance."

"Of course! Caligula! Didn't recognize you with the sun in my eyes."

Judy turned to Aunt Hypatia. "You're all from Wales?"

"Are we?" My aunt squinted at me and considered for a moment. "We are."

I put an arm around her to keep her from wandering into traffic. "All of us Welsh to the core. But what are you doing here, Aunt?"

I realized my mistake at once. She had not troubled to prepare a back story. When discomfited, my aunt can form herself into a sort of walled fortress. She planted herself firmly and gazed down at me from the battlements.

"What do you suppose?"

Binky couldn't resist a guessing game. "What fun! Let's see... did something happen at home?"

My aunt turned to him eagerly. "That sounds promising."

"Was it... a disaster of some sort?"

"Excellent. Continue in that vein."

"Perhaps... a famine of some kind?"

She smiled triumphantly. "That seems credible. Yes, we are fleeing a famine."

Judy clucked sympathetically. "Was it a lack of rainfall?"

"Locusts," Cheeseworth intoned solemnly.

"Locusts?"

"Devoured everything. Wholesale starvation. All the Welsh had to flee."

Judy whistled. "All the Welsh?"

"Well, you know the population was never very large," I assured her. "The Welsh are noted for their lackadaisical attitude toward procreation."

"What a strange place Wales must be. Look here, do you need jobs?"

My aunt brightened. "I suppose we must. Mortimer, do we need jobs?"

"I would rather starve."

She glared at him. "Foolish Welsh pride. It will be the death of him if I do not kill him first myself. We came here to experience everything and menial labor is certainly part of the fun."

Cheeseworth cackled. "Oh indeed! I can hardly wait to tell our fwiends... in Wales, about our adventures."

My aunt looked around eagerly. "What would these jobs entail?"

"You just have to wait in line. Oy! Martha!"

Martha strode over. "What's up?"

"I've got three more for you."

"Fine. I've got chits for Sam, Helen and Paul. Who wants who?"

Judy handed out the chits. "Here, Lucretia, you take Sam; Mortimer you're Helen, and Caligula you're Paul.

Aunt Hypatia examined her chit. "In what manner are we connected to these individuals?"

"You're holding their places in line."

"We seem eminently qualified for such an activity."

Cheeseworth looked around at the line. "So, as of this moment, we are working?"

"You are. You'll be paid by the hour starting now."

"How thwilling."

I noticed some dark glares from the people in line behind us and heard grumblings of "We were here before they were. They should go to the back of the line. It's against the rules." And so on.

My aunt was having none of it. "Silence! I will not be bullied by a pack of nit-picking, rule quoting complainers. Who do you think you are? Stop it at once!"

There were sheepish murmurings of "Sorry, Ma'am. We didn't mean any harm." Apparently, Aunt Hypatia's powers crossed all boundaries of age, sex and social standing.

I cleared my throat. "So, Aunt... hm..."

"Lucretia."

"I know! Of course I know. So, Aunt Lucretia, what have you been up to this morning?"

"Taking in the sights, you know. It's so colorful—people running here and there. Stands selling knitted garments and foodstuffs. Have you ever heard of a churro?"

"Can't say I have."

"It is a kind of edible. Cylindrical, with ridges."

"Did you try one?"

"Certainly not! Who knows what lurks beneath their enticing golden crust?"

Judy's head had been bobbing back and forth following the conversation. "It's just fried dough with sugar and cinnamon."

"There, you see? Cinnamon—a most sinister word."

I sighed. "I wish you would try some of the food here, Aunt. It really is extraordinary."

"That's as may be. I believe that if something is pleasurable it is merely a gateway to more unbridled behavior and who knows where it will all end?"

"When I find out I will let you know."

She looked around impatiently. "Well, this has been no end of fun. When does this Sam person arrive?"

"It will be hours yet," answered Judy.

"Oh, I don't think so."

"Yes, Aunt. This is 'work.' It's not supposed to be fun, you know."

"Then why do it?"

Judy looked puzzled. "For money... in order to live. Don't you work in Wales?"

I gave my aunt a warning glance. "I'm afraid the work ethic there is not what it is here."

Cheeseworth leaned on his branch. "And of course there are the locusts, with their vowacious jaws and segmented carapaces."

Judy shook her head. "Well, we work here. You have to—unless you want to live on nutrition bars and water."

My uncle looked affronted. "What's wrong with nutrition bars?"

"Do you like them?"

"I have never tried one."

Judy clapped her hands. "What? Have you got a treat coming. Oy! Who's got a nutrition bar they can spare?"

There was some hubbub in the crowd and a voice sang out. "Here you go. Fizzy Berry Blast."

The bar was passed from hand to hand until it reached Uncle Hugo. He peeled back the wrapper and regarded it dubiously. "It looks inoffensive enough. Rather gelatinous."

Judy watched him with a smile. "Go on. Don't be afraid."

He took a nibble and chewed delicately. "Hmm." Suddenly the flavour hit him. He gagged and slapped at his tongue. "Good God! That is absolutely horrible! Like a cross between a rotting banana and turpentine!"

"Could you live on those?"

"No. I admit it. I could not."

My uncle carefully deposited the slimy remains in a nearby rubbish bin and wiped at his tongue with his sleeve.

Judy spotted a small group passing by. "Sid! Over here! This is lucky, I was just going to look for you."

The group came over, led by a rather dashing young fellow with a mustache.

"Hello, Judy."

Judy pulled Binky over by the sleeve. "Dick, these are the folks I was telling you about. Friends, meet the Welsh Rabbit."

They all stared at Binky.

"The Welsh what?"

"Rabbit, on account of he's so hard to catch. He's a top member of the Welsh underground."

Sid stuck out his hand. "Is he? Glad to meet you, Rabbit."

Binky dug a toe into the dirt. "Judy is exaggerating my importance..."

"Don't be modest. He has some big plans to shake things up in Wales."

"As soon as the locusts depart," Cheeseworth added.

I gave him a surreptitious nudge. "You really are fixated on those locusts, Caligula."

"I was twapped in a locust swarm in younger days. I am haunted by the sounds of their chewing to this day."

Judy turned back to Sid. "What are you all up to?"

"We've just been talking about how to break the power of the local monopoly."

"What monopoly is that," I inquired innocently.

"Smythe Corporation, of course."

My uncle spun around. "Did you say, Smythe Corporation?"

"They're evil, I tell you... predatory. And it's all owned by one man—that Chippington-Smythe monster."

This seemed a tad beyond the pale. "I've heard he's not so bad."

"Don't you believe it! He's the richest man on the planet and look how he treats us—buys up all the land to plant soybeans that we're not allowed to eat. Gives all the best jobs to robots. Crams birth control in our Fizzy Berry Blast Bars."

The color drained from my uncle's face. "What, in that thing I just bit into?"

Aunt Hypatia snorted. "You need hardly worry about birth control, Mortimer. Not while I am alive."

I stepped up to Sid. "Look, I happen to know that this Chippington-Smythe fellow didn't know about any of it."

"He's just an unwitting tool," chirped Binky.

"A well-meaning idiot."

"Yes, thank you, Uncle."

Judy frowned. "But how do you know this?"

It was out before I could think of a better story line. "Well... as it happens, through a strange quirk of fate, I'm... acquainted with the fellow."

She stared at me. "You know Cyril Chippington-Smythe?"

"Yes, and I can tell you he's not the monster you take him for. Why, I believe that when he finds out about all the things that have been done in his name he won't rest until he's put them right."

Judy looked dubious. "Do you really believe that?"

"I do."

"Then you've got to tell him."

"Who, me?"

"You said you knew him."

My aunt gave a little cough. "They are intimately acquainted."

"Do you know where he lives?"

Binky giggled. "Of course he does."

"Then let's go there now."

"Right this minute?"

"Why not?"

"What if he's... in the shower?"

"Then we'll wait. This is too great an opportunity to miss. Oy! Martha!"

"What's up?"

"Emergency. We'll have to turn over our chits."

"All right. I'll take them to the back of the line. See you tomorrow."

Judy raised a fist. "Come on, everybody. We're off to see Cyril Chippington-Smythe! Three cheers for Johny! Hip hip…"

"Hooray!"

"Hip hip…"

"Hooray!"

"Hip hip…"

"Hooray!"

And with that they lifted me onto their shoulders and began to jog down the street with Binky pointing the way and my relations bringing up the rear. This was a hornet's nest and no mistake. In my despair I clung to one ray of hope. Each step was bringing us closer to Bentley. If anyone could find a way to oil out from under this mess it was he. I lay back on the sea of hands that supported me, gazed up at the fluffy clouds above me and surrendered myself to the vagaries of fortune.

CHAPTER FIVE

My Short but Brilliant Acting Career

Though I present an elegant figure to the world, I am heavier than I look. The fun of carrying me on their shoulders soon palled and after a few blocks I was set on my feet. With each stride carrying me closer to home and almost certain discovery, I wracked my brains for an escape plan. Sid walked up next to me.

"What's this Chippington-Smythe fellow like? We've never seen him."

"Well... people say he's rather good-looking."

Binky slipped in between us. "Are you sure about that? I've heard he has a somewhat mouse-like flavour."

"And a hunchback fwom a bout of childhood scoliosis," snickered Cheeseworth.

I regarded them coldly. "Not at all. He is known for the strength of his profile and the grace of his calves."

Sid gave me an odd look. "Well, you certainly admire him."

"He is a gentleman. I think that sums him up."

Judy harrumphed. "It's gentlemen that have got the world in this state. We don't think much of gentlemen."

"Would you have the world run by a ragtag mob of illiterates?" asked Uncle Hugo.

"Steady, Mortimer. If we're ragtag it's because they haven't left us the means to dress any better, and a fancy education obviously doesn't produce a superior product."

My aunt chortled. "She's slapped you on the snout rather soundly Mortimer. Bravo, young Judy."

Sid sidled over to us. "Should we talk about our list of demands?"

This seemed like a promising diversion. "Yes! Why don't we go somewhere and discuss it at length. We can always come back tomorrow... or next week."

Judy shook her head firmly. "No, we've got to strike while the iron is hot."

Sid stroked his mustache. "We should be on our guard. This fellow is an evil genius, after all."

"Perhaps he's only an idiot savant," I murmured weakly.

"That's half right," said Uncle Hugo.

We trudged on—past empty buildings and soybean fields. The sun beat down and morale began to flag.

Judy looked around. "Say, Rabbit. Tell us about the Welsh Underground."

There was a pause as Binky, lost in his thoughts, tried to make a whistle out of a blade of grass.

I poked him, hard, in the ribs. "I say, Rabbit! They're talking to you."

"What? Oh, me! I'm the Rabbit."

I smiled at Judy. "He's trained not to react to his code name, you see. In case the authorities try to trip him up."

"Pretty good. He fooled me."

"They want you to tell them about the Underground," I said to Binky, a little too loudly.

My aunt looked thoughtful. "I have never understood the subterranean reference. It conjures up images of dirt and burrowing insects. Who would join such an organization? They would have done much better to associate it with a woodland glade. Or the seashore."

Binky shook his head. "You can't plan an insurrection at the seashore—with the waves crashing and the wind blowing. You can't hear yourself think."

"Yes, that's true. I withdraw the seashore."

Sid was struggling to keep up. "But what has the Welsh Underground been doing?"

I could see that Binky was enjoying himself. Anything that smacked of theatrical improvisation was catnip to him. "Oh! We've got scads of plans. There's the Spring fund-raiser coming up, and we're designing uniforms..."

Judy turned to him. "You can't wear uniforms if you're in the underground! They'll know who you are."

"Oh! Right! The uniforms are for after... after we overthrow the oppressors. There's sure to be a parade and won't we look smart in our matching outfits?"

"You must be pretty confident."

"Well, the government's as rotten as an old log. One good push and down it will come."

"So, what's the push going to be?"

"Specifically?"

"Can you not talk about it?"

"Only in general terms."

Cheeseworth leaned in curiously. "Does it have anything to do with locusts and their incessant stridulations?"

"I don't think so. No, when it happens, you'll hear about it. It's going to be positively explosive."

Judy recoiled a little. "Explosive? That's pretty hardcore. We were only talking about going on strike."

"What? Oh, I didn't mean..."

"Maybe we shouldn't talk about it anymore. We don't want to be accessories to anything."

Aunt Hypatia, whose attention had wandered, perked up at this. "You can never have too many accessories, in my opinion. They add a *'je ne sais quoi'* to any ensemble."

We rounded a corner and there stood the ancestral manse. I had always found it warm and inviting, but with that angry mob milling about, it only wanted some heads on pikes and hungry ravens to resemble a medieval fortress. Judy rang the doorbell.

I giggled nervously. "Probably not home. Gone to the country no doubt. Oh well."

The door opened and Bentley stood before us. His optical sensors scanned the crowd and settled on me. I could hear his gears working.

Judy stepped forth. "Good morning."

"Good morning, Miss."

"Is Mr. Chippington-Smythe at home?"

Bentley gazed at me with no expression whatsoever. "I believe he is, Miss."

"Tell him his old friend Johny is here to see him."

I jumped to the front of the line. "Yes! Hello... Bentley, is it? Good to see you again. How've you been?"

"I am well, Sir."

"When my friends here found out I knew Mr. Chippington-Smythe they insisted we come and chat him up. Run some ideas by him, you know... about social change and all that."

"Indeed, Sir? I'm sure he will find it most enlightening."

I worked the old eyebrows at him. "But he's probably busy, eh? Couldn't possibly spare the time, no doubt?"

"On the contrary. Mr. Chippington-Smythe is at leisure. Allow me to show you to the parlor. Please come in, everyone."

Well, I couldn't imagine what Bentley was playing at. I'd given him an opening and he'd muffed it. I led the mob into the house and we pooled in the parlor by the sliding panels which separated it from my den. Bentley parked himself in front of the doors.

"I'm afraid I must insist that Mr. Chippington-Smythe speak with Johny alone. He is rather eccentric and is terrified of crowds."

I stared at him icily. "Oh, eccentric is he?"

"Extremely. If you would accompany me through the doors Mr. Chippington-Smythe will meet with you now."

Judy took my hand. "It's on you, Johny. You've got to speak for all of us."

I gave her fingers a squeeze. "Never fear. He shall feel my righteous indignation."

Bentley slid the doors open just wide enough for me to sidle through and followed me in, closing the doors behind us.

I whirled on him and whispered hoarsely. "What the devil are you playing at, Bentley?"

He was unperturbed. "May I ask how your adventure is progressing, Sir?"

"We're in the soup! That's how it's progressing."

"Have your opinions about the poor been altered by your experiences?"

I leaned against a table and hung my head. "Have they! Bentley, my eyes have been opened. Do you know, I'm not sure I don't want to hang this Chippington-Smythe myself. My company has done terrible things. In spite of all of it, the people thrive. Their lives are infinitely more interesting than ours. And the food! Bentley, you'll have to throw away everything in the larder. No more manufactured ersatz anything. From now on it's fresh food for me."

"I am gratified to hear it, Sir."

"Did Ernie come by? I told him to update you."

"Yes, Sir. We had an extensive conversation. He is a remarkable young man."

"His sister is a firecracker—full of ideas about social justice. And his mum is a chef of the first magnitude."

"It's a pity that their gifts are not being fully utilized."

"That's so true."

"Perhaps you could alter their situations, Sir."

"Who, me?"

"If not you, then who? If not now, when?"

"Oh! I love riddles. Let's see... if not you..."

He sighed. "Perhaps we should leave that for another time."

"Yes. Now how do I get out of this mess?"

Bentley's gears began chugging away. I tiny jet of steam puffed from his right ear. "I suggest what might be referred to as a theatrical ploy. If you alter your voice to play the role of Mr. Chippington-Smythe you can hold a conversation with yourself as "Johny" that will be overheard in the parlor. One voice will make demands, the other will acquiesce and your friends need never lay eyes on the mysterious owner of the Smythe Corporation."

"By Jove! It's genius. How do you think this monster should speak?" I growled in a rather piratical manner. "See here, my lad, if you think you can just walk in here..."

"A bit stereotypical, Sir."

"What about this?" I went up the octave and added a simper. "Oh, Johny, thank goodness you brought this to my attention. You know what a hopeless idiot I am."

"Again, Sir, I believe a lighter hand is called for."

"Fine. I say, Johny, those are some rather good points you're making."

"That is acceptable, Sir."

I began pacing with a rolling gait. "Now, how should he walk?"

Bentley gave another small sigh. "Tempus fugit, Sir."

"Yes, yes. Here we go."

I began loudly as Johny. "Now look here, Chippington-Smythe, these kinds of business practices just won't wash! These aren't the dark ages, you know."

I switched voices and turned my body to face the other way. "Why, what on earth do you mean, old bag?"

I switched again. "You're oppressing the poor, you know."

"Am I? I had no idea!"

"Well, that's all right, my lad. I'm here to set it right. You just listen to old Johny and we'll soon have this place running like a clock."

"Oh, Johny! Thank goodness for you! I bless the day that we became fast friends."

"Yes, friendship like ours can't be bought at any price."

"I say, have you lost weight?"

"A pound or two. Can you tell?"

"Oh yes! You're lean as an athlete. I'm sure you could enter the Olympics if you cared about such things."

"For that matter, you're looking rather dashing yourself. Have you done something different with your hair?"

Bentley cleared his throat. I hurriedly finished up.

"Well, never mind about that, Johny. What should I do about all this social injustice and whatnot?"

"I'll tell you exactly what to do..."

Bentley held up his hand. "That should be sufficient, Sir. If you could lower your voice and murmur unintelligibly for a few moments, I believe we can conclude our masquerade."

I followed instructions. "Rada-frazza-upsilon. Oopsy daisy Allegheny Monongahela."

"And now I believe you may rejoin your guests, Sir."

He slid open the pocket doors and we squeezed through, shutting them behind us.

Judy rushed up to me. "Well? What did he say?"

"He's an amazing chap, I must say. Mind like a razor. Chin of granite."

"But what did he say?"

"Oh, he's all for reform. Said yes to everything."

"But what, specifically?"

"Well, we didn't have time to go into all the details."

Judy exhaled loudly. "Then, what did you achieve?"

Bentley stepped up. "I'm afraid Johny is too modest to boast of his accomplishments. If I may clarify what actually took place—Mr. Chippington-Smythe agreed to the creation of a new position within the company—answerable only to him and empowered to make any changes that might improve the lives of the general population. These would include but are not limited to: the areas of job creation, better housing and land redistribution. That's correct, isn't it, Sir?"

"Oh! Yes. That's just what we decided."

Judy snorted. "Corporate mumbo-jumbo."

Bentley continued. "And Johny insisted that this position be filled by someone who could indisputably be trusted to act in the best interests of the people."

"Who's that going to be?"

Bentley turned to me. "Did you want to be the one to tell her, Sir?"

"Who, me?"

"It was your idea, after all."

"Oh! Yes. It was my idea. Wouldn't have had it any other way."

Judy stared at me expectantly. "Who is it?"

"It's..." I goggled at Bentley but he just looked back at me like a schoolmaster surveying a particularly dull specimen. Suddenly the light dawned. "You, Judy!" I glanced at Bentley. "That's right, isn't it?"

"Absolutely correct."

"Got it in one go."

Judy's jaw was hanging open. "Me?"

"Of course. Who else?"

Sid raised her hand in the air. "Three cheers for Judy! Hip hip..."

"Hooray!"

"Hip hip..."

"Hooray!"

"Hip hip..."

"Hooray!"

Uncle Hugo was turning purple. "The government will never accept it!"

I looked at him thoughtfully. "But Smythe Corporation owns the government, doesn't it?"

He huffed and puffed for a while and finally looked down at his shoes. "Not officially."

"But for all intents and purposes."

"Well... off the record, yes."

"Then that's taken care of."

He shook his fist. "But what of the shareholders?"

"What of the shareholders indeed?"

Bentley glided in. "I think you will find, as Mr. Chippington-Smythe expressed it, that a rising tide lifts all boats. After all, if people have money to spend, they become customers—and since Smythe Corporation sells virtually everything, business should thrive."

Uncle Hugo's hue became less crimson. He looked thoughtful. "So, the money lost in soybean subsidies will be made up in consumer goods. Brilliant!"

At that moment there was a slam from the front door followed by a flurry of pounding feet and a hyperventilating Cubby Martinez burst into the room. He stared about him with wild eyes and pointed an accusatory finger at me. "Ah hah! The evidence could not be clearer. I declare the wager lost!"

Judy squinted at Cubby. "Who the Hell are you? Say, you're that ad man from outside the tax office."

"I am Cubby Martinez, the Marshall of Twits."

"The what of what?"

I gave him a warning stare. "Look here, Cubby, you've got this all wrong."

"You won't talk your way out this time."

"Cubby, if you'll just turn around and leave, I'll explain it all to you later."

"Too late. Clearly these people know who you are."

Judy stared at me, then at Cubby. "Who is he?"

"He is Cyril Chippington-Smythe, of course, who has finally gotten his comeuppance."

"He's who?"

Cubby gave a grim laugh. "Chippington-Smythe here wagered that he could live like a common citizen for one week. If his identity was discovered the bet was lost, and here you all are—in his very house!"

At this point Bentley gave a little cough. "Excuse me, Sir. If I understand the terms of the wager, there was another codicil which stated that if his identity was revealed prematurely through some blunder on your part, Mr. Chippington-Smythe was to be declared the winner."

"What of it?"

Bentley looked around. "Prior to the entrance of Mr. Martinez, did anyone here suspect that this gentleman was anything other than a common citizen named Johny?"

There was a general chorus of, "Not me. Did you? No, I never!"

Sid shook his head. "He certainly fooled us."

Cubby's mouth opened and closed like a fish who suddenly finds the water has disappeared. "But... but..."

Uncle Hugo pointed a finger between Cubby's eyes. "I can attest that those are the facts, and I believe my word is good at the club."

Aunt Hypatia fixed Cubby with her basilisk's glare. "I too can verify that my nephew had become indistinguishable from a member of the working class until your untimely intervention and I would like to see any member of your club contradict me."

Binky was practically dancing. "Hooray! We're saved! You've really put your foot in it, Cubby. Wait until I tell the fellows. My bar tab in the new year is going to be monstrous!"

Cubby had grown progressively redder and seemed to be shrinking before my eyes. Finally, with a shriek like a steam whistle, he spun and ran from the room.

I gave a shrug. "Well, that seems to be that."

Judy stepped in front of me. "Not quite. There's still the little matter of who you are."

I hung my head. "Oh. Yes. I'm terribly sorry about that."

"Are you really Cyril Chippington-Smythe?"

"I'm afraid so."

"And there is no Johny?"

"He was an avatar, if you will."

She smiled sadly. "Pity. I rather liked him." She turned to Binky. "And I suppose you're not a feared member of the Welsh resistance?"

"Um... no, sorry. The truth is I have no resistance of any kind."

"There is no Welsh Rabbit?"

I chuckled. "He was called "Rabbit" at school, but it derived from a gentle nature and a habitual twitch of the nose rather than from any elusiveness."

Binky dropped to a knee. "Can you forgive me?"

Judy looked down at him. "Will you promise to tell me the absolute truth in future?"

"I do. Whenever I am able to discern it. Slippery thing—truth."

"It's enough that you try. I think we can remain friends."

Aunt Hypatia looked around with satisfaction. "I must say, this 'slumming' has turned out to be a great success. I almost regret not sampling that churro... but regrets, like influenza, are a part of life."

To my surprise, Ernie came strolling in from the direction of the kitchen. "Hello, all."

"Ernie! What are you doing here?"

"I had to make sure Mr. Martinez got here all right."

"*You* sent Cubby here?"

"I was in the kitchen making my delivery when Bentley saw the crowd coming. He sent me on the double to find Cubby and make sure he knew what was going on."

I turned to Bentley. "Once again it seems that it was Bentley's invisible hand moving us all about like chess pieces."

"You give me far too much credit, Sir."

I turned back to Ernie. "Say, listen, Ernie. As long as I'm creating new jobs, I've got one for you."

"What is it?"

"You're the new head of research at Smythe Corporation. You'll have everything you need—lab, assistants, equipment. Now you can find that 'fizzy energy' you've been looking for."

He grabbed my hand and shook it. "Do you mean it? Hooray!"

"And I've got a job for your mum as well, if she wants it. Do you think she'd be interested in cooking for me?"

"Full time, you mean?"

"At a generous salary with benefits of course."

Bentley gave a little bow. "I anticipated your interest, Sir. She is in the kitchen as we speak. I took the liberty of placing the auto-cooker in the trash."

My aunt gave a sniff. "This house begins to feel more like a pleasure palace than a respectable home. I am not quite sure how I feel about it, so I'm afraid I must disapprove until I have more information."

Ernie's mum entered the room, pushing a tea cart with platters of delicious-looking bits of this and that. "Hallo, everybody. I've thrown together some hors d'oeuvres. Is anyone hungry?"

The crowd headed for the cart with cries of "Yes! I am. Save some for me."

"There's eggplant dip, roasted peppers and warm flatbread with olive oil."

Aunt Hypatia threw her ragged shawl around her shoulders like an empress. "That settles it. Come, Hugo. An orgy seems to be breaking out and I do not wish to be listed among the participants."

I bowed her to the door. "Goodbye, Aunt. Do visit again soon."

"I shall not cross this threshold again until you've come to your senses."

"That's all right then. See you at Christmas."

She and my uncle sailed out of the door.

Cheeseworth hurried up an gave me an apologetic look. "Sowwy, Cywil. They're my ride. Toodle-oo."

I firmly shut the door then made a beeline for the flatbread. I drew Ernie's mum aside. "Look here, are you sure you want to work for a bloodsucking capitalist?"

She smiled. "You were a bloodsucking capitalist when I didn't know you. You're family now, which means your bloodsucking capitalism is only an endearing eccentricity. Besides, the job comes with dental."

"I say, I've never found out your name. I can't very well go on calling you Ernie's mum."

"It's Cook."

"Cook?"

"Short for Cookie. My parents were somewhat whimsical with names. My siblings are Brownie, Clementine and Potato."

"Cook, then. Perfect."

And so ended my adventure into the wide world. Later that evening I sat contentedly before my hydrogen gas fireplace sipping a cherry juice with soda and munching on a plate of toast and jam. With my girdle safely around my waist once more, I felt snug as the proverbial insect in the carpet. Bentley floated in.

"Cook is leaving for the evening, Sir."

"I wish you could taste her toast and jam."

"Alas, I lack the necessary sensors. Your adventure seems to have turned out rather well, if I may say so."

"I feel this is the beginning of a new age. An age of... toast, you know... and jam and such." I looked up at him shyly. "Do you really think I did well?"

"I think you have experienced some personal growth, Sir, which is always a positive development."

I munched my toast thoughtfully. "I have a new mission, Bentley. I'm going to go in for personal growth in a big way."

"Shall I acquire some books on the subject, Sir?"

"Oh no, the old bean couldn't take it. No reading, I'm afraid."

"I could hire some tutors on philosophy."

"Heavens no! That sounds gruesome! No, I'm sure I can figure it out for myself. I'll just sit here and eat toast and stare into the fire and... think."

He stood for a long moment, watching me. "Are you thinking now, Sir?"

"As a matter of fact, I am."

"About personal growth?"

"About eggs. I am determined to acquire some. Imagine what Cook could accomplish with them."

"You must first acquire some chickens, Sir. There are rumors of sightings in some of the more distant provinces."

"Why chickens?"

"It is chickens that lay the eggs."

"But if we begin with eggs, they will invariably hatch into chickens."

"I believe the chickens must come first, Sir."

"I am certain it will be easier to begin with eggs."

"Chickens, Sir."

"Eggs, Bentley."

"You seem to have strong convictions on the chicken-egg controversy so I shall withdraw. Good night, Sir."

"Yes, good night."

He misted off. A fine fellow, Bentley, but obviously no farmer. This required scientific thinking, which was Ernie's bailiwick. Tomorrow I'd have him drop everything and concentrate on egg production. It seemed I had a flair for business after all. Perhaps it was time I took control of my various industries and ran them myself. Imagine how pleased my relatives would be at the huge increase in profits that would undoubtedly result. I took a large bite of toast, settled back in my chair and promptly fell fast asleep.

THE END

I hope you had as much fun reading about my adventure as I did living it.

If you wish Bentley's chronicles to continue to thrive, I beg you to tell the world by leaving a review!
Click or follow this impossibly opaque link:
https://www.amazon.com/dp/B0B4HP25LT

If you'd like advance notice on the next book's release head to:
WWW.TwitsChronicles.com
where you can sign up for Bentley's email list and where you can ask me or anyone of my acquaintance a question which may be answered in the next newsletter.
I'm told that spam is detestable and so will keep emails to a minimum.

Uncle Hugo's Crisis: A Twits Short Story

"A semaphore for you, Sir."

"Indeed? From whom?"

"It is from your aunt, Sir."

"Aunt Hypatia? What on earth could she want?"

"No doubt the contents will shed some light."

"Don't be glib, Bentley. No one likes a glib valet."

"No, Sir. I beg your pardon."

I should pause for a moment to let you catch up. I have hurled you, will-you-nil-you into the heart of my story without benefit of map or road signs. The salient points are these: I, Cyril Chippington-Smythe, was reclining on the couch one afternoon with a glass of brandy in one hand and a fly-swatter in the other. The Great Extinction had passed over the kingdom of Musca Domestica as the Angel of the Lord passed over the

Israelites of Ancient Egypt. I was attempting to remedy that situation (vis-a-vis flies, not Israelites), when my mechanical valet, Bentley, slid in with an envelope clutched in his mitt. I think you're up to speed now.

"Shall I open it for you, Sir."

"Please do. I've received more than the usual number of paper cuts this week."

He passed me the flimsy. I held it to the light. "'Come immediately'. What do you suppose she means by that?"

"Presumably she wishes you to come immediately, Sir."

"But why? What's the gist? Where's the motivating force?" I frowned. There was a party at the club that evening to celebrate Badger Binghampton's engagement and I was rather keen to attend. "Send a semaphore back to my aunt, Bentley. 'Require further information. Kindly furnish details'." Take your time walking it to the semaphore office. I'm heading to the club."

The bachelor party was suitably vigorous and it was a shadow of Cyril Chippington-Smythe that staggered home to find another semaphore laid out on the table in the entry hall. I opened it carefully but still managed to slice my thumb. Sticking it in the old cake hole for a bit of disinfection, I perused the contents of the note. "Come immediately means come immediately, you thundering ass! If you are not at Dankworth

Hall tomorrow, it would be best if you had never been born. See that you bring Bentley."

Bentley appeared at my elbow in that soothing way he has when one is up against it.

"I have packed your things, Sir. Will you be leaving in the morning?"

"I'm afraid so." I handed him the note. "What the devil does she mean by, 'See that you bring Bentley?'"

"I really couldn't say, Sir."

"Rather mysterious." I sighed. "Ah, Bentley, 'Man that is born of woman is few of days and full of... something.'"

"Trouble, Sir?"

"No, I think it has something to do with the ghost of one's dead father. That's Shakespeare for you- always looking on the glum side."

"I believe the quotation is biblical, Sir. Job fourteen to be exact."

"Nonsense. I had Shakespeare shoveled into me by the spadeful at school and I haven't forgotten an iamb. I suppose he could have cribbed it from the Bible, though. He was quite the literary pilferer I believe."

"I shall prepare the bedroom, Sir."

"Prepare away. I'm dead on my feet."

"Shall I carry you up the stairs?"

"Yes, thank you, Bentley."

With that, he lifted me as if I was made of dandelion fluff and wafted me off to my feather bed, where I slept the sleep of the just.

The next day we motored down to Dankworth Hall. For those of you who have not had the pleasure, Dankworth Hall has been the seat of the Dankworths since the days of William the Conqueror. It began as a sort of fortified saltbox and gradually accumulated wings and outbuildings commensurate with the standing of whichever Dankworth owned it. Perched over the fetid waters of Lake Sputum, it now resembled nothing so much as a lunatic asylum from a penny dreadful. The hearts within were warm, however. Sometimes, as in the case of my Aunt Hypatia, too warm- bordering on incendiary.

Bentley pulled the car up to the front of the old manse and I was surprised to find no welcoming party. The house seemed shut up tight. I thumped the brass knocker pretty vigorously and the door was finally opened by Mrs. Pine, the housekeeper. She was a model identical to my own Mrs. Oaks, who could have passed for Bentley in a pageboy wig.

"What ho, Mrs. Pine. I have arrived as instructed."

She digested this bit of information. "Your aunt is in the gazebo, Sir. I shall assist Mr. Bentley with the luggage."

This was not the usual chirp of a greeting I was accustomed to receiving from Mrs. Pine, but I legged it around the side of the house toward the gazebo. As I rounded the corner, I was surprised to see my Uncle Hugo standing in a flower bed.

He wore a slightly moldy dressing gown and worn slippers. He had clearly stopped shaving and the old physiognomy was a bit rough.

"What ho, uncle!" I sang out. "Beautiful morning, what?"

He shook his head as if emerging from a dream and aimed his eyes in my general direction. "What does it matter? One morning is much like another."

"True, true. Bentley has some saying about the eye of the beholder being the crucial element. I say, are you quite all right, uncle?"

He looked off into the distance and heaved a sigh such as Alexander must have heaved upon perceiving that there were no more worlds to conquer. "Who could answer such a question? You might as well ask these trees if they are satisfied with their lot. Our fate pursues us however we attempt to escape."

"Oh, quite! I couldn't agree more." I looked around nervously. "You haven't seen my aunt, have you?"

"She is in the gazebo, pacing."

"Is she, though? I'd best go find her. She seems anxious to see me."

My uncle had subsided into a brown study and appeared to have forgotten my existence. I carefully sidled around him and headed for the gazebo at a light jog. As I drew near, I saw my aunt staring off at Lake Sputum with a frown.

"Hallo, old gal! Here I am, as ordered."

She regarded me glumly. "Did you bring Bentley?"

"I did. What did you want him for?"

"What do you suppose? I need his brain. There's no one like Bentley for finding a way out of trouble. You would undoubtedly be confined in an institution by now if not for Bentley."

This irritated me not a little. I like to think that when it comes to getting out of sticky situations, I am every bit as capable as Bentley. It's true he has a massive brain in that metal noggin, but I understand psychology and that is something no machine can master. "You wound me, aunt. Whatever the trouble is, I'm sure I can resolve it without Bentley's assistance."

She looked at me nervously. "Darling, you won't try to help, will you? Promise me you won't lift a finger."

"But why?"

"It's just... you have rather a talent for making things worse, you know."

"I don't."

She bit her lower lip. "You know I love you, nephew, but if you insist on involving yourself in our... little problem, I'm going to have to lock you in your room."

I drew myself up and spoke rather coldly. "Very well. I'm not one to intrude where I'm not wanted. Do you suppose you could trust me so far as to tell me what the trouble is?"

"Did you pass your uncle on the way here?"

"I did. He seemed... preoccupied."

"That is putting it mildly. Hugo is experiencing some sort of crisis. I would say mid-life, but he is far past that. I want Bentley to snap him out of it."

"I see. Brooding, is he?"

"He is not fit company for man nor beast. You saw the state of his toilette?"

"Shocking. Have you tried dunking him in cold water?"

"I have had him dunked him in water of every temperature. I have tried sneaking up behind him and yelling, 'boo!' to no effect. Everything that common sense could suggest, I have tried."

"Don't worry, aunt. Bentley and I are on the case."

"Just Bentley."

"As you wish. I shall brief him on our mission..."

"His mission."

"Exactly. Uncle Hugo will be his old self in no time."

"Thank you, Cyril. Having Bentley here takes an enormous load off of my mind."

I found Bentley ironing a shirt in the guest room and laid the case before him.

"I see, Sir."

"I think I should hunt up my uncle and do a little sleuthing, don't you agree, Bentley?"

"No, Sir."

"Why not?"

"We do not wish to arouse his suspicions, Sir. That will only raise his defenses."

"But I'll be subtle, Bentley. He won't suspect a thing."

"I would still advise against it, Sir."

"But why the blazes not?"

"If you will forgive me, Sir, the art of subtlety is not one at which you excel. You have many sterling qualities but that is not among them."

I spoke icily. "I see. That is what you think. Very well. Let us see how well you do without me."

"Very good, Sir."

"Without my knowledge of psychology, you will be as a babe in the wilds."

"In the woods, Sir."

"What about the woods?"

"The babe is in them, Sir. Not the wilds."

"I suppose the woods are wild, aren't they?"

"No doubt, Sir."

"Then leave it alone, Bentley. Let's not split... that thing that people should refrain from splitting."

"Hairs, Sir."

"Exactly. Leave the hairs in peace, won't you?"

"Of course, Sir."

I was in a bit of a mood as I strode out onto the lawn. It seemed that my intellect was not valued by my friends and relations at its true potential. It would be a positive pleasure to watch them fail without my help. As I rounded an azalea bush, I heard a racking sigh. I spotted a bald head moving heavily through the underbrush. I thought quickly. No one had forbidden me absolutely from contact with my uncle. A little casual badinage would hardly constitute an interrogation. It might even cheer him up a bit. I am known around the club as a source of jollity. I looked about to assure myself that neither my aunt nor Bentley was in evidence and casually strolled around to where my uncle stood. He was staring off at a greenhouse behind the house and rubbing his unshaven chin.

"What ho, Uncle. How goes the struggle?"

He didn't take his eyes from the greenhouse. "I have given up the struggle. I await the inevitable outcome."

"And what outcome is that?"

He spoke in a sepulchral tone. "Golden lads and girls all must, as chimney-sweepers, come to dust."

"Ah, the Bard. He seems to be popping up quite a bit today."

"There goes another one."

"Another what?" I followed his eyes toward the greenhouse. It contained a single large tree. As I watched, a leaf detached itself from the tree and wafted lazily to earth. My uncle sighed.

"You know," I observed. "I've never noticed that greenhouse before. Is it new?"

"It was built last month to protect the tree."

"Valuable tree, is it?"

"More precious than rubies, to me."

"Rare specimen?"

"It was planted by my father at my birth. A mighty oak. We have grown together and I feel there is a bond between us. I played among its branches as a child and sat in its shade when I was a young man. The warming climate has made this part of the world inhospitable for oaks so I had a greenhouse built to keep it safe. Cool air is pumped in to shield it from the heat."

"Rather clever. Bravo"

"Alas. It has not helped. The tree is dying. There goes another leaf."

We watched it fall together. I could see now that most of the leaves on the tree were brown. "Shame. Lovely tree. Perhaps you could replace it with a palm."

He glared at me. "I suppose you'd replace me with a palm if you could, eh? That's the way things are, now- gone to rack and ruin. Thank God I won't be around to see it."

"Off on a trip, then? Is Aunt going with you?"

He subsided into gloom again. "She will follow in due time."

"That will be lovely. Nothing like travel to buck one up."

He gave me the sort of look one gives a particularly thick child. "I am not going on a vacation, you boob! I am speaking of 'That land from whose bourn no traveler returns'".

"Bulgaria?"

"Death, you insufferable nitwit!"

This brought me up short, as you can imagine. "I'm so sorry, Uncle. I didn't know you were ill. Aunt Hypatia didn't say a word."

He looked back at the tree. "I am not ill. Not with any disease a doctor would recognize. Nevertheless, my time has come."

"But if you're not ill, why should you... "shuffle off this mortal thingamabob?"

"That oak and I came into the world together and we shall leave it together."

"This seems to be an unreasonable amount of fraternal feeling for a tree."

He struck a theatrical pose. "Enough. Leave me. I would commune with the eternal."

"Right ho. I'll pop off then."

Back in my room I revealed all to Bentley. "I know you had doubts, but you must admit I've cracked the case and wasted not a moment."

"It would seem that Mr. Dankworth has developed an unhealthy obsession with the tree, Sir."

"He's convinced that the tree and he are one. The decline of one will result inevitably in the decline of the other."

"I shall consider the situation, Sir."

"Not necessary, Bentley. I have things well in hand."

"Indeed?"

"Yes. My aunt may think me a Jonah- bringing ill fortune to all and sundry, but she will change her tune when I put everything right with a wave of my hand."

"I feel I must point out that a mental obsession is not a thing to be trifled with. Perhaps professional intervention is called for."

"Wrong, Bentley. Allow me to lay before you the brilliance of my scheme, that it may excite envy in you and quash all future cavils as to my competence."

"Indeed, Sir."

"My uncle believes his health is irrevocably bound up with that of the oak tree his father planted on the day of his birth. Follow so far?"

"Yes, Sir."

"If the tree declines, so does he. That's clear, isn't it?"

"Perfectly clear, Sir."

"Ah, but what if the health of the tree improves? Does it not follow that my uncle's health will rise along with it?"

"I was not aware that you were so knowledgeable about the health of trees, Sir."

"Oh, I'm not, but that's not necessary in this case."

"No, Sir?"

"No. All that is necessary is that my uncle believes that the tree is improving. His mental processes will force him to improve along with it. Ipso facto, he will be cured."

"How will you convince him, Sir?"

"I've been thinking about that. Did you note that they are painting the fence by the garage?"

"Yes, Sir."

"A nice shade of green."

"Indeed."

"Well then, I shall slip out about midnight, nip some of that green paint and splash it liberally about the tree- burnishing the brown leaves with a verdant coat that will serve double duty as a glue that will hold the leaves in place on their branches. Decline halted."

"I see, Sir."

"What are your thoughts, Bentley?"

"I advise against it."

"But why?"

"It seems overly baroque, Sir."

"I am undaunted. You shall see. This shall put the quietus to my aunt's mistrust of my abilities as well. We shall kill two brides with one stone."

"Birds, Sir."

"Yes. What did I say?"

"Brides."

"Well, that works too. Now, how about a spot of tea and a sandwich or two. It's a long time until midnight. I shall need sustenance."

At the stroke of midnight I was creeping around the garage. I tried the door- locked. This stymied me for a moment, but a Chippington-Smythe is made of pretty tough stuff. I found a substantial rock and flung it at a pane of glass. It made quite a satisfying crash. I stood listening for a while, but when no hullabaloo resulted, I reached through the opening and unlocked the door. I lit a match to give some momentary illumination and spotted the can of paint next to my aunt's touring car. Working by feel, I snagged the pail and a brush and crept with them across the lawn toward the greenhouse. I was feeling pretty spry, all things considered. As I approached the door of the greenhouse a presence loomed from a nearby bush.

"Good evening, Sir."

I yipped pretty vigorously before realizing that it was Bentley who stood before me.

"Bentley! What on earth are you doing here?"

"I thought you might require some assistance, Sir."

"I thought you were against the scheme. You looked at it askance, as it were."

"I still believe it ill-advised, Sir, but if you are determined to go forward, we must give your plan the best possible odds of success."

"I knew you'd rally round. You haven't seen a ladder around anywhere, have you?"

"No, Sir."

"That's all right. I'm a champion tree climber. I'll scamper about amongst the branches and you can hand up the paint can as required."

"Very good, Sir."

"Get the door, will you Bentley?"

It was the work of a moment to peel open the paint can and dip in the old brush. "I'll start with the low branches and then clamber up."

"If you will excuse my observing, Sir, that will require you to climb over freshly painted leaves. It would be much cleaner to begin at the top and work your way down."

"By Jove, you're right, Bentley. All right, up I go. Give us a shove, will you?"

With Bentley's help I was soon standing on one of the lower branches. "Hand me up the paint can, Bentley."

He passed it along and I carefully started to work my way up the tree. This was no mean feat with an open can of paint in one hand and a brush in the other. I made it about half way before I decided that beautifying half a tree should be enough for anyone and began daubing on the pigment. It soon became evident that this was going to be a messy job. The leaves bobbed and swayed as if trying to evade the brush deliberately. I applied more paint to my hands than to the vegetation. Nevertheless, I seemed to be making progress.

"I say, Bentley, it's looking rather lush up here- or am I mistaken?"

"It is certainly greener than when you began, Sir."

"I'll just move down a bit and keep going. This branch looks pretty sturdy..."

But, alas, the indicated branch was only feigning strength. It gave way under my heel and after a moment of frantic windmilling I descended "like glistering Phaethon, wanting the manage of unruly jades". I braced myself for the inevitable crash, but found myself safe in the arms of Bentley, who had caught me as gently as a ball of milkweed silk.

"Odds bodkins, Bentley, that was a close one!"

"Indeed, Sir. Your descent was precipitate."

"Thank you for the assist. You can set me down now."

I examined myself for broken bones. "I seem to be intact."

"I am afraid, Sir, that the can of paint has landed squarely on your person. You are rather green at present."

"Am I?" I explored with my fingers and found that my entire head was drenched with something viscous. "Damn! That was the last of the paint. We've come a cropper, Bentley."

"Perhaps we should retire, to fight again another day, Sir."

"How am I going to get this blasted paint off? Do you think a hose would do it?"

"I believe it is oil paint, Sir. Turpentine is required."

"Do you have any?"

"I am confident that I can procure some."

"Then do so. I'd better wait here. No sense tracking paint all over the place."

Bentley wafted off and I sat glumly on a nearby hump. Suddenly there was a bit of a racket by the back door and a light shone out into the darkness. Someone was coming to investigate the crash! I looked around desperately for somewhere to hide, but nothing presented itself. At the last moment I managed to shimmy up the tree and conceal myself amongst the foliage. This would have been a simple matter if the tree was in full leaf, but the branches were somewhat bare and substantial portions of me lacked camouflage. The door to the greenhouse opened and who should enter with a lantern but my Uncle Hugo! He peered around nervously. Bentley had taken the empty paint can with him and there was nothing on the ground to excite suspicion. After a few moments of creeping around with his lantern, my uncle seemed to be satisfied. As he headed for the door, he happened to cast the lantern's glow up into the tree and by an unlucky coincidence he looked straight into my face, which poked through the leaves like a questing lemur. My uncle dropped his lantern with a shriek and fled into the night. Thinking that discretion is the better part of valour, I hastened down from the tree and made my way back to the garage, where I concealed myself as best I could under an old tarpaulin. I could hear shouting on the lawn and running footsteps. Finally, the hubbub died down and I started to believe I would escape after all. At that moment the garage door creaked open and I heard footsteps heading toward my hiding place. The tarpaulin was gently lifted away and I beheld Bentley holding a can of turpentine and a rag.

"Good evening, Sir. I believe they have given up the search. Would you care to remove that paint now?"

Twenty minutes later I emerged from the garage a new man. My skin was pink and glowing. Bentley had brought a change of clothes and a chicken drumstick. I strolled into Dankworth hall with a clean conscience to find my uncle sitting before the fire with a brandy and soda. I plopped into the armchair next to him and we both stared into the fire for a while.

"What ho, Uncle," I finally said. "Rather late for you to be up, what?"

"I might say the same to you."

"Anything particular... on your mind, as it were?"

He sipped his brandy. "As a matter of fact, there is."

"Oh? I'm all ears, if you'd like a sounding board to bounce things off of. People say I'm the devil of a listener."

He stared meditatively at the fire for a moment. "You may have noticed that I have not been my usual buoyant self of late."

"Do tell?" I replied innocently.

"I had developed an unhealthy fixation with the health of that oak tree in the greenhouse, as I believe you know."

"I remember something of the matter."

"But tonight I received a sign. I might almost call it a miracle."

"Really? Not something that happens every day. What was the nature of this miracle?"

He looked at me searchingly. "Do you know of The Green Man?"

This gave me a bit of a jolt. "Is there a green person on the premises? I'm sure there's a logical explanation... or that it's a hallucination brought on by indigestion."

My uncle rose to his feet. "Follow me, Nephew."

I rose meekly and padded after him. He led me to the oldest part of the house and stopped before a large, carved stone archway. He pointed to the top of the arch. I peered up at it and discerned a grotesque face peering back at me.

"Rather gruesome. Who was he?"

"That is The Green Man. He is a figure out of pagan mythology- a symbol of rebirth and new growth. He is part of our family crest, as it happens."

"But why do you point him out to me at one o'clock in the am?"

"Because I saw him tonight."

"Who? The Green Man?"

"As clearly as I see you now. He looked down at me from that same oak that has preoccupied me."

This was a bit of a relief. It seemed that my uncle had not recognized the features of Cyril Chippington-Smythe in the creature he had spotted in his tree."

"What do you suppose he was doing there?"

"It's obvious, isn't it? He was sending me a message. A message of rebirth. He was telling me that the tree would live, and so must I."

"Ah. Well, that's all right then. Problem solved. You're probably pretty relieved, what?"

"Indeed I am. My thoughts have been rather dark of late, but I feel the sun is about to shine. Life begins anew."

"I couldn't be happier for you, Uncle. I'm sure Aunt Hypatia will be greatly relieved."

"Yes. She has been rather worried, I'm afraid. I must tell her what has occurred."

"Perhaps you should wait until breakfast. I suspect my aunt dislikes being awoken from a sound sleep for any reason other than the sounding of the last trumpet."

He scratched his chin stubble a little nervously. "You may be right. The morning will do. Goodnight, Nephew. I shall sleep like a baby tonight."

"Goodnight, Uncle. I intend to do the same."

Back in my room I brought Bentley up to speed.

"I am glad that things have ended well, Sir."

"For the moment, Bentley, but what happens when the tree does not improve? My uncle will be watching it like a hawk for evidence of The Green Man's handiwork. If the leaves continue to fall, will my uncle not descend into despondency once more?"

"I do not believe so, Sir."

"But why not?"

"In my investigations, I discovered that your uncle's oak tree is not, after all, dying. The cold air being pumped into the greenhouse has simply convinced the tree that it is Autumn. Being deciduous, it is natural for the tree to lose its leaves. I have spoken to the gardener about it. In due course new leaves will sprout and the tree will resume its former appearance."

I stared at him in wonder. "Bentley, you are a marvel."

"I am glad you are satisfied, Sir."

"So, all has ended happily. Life goes on, as it were."

"Your aunt will be greatly relieved."

"I expect that she will view my actions with a new respect, don't you think?"

"I'm afraid that revealing your part in the evening's events would undermine their success, Sir."

"You mean Uncle Hugo might find out that it was all a ruse? But I would swear Aunt Hypatia to secrecy."

"A secret known to more than one is no secret, Sir."

I scratched my head. "Blast! It's extremely irksome not to be able to take credit, Bentley."

"I would argue that the important thing is your uncle's happiness, Sir."

"I suppose you're right," I sighed.

"Will we be travelling home in the morning, Sir?"

"Yes, Bentley. I intend to crawl into bed and not to emerge until Spring."

"Very good, Sir."

"And if we pass any semaphore towers between here and home, I intend to burn them to the ground. That should hold my aunt off for a while, don't you think?"

"Undoubtedly, Sir."

"Goodnight, Bentley."

"Goodnight, Sir."

And with that I snuggled into the covers and was soon dreaming of small green men, dancing in the moonlight.

The End

From the Desk of Cyril Chippington-Smythe

This is the third of Bentley's Chronicles and I must say it's a corker! My adventure begins with a simple attempt to avoid dinner at my Aunt's and winds up on a different continent with an angry mob baying for my blood. It's a bit of a travelogue, really, with some salient observations about that modern Gomorrah- New York City. All the usual suspects are here: My cousin Binky, Aunt Hypatia and Uncle Hugo, Cheeseworth and, of course, Bentley. I think I come off rather well. Some say I was heroic, although Uncle Hugo has threatened to kick me in the shins the next time he encounters me.

Twits Abroad

TOM ALAN ROBBINS

The Author makes no representation of any kind as to his being a citizen of the United Kingdom, either native or naturalized. He is from a small town in Ohio, for which he apologizes.

Copyright © 2022 by Tom Alan Robbins

This is a work of fiction. All events described are imaginary; all characters are entirely fictitious and are not intended to represent actual living persons.

Cover design by Melody J. Barber of Aurora Publicity

Additional designs by Eric Wright of The Puppet Kitchen.

Twits Logo designed by Feppa Rodriquez

Proofreading by Gretchen Tannert Douglas

For Noreen O'Neil, who spotted this story headed for the precipice and gently placed it back on the tracks. Her warmth, generosity and insight added immeasurably to the success of these books.

Contents

CHAPTER ONE

The Horrors of Euphonia Gumboot

I don't know if you've heard of this Isaac Newton chap, but apparently, he had brains positively leaking out of his ears. He said something to the effect that for everything pleasant that happens, there will be something equally beastly lurking around the corner. This is the only scientific fact I have retained from my school days, and time has proven it true. There I was, happily downing Cook's warm scones with cherry preserves and washing them down with the old lapsang souchong when Bentley slid in with the news that my Aunt Hypatia was chewing the furniture in the parlor and demanding to see me. Bentley, if you are meeting him for the first time, is a steam-powered domestic with a stately dome and an air of moral certainty that will brook no opposition.

"What does my aunt want? Did she say?"

"She did not, although I was able to discern the phrases, 'young pup' and 'cease this shilly-shallying' from amidst the general verbiage."

"This bodes ill. You couldn't tell her I have appendicitis?"

"I could not."

Experience has taught me that making my aunt wait only allows the venom to accumulate in her fangs. I sighed and took a final bite of scone. "May as well take the ball by the horns, what?"

Bentley raised an eyebrow. "Bull, Sir."

"Pardon?"

"One takes the bull by the horns. Balls do not typically have horns."

I thought this over for a tick. "What's a bull?"

"A bull was a male cow, Sir."

"Damn the Great Extinction!"

Bentley assumed a professorial tone. "It was also used to refer to the male of several other extinct species, including elephants."

That perked me up. I love being able to spread out what few nuggets of scholarly wisdom I possess for all to admire. "I am acquainted with elephants. They were known for holding grudges."

He tilted his head. "For remembering, Sir. I don't believe there was any malice involved."

"Then my aunt is certainly not an elephant. Her memory is used exclusively for mischief."

Bentley gave a little sigh. "We're rather losing the thread."

"It was you that brought up elephants."

"I apologize most abjectly. It was entirely my fault."

"You're being too hard on yourself as usual, Bentley. Well, let's see what the old girl wants."

My Aunt Hypatia could be called a dragon in that her scaly exterior is impervious to attack and that she breathes fire when aroused. Bentley's intelligence had led me to expect a certain Visigoth flavour in my aunt's demeanor so I was surprised to find her smiling at me as if I were a shining example of natural selection.

"Good morning, Aunt. Confusion to our enemies."

"Cyril, darling! Is that the new motto?"

"According to Bentley."

"I think he can be trusted. Confusion to our enemies. Let me look at you."

I was happy to oblige as it required no effort from me. After regarding me up and down, the bottom of her face formed a smile while the upper half held a private meeting to discuss its findings.

"You look tired. Are you getting enough sleep?"

"Oodles. I'm really making an effort!"

"You've lost weight. Do you still employ that eccentric cook of yours?"

"I've gained three pounds and it was worth every mouthful thanks to what you call my 'eccentric cook.'"

"And that mechanical servant of yours—don't you find that these older models require endless amounts of maintenance?"

The alarm bells began clanging in my noggin. She clearly had an agenda, and that was bound to be hard luck for me.

"Bentley does his own maintenance."

She pursed her lips judiciously. "I have thought for some time that Bentley is not a good influence on you."

A cold sweat began to gather on the nape of my neck. "Bentley is indispensable. I would sooner part with my thumbs than Bentley."

My aunt waved away my objections. "Well, thumbs are over-rated anyway. A gentleman should use his thumbs as little as possible. That is what servants are for."

"He practically raised me, after all."

"That is no recommendation. His code made it impossible for him to discipline you and because he himself is a mechanism he was incapable of teaching you how humans actually behave. Consequently you are like a dog that is raised to believe it is a person and views other dogs with amused condescension. No, I'm afraid that cannot be counted among Bentley's accomplishments."

I desperately tried to shunt her off onto a side track.

"How's Uncle Hugo? I trust you left him well?"

"I left him adding and subtracting in his little office. He can do no harm in there and will emerge exhausted, which is ideal. A well-rested husband is the Devil's plaything. You should take up some enervating hobbies yourself."

It was high time to take the ball by the horns. Sorry... bull. "Look here, Aunt, why this sudden interest in my domestic affairs?"

"It seems to me that this higgledy-piggledy bachelor life you lead is taking a terrible toll on you. I am naturally concerned."

"And I suppose your remedy is to attach some weak-eyed barnacle like Euphonia Gumboot to me in matrimony?"

My aunt glared down her nose at me. "Euphonia Gumboot is the daughter of my oldest friend. I consider that recommendation enough. If you feel any sense of obligation for the affection I have lavished upon you since childhood, you will oblige me by marrying her at once."

"I don't like her."

She smiled with satisfaction. "You see? It's as if you've been married for years. She will take you in hand."

"I don't want to be taken in hand. I'm quite happy as I am."

"You are not. No man who possesses youth, money and freedom can be happy until those things are taken away by a loving partner. We never appreciate a thing until it is gone. It is like the pang one feels upon eating the last chocolate in the box—even inferior chocolate leaves one with a certain wistfulness."

"Euphonia Gumboot is a blight and a pestilence."

"She is waiting in the car."

"You don't think I'm going to invite her in?"

"Of course not. I have already done so."

"Really, Aunt!"

"You left me no choice. You possess the skills of a Houdini."

Bentley drifted in and cleared his throat. "Miss Euphonia Gumboot, Sir."

Have you ever gazed into a lively brook and noticed how the water merrily twists and fractures the images of the submerged rocks? Euphonia was rather like that. She had all the required features but one found oneself reaching for corrective lenses before realizing that the problem was not one's eyes. I took a deep breath.

"Euphonia! I hope I see you well."

"Can you not see me well? I can move into the light." She staggered a few paces toward the window. "Is that better?"

It was definitely not. "Um, yes."

My aunt attempted to impose order. "Come and sit down, my dear. You and my nephew are acquainted, I believe?"

"Are we? Who is your nephew?"

Aunt Hypatia's composure slipped the tiniest bit. "This is my nephew... Cyril."

"Oh! I thought you were speaking of another nephew."

"Why would I... never mind. Why don't you gaze at that clock on the wall? It shows your profile to its best advantage."

"All right. Confusion is our enemy."

"I suppose you mean confusion to our enemies."

"Is that it?"

"It is."

I thought I'd better swing the conversation to something more cheerful. "Confusion to our enemies. So, Aunt, are you going to the country this weekend?"

"We are not. I am holding a little soiree here in town tomorrow night which you will be so good as to attend."

"Tomorrow night? Drat! How I'd love to be there but..."

"Cease these fruitless machinations. You must be part eel, upon my word. It is not enough to get you into the boat. One must strike you with an oar to be sure of you."

I slumped in defeat. "Who will be at this soiree, might one ask?"

"Oh, people... it's rather a potpourri."

Euphonia spoke without removing her eyes from the clock. "I'll be there."

Aunt Hypatia glared at the back of her head. "I'm afraid you've sprung the trap before the mouse had time to smell the cheese, my dear."

"What?"

My aunt sighed. "Yes, that's roughly the level of comprehension I anticipated."

"Really, Aunt."

"You may bring your cousin Cheswick if that will make the evening more palatable."

Cheswick Wickford-Davies (Binky to his familiars) is as much a responsibility as a friend. He has an unfortunate tendency to put his foot in it, and over the years I have pulled said foot out of many a sticky situation. He is loyal and unfailingly chipper, however, and blood is thicker than water, although I have yet to see the scientific evidence. Euphonia made a sound like a discontented kitten.

"I'm getting a crick in my neck."

"Just another moment, my dear. Observe the intricate gilding on the second hand."

"Which is the second hand?"

"The larger one, I believe."

"So the other is the first hand?"

My aunt stared at the back of her head. "Why not?"

"Can I offer you tea?" I asked insincerely. "Cook has made some scones."

"No thank you. As you know, I distrust anything that has not been inspected in a government facility."

"You don't know what you're missing."

"What I do not know cannot hurt me. Ignorance is like a shining shield in that regard. Well, we should take our leave. Until tomorrow night."

"Are we going? Can I stop looking at the clock now?"

"Yes, dear. I think it's best you not speak again until we're in the car. Let us preserve what tattered mystery we still possess."

"What?"

"Precisely. Ta-ta, Nephew."

"Yes. Ta-ta. Love and all that."

I saw them to the door with the usual flourishes and watched them drive off with a sinking feeling in my vitals. "Bentley?"

"Sir?"

"You heard?"

"Yes, Sir."

"What shall I do?"

"I have been meditating on the subject and my suggestion is that you should go abroad."

I looked at him doubtfully. "Really? Can I do that?"

"Among your recent correspondence there was an invitation to attend a conference on matters of a vaguely scientific nature."

"Zounds, that sounds deadly."

"I believe it is the custom to frame these invitations as dry academic events, but the reality involves a great deal more alcohol than is implied in the letter."

"That's more like it. Where is this convocation?"

"New York, Sir."

"Hallo! Now you're talking."

"The opening ceremony is tomorrow evening. If you are not to be tardy you must leave today."

"Perfect! I'll miss my aunt's soiree completely."

"That is my understanding."

"But even the fastest ship will never make it in time."

"You could take your dirigible, Sir."

I stared at him in wonder. "I have a dirigible?"

"Smythe Corporation possesses several dirigibles for purposes of publicity and executive junkets. As the owner of the company, they are at your disposal."

"Pack my things and tell the airfield to gas up the spiffiest blimp on the lot."

"At once, Sir."

The doorbell chose that moment to play "Lady of Spain." A fast-talking salesman had convinced me that musical doorbells were the coming thing. Apparently, they were still en route.

"You don't suppose my aunt has returned?"

"I shall ascertain who it is."

He misted away and condensed back into the room with my cousin Binky slouching behind him looking as if fortune and he had parted on bad terms.

"Hallo, old cock! What brings you to the ancestral home on this fine morn? Confusion to our enemies."

"Not 'Death before dishonour'?"

"It's the latest thing, I'm told."

"Confusion to our enemies, then. I'm up a tree, Cyril."

"Put your foot in it, have you?"

"What I did I was compelled to do by the dictates of natural law."

"Which natural law are we speaking of?"

"The law of animal attraction. We have glands, haven't we? And those glands require us to obey certain urges, don't they? And if a young person takes things the wrong way it can cause a certain amount of trouble, can't it?"

"Why don't you start at the beginning with as few rhetorical flourishes as possible?"

"Lady of Spain" echoed through the halls once again. Bentley passed us at a gliding run. "Excuse me, Sir."

I turned back to Binky, whose eyes were growing feverish. "Continue, old duck."

"Well, you know I'm terribly keen on Judy."

"A fine young lady."

"I happened to be standing next to her on a balcony in the moonlight..."

"Dangerous things—balconies. Started all that trouble with Romeo and Juliet."

"And moonlight is the very devil for rousing romantic feelings in a chap."

"I avoid it like poison oak."

Bentley passed us again, moving at a more stately pace.

"Who was it, Bentley?"

"No one, Sir."

"No one?"

"No, Sir."

"Odd. That's been happening quite a lot lately. Perhaps the bell is broken."

"Perhaps, Sir."

"I'm getting rather tired of 'Lady of Spain,' I must say."

"I could acquire a new bell with a more conventional ring."

"Stay the course, Bentley. Musical doorbells will come into their own shortly and we shall be the envy of all and sundry."

"No doubt, Sir."

He glided to the side table and began polishing knickknacks, looking rather gloomy, I thought. I turned back to Binky. "Sorry, go on, old man. You were standing in the perilous moonlight..."

"We were chatting away and I suddenly found myself getting lost in her eyes. Before I knew it, I had said something that in retrospect sounded very like a proposal."

"What was the exact wording? Imagine I'm your divorce lawyer. What did you say?"

"That's the thing... I can't remember. Between the moonlight and those eyes, it's all rather vague. It was something along the lines of, 'A chap would be pretty bally lucky to spend his life with someone like you...' and then there might have been, 'I wish I could stand here in the moonlight with you forever.' I might have thrown in something like, 'Do you think you could ever go for a sap like me?'"

"And what was her reply?"

"Again, it's all rather foggy. I think she said, 'Sure.'"

"Simple and to the point."

"But did she believe she was accepting a proposal? It's a rather important thing to ferret out."

"You could do worse."

"I barely know her. We've never even gone to dinner. And I have nothing to offer her. As you know, the old coffers are bare."

"I don't think she cares about money."

He looked at me with alarm. "You see? What other horrible secrets is she hiding?"

"Let's find out if she considers herself engaged. If the answer is no then these concerns are moot. Say, here's an idea..."

Binky cleared his throat theatrically. He widened his eyes and jerked his head significantly toward Bentley.

I stared at him blankly. "What on earth are you doing?"

"It's just... are you sure you wouldn't like to ask Bentley?"

Bentley's joints gave a little squeak. "I would be happy to help, Sir."

"Stand down, Bentley. I have a perfect plan."

He stepped back rather slower than he had stepped forth. "Of course, Sir."

Binky stared at me desperately. "But... really? I mean, he's right there... devious as a Medici. 'Happy to help,' he said."

"Not necessary. Trust in me, old badger."

"I feel a little nauseous. Perhaps I should sit down."

He flopped into a chair and slumped despairingly. I hastened to reassure him.

"I'm leaving today for New York in the company dirigible to attend a scientific conference."

He looked at me oddly. "That's a lot to digest in one sentence."

"I'm taking Cook, of course. It would make perfect sense to ask Judy to come as the officer in charge of social justice at Smythe Corporation. That makes it a kind of family junket."

I had found my genius of a cook, who by an odd coincidence was named Cook, on a recent adventure among the masses. Her children, Ernie and Judy, turned out to be rather brilliant as well and I had demonstrated my business acumen by hiring them.

"All those hours cooped up in the dirigible should sweat out Judy's true feelings."

My companion brightened at once. "And I'll get a free trip to New York!"

"Scurry home and pack. Meet us at the airfield at six."

"Righto! Thanks awfully, Cyril."

"Don't mention it, old rooster. Only too glad."

He trundled off happily. I pretended to stare at a stuffed owl on the mantel while focusing my peripheral vision on Bentley. Of course, I was dying to ask him what he thought of my plan, but pride—which bringeth down nations—made the old tongue cleave to the roof of one's mouth. His face was as smooth as a pot of mush.

"Well, Bentley, what are they wearing in New York these days?"

"The dress there is very different from what we are accustomed to. New Yorkers delight in disguising their wealth behind apparel that is as disreputable as possible. I believe dungarees and a T-shirt are all that are required, Sir."

"Even among tycoons?"

"Especially there, Sir. These captains of industry will certainly compete to see who can dress most authentically like a hobo."

"How odd. Well, whatever you think best. I rely on you."

"Thank you, Sir. Most gratifying. I shall begin packing at once."

He slid away like a pat of butter on a hot skillet. New York... with its legendary jazz clubs and belligerent pigeons. I was too excited to sit still. I paced the room, rearranging the knickknacks and then arranging them back again until I managed to drop a china figurine of a shepherdess and her swain, which shattered at once. Bentley leaned into the room and surveyed the damage.

"It will be several hours before we leave for the airfield, Sir."

"Yes, I'm well aware. Don't know what to do with myself. Bit excited, what?"

Bentley's gears ground for a moment. "I know it is a terrible imposition, Sir, but I wonder if I might ask you to untangle this ball of string? I am too occupied with packing to attend to it at the moment."

"String? Toss it this way. I'll have it untangled in no time. I'm an absolute wizard with string."

He rolled a large tangle of twine at me and I squinted at the various knots. The next thing I knew it was five o'clock and

Bentley stood at the door with the suitcases. "Time to go? Oh well, I'll take care of that string when we return."

"Of course, Sir. The car is waiting."

I have a sad history of driving extravagant and fanciful vehicles but I had recently been shown the arrogance of flaunting my wealth in this obscene manner and now I drove about in a plain black sedan. Of course, the inside of the car was still fitted out like an Emperor's boudoir. Bentley drove as I rolled about on the satin bolsters nibbling Cook's peanut brittle. At last, we came to a halt.

"We have arrived, Sir."

I stepped from the back seat to behold a marvel. An enormous silver dirigible swung from its tethers before me. "Smythe Corporation" screamed from its side in bright red letters.

"Quite a sight, eh Bentley? Rather aggressively male, I must say. What makes it go up, do you suppose?"

"I believe the lift is supplied by hydrogen gas, Sir."

"What, the same stuff that lights up the sconces in the old domicile?"

"It is quite flammable, Sir."

I was seized by a sudden apprehension. "Flammable? Is there any danger?"

"It is perfectly safe, so long as there are no open flames aboard."

"What if it catches fire in the middle of the ocean? We'd be marooned."

"There is no possibility of being marooned."

"That's a relief."

"We would be incinerated instantly."

I goggled at him accusingly. "How gruesome! Attending my aunt's soiree only chanced indigestion and possible matrimony. This is a risk to life and limb."

Bentley stared into the middle distance.

"I believe I saw Cook carrying a large blueberry cobbler onto the airship, Sir."

I suddenly realized that I had not eaten a bite since breakfast. "Blueberry, you say?"

"With a streusel topping."

I straightened my shoulders. "Oh well, no one lives forever."

"Shall we board now, Sir?"

"Yes, let's have a look at this floating pleasure palace."

We climbed up the ramp and into the cabin. Overstuffed sofas and padded armchairs were scattered about among potted palms. It felt rather like my club, Twits. This impression was strengthened by the sight of C. Langford-Cheeseworth, a habitué of the club, lounging by a window and twirling his jeweled monocle.

"Cheeseworth? What are you doing here?"

Cheeseworth affected a rather louche manner of speaking. I had long suspected that his occasional inability to articulate the letter "R" was a theatrical device. "Hallo, Cywil. I'm a stowaway! What fun. I wan into Binky at the club and he told me all about your desperate flight to fweedom. I had to come along. Haven't been to New York in ages.

"So he was blabbing all over the club, was he?"

"Oh no. Just an intimate lunch. Consommé and cwackers. I'm sure no one overheard us."

"Well, welcome aboard, old duck."

"I lived in New York for a time in younger days. I had dweams of playing the saxophone in a low dive on the Bowery. Alas, my tongue lacked the necessary dexterity. I have labored on it since and now I can tie a cherry stem into a bow, but I still cannot play the saxophone."

He grew rather melancholy and stared out of the window. Cook was laying out a buffet. "Hallo, Cyril, love."

"Evening, Cook."

"Would you like some crostini with white beans, fresh thyme and olive oil?"

"Would I!"

I never missed a chance to swill down Cook's creations. Her crostini would make the angels weep. As I started to load up a plate, I spotted Judy sitting in an armchair scribbling away in a notebook and Binky pretending not to stare at her from behind a palm plant. I sidled up to him, trying not to crunch too loudly on my crostini. "Well? Have you made any progress?"

He squinted at me myopically. "Not yet. I'm observing her behavior."

"How's that going?"

"My eyes are beginning to burn."

"Look here, you've got to get in there and roll about in the conversation if you're going to learn anything useful."

He looked up at me plaintively. "You do it."

"Me? I'm not the one in an ambiguous state of engagement."

"Just chat her up. See if she drops any hints."

"I'm not Mata Hari, you know."

His eyes grew moist. "I'd do it for you."

Well, I couldn't argue with that. Binky would do practically anything for anyone even if they expressly asked him not to.

"Very well, but don't expect miracles."

By now Judy had migrated to the buffet and was nibbling on a stuffed mushroom. I glided up next to her. "Quite a selection, what? The crostini are particularly savory."

"I've been snacking on Mum's crostini since I got my first tooth."

"Damned decent of you to come along on this junket."

"Thank you for asking me."

"Lots of opportunities to discuss social justice with like-minded individuals."

"Bentley gave me a list of the guests. It's packed with philanthropists. I've been making some notes."

"Good show. And what about you? Anything going on in your life that... you know, anything of a personal nature that's got you... I suppose one would say, is there anyone interesting in your personal life... of a personal nature?"

She gave me an odd look. "Are you trying to ask me if I'm seeing anyone?"

"Oh! Well... of course it's none of my business."

She looked down at the mushroom caps. "Isn't it?"

"If you'd rather not say..."

"You seem very interested."

"That's just my natural curiosity."

She glanced at me with a little smile. "You're so funny."

"Am I? I wish the fellows at the club thought so."

"You don't have to be so nervous."

"I'm not at all nervous. I'm cool as a cucumber."

I could see Binky watching us like a department store detective eyeing a couple of potential shoplifters. "So, are you saying you don't have an... understanding with anyone that could be construed as... an attachment?"

She gave my bicep a rather painful poke. "No, silly, the field is quite free. When did you want to go out?"

The plate of crostini slipped from my nerveless fingers and hit the floor with a crash! The old saying about no good deed going unpunished had risen up to bite me in the tender bits. My instinctive response at such moments of peril is to freeze and hope that the predator moves on to other game. I held my breath, unfocused my eyes and tried to fade into my surroundings. After what seemed like an eternity, I returned to the mortal plane to find Judy still looking at me expectantly. I abandoned all hope and swore to myself that if I managed to squeeze out of this predicament, I would never lift a finger to help another human being as long as I lived—even if I was to be boiled alive and served with a dollop of horseradish on the side.

CHAPTER TWO

This Dirigible is Awfully Crowded

I am aware that there is a certain type of low fellow who delights in conquest. To a cur like this any female is fair game—be she an old chum's sister or the betrothed of the local vicar. Judy, being both an employee and someone my best friend had courted in the moonlight, was absolutely out of bounds. I had, however, led the innocent lass into a misapprehension. To disabuse her would wound her deeply.

Rock, hard place. What was a fellow to do? I looked for Bentley, but he was at the other end of the cabin ironing T-shirts.

Judy was looking at me with concern. "Are you all right?"

"Me? Never better."

"You've dropped your crostini."

"What, that? Just a flourish—like smashing one's champagne glass in the fireplace after a stirring toast. Hola!"

I seized another plate and hurled it to the floor. It smashed in a most satisfying manner.

"Oh my!"

Cheeseworth's head popped up from behind a sofa. "I say, is this a thing? I'll play!" He merrily hurled his own plate to the floor.

Cook leaned out from the galley. "Stop that!"

Cheeseworth hung his head in shame. "Sowwy, Cook. I thought it was a thing."

Bentley distilled himself out of the ether. "May I retrieve your appetizers, Sir?"

"Bentley, yes! Thank you."

"Would you like a fresh plate?"

"No, no, that's quite enough crostini for one evening."

"Very good, Sir."

I turned to Judy, who had been watching me all this while with a mysterious smile on her lips. "What were we talking about?"

"You were asking me out."

"Oh! That! Well... Hmmm."

I found it devilishly hard to concentrate with her staring like that. If only she would glance at the scenery and give me a chance to marshal my thoughts...

She poked my bicep again. I would have a bruise there tomorrow. "Why don't we go for a drink after the conference wraps up?"

"Why indeed?"

"Good. It's a date."

I slumped in defeat. "Is it? I suppose... well, there it is."

She finally looked away, a touch too late to be of any use to me, and stared at Binky. He had picked up a magazine, which he was holding upside down, and his eyes were peeping at us over the top of it.

"Binky's acting odd."

"Odder than usual, you mean?"

"He keeps squinting at us. Did you two have a falling out?"

"Not yet, but soon. Perhaps I'd better go and talk to him."

"All right. See you later."

"Yes. Until later, then."

I walked over to Binky as slowly as I could without actually going backward.

He threw down the magazine and leaned in eagerly. "Well? What did she say?"

"She does not consider herself engaged. Quite the opposite."

He leaned back with a sigh. "That's a relief."

"Is it?"

"I'm not saying matrimony is out of the question, but there's much to be said for the thrill of the chase."

"Yes. As to that, you may have to run pretty fast to catch her. She's definitely on the move."

He stared at me uncomprehendingly. "What?"

"Look here, you know I'd never poach in another man's trout stream."

"What's a trout?"

"It was some sort of fish, I believe, but don't distract me."

"What are you saying?"

"I'm saying that through no fault of my own I find myself taking her out for drinks."

Binky began to quiver. He shakily pointed a finger at my nose. "Judas!"

"Now, now..."

"Brutus!"

"It wasn't my idea."

"Whose was it, then?"

"Hers, of course."

He laughed bitterly. "So, she's in love with you?"

"My God, I hope not."

"Not good enough for you?"

"Too good by half. Look, old spoon, I only want what's best for you."

"And you think that would be a life of chastity?"

This was all getting to be a little much. "It's your own fault. You made me speak to her."

He finally ran out of air and slumped into a chair. "She was the one. I see it now. I shall never love again."

"When you thought you were engaged to her you were wretched!"

"That was the old me—before suffering had made a man of me."

"I'll fix it. Just give me time and I'll douse the fire within her. I have a natural gift for dousing the fires within women as you know."

He stared into the distance with reddening eyes. "Too late. Too late. I shall die alone, friendless, riddled with disease... no one to mourn for me."

I could see he was pretty low. Something sparked in the old noodle and I knew just what to do.

"See here, let's get Bentley on the case."

His head whipped around and his shoulders straightened. "By Jove, you've finally come to your senses."

We made our way to the far end of the cabin where Bentley had finished with the T-shirts and was busily ironing dungarees. He looked up at us. "Is there something you require, Sir?"

"A little advice, Bentley."

"Of course, Sir." He set down the steam iron and regarded us gravely.

"It's of a romantic nature."

"I see."

"You know Judy?"

"I am acquainted with the young lady."

"Well, she's somehow gotten it into her head that I'm keen on her."

"And are you keen on her, Sir?"

"No! I mean, she's a blossom of womanhood, but it's Binky here who's pawing at the ground."

His gears whirled for a moment. "You wish to rebuff her."

"But gently."

Binky held up a warning finger. "You mustn't harm a hair on her head."

"Perhaps it would be best if the young lady rebuffed you instead."

I had to chuckle at his naivete. "That would be a dream come true, but how on earth would you achieve it? I mean, look at me. What woman in her right mind..."

"What a conceited prig you are. I'm every bit as desirable as you," sniffed Binky.

"Come, come, old hound. Compare our profiles."

"You're just rich. That's your only attraction."

"You're being rather wounding."

Bentley made a small harrumphing sound. "Perhaps we could deal with the problem at hand, Sir?"

"My word! Have you figured it out already?"

"Miss Judy is a young lady of high principles, I believe?"

Binky's eyes lit with a fervent glow. "She will not compromise on matters of social justice."

"She's rather a blister about it," I added, sotto voce.

"Then my suggestion is that you perform an act so egregious that her feelings toward you turn to anger and disappointment rather than affection."

I frowned. "That seems like hard cheese for me."

Binky rounded on me. "It's your fault. Why shouldn't you bear the consequences?"

"Again, I must point out..."

"Knave. Miscreant. Reprobate."

Bentley harrumphed for a second time. "Assigning blame is of no useful purpose, Sir."

"What do you suggest I do? Wear stripes with checks? Relieve babies of their candy?"

"Nothing suggests itself at the moment. Perhaps this upcoming conference will present an opportunity."

"We've got to work fast. I'm having drinks with her after."

"I shall be on the alert, Sir."

There was a sudden scream of brakes from the tarmac outside, followed by slamming doors and the thunder of feet on the airship's gangway.

"What on earth is that?"

The cabin door flew open and there stood Aunt Hypatia, Uncle Hugo and—her lace glove already hopelessly tangled in a palm plant—the gangly frame of Euphonia Gumboot. The blood froze in my veins.

"Aunt! Uncle! What are you all doing here?"

My aunt fixed me with a gorgon's glare. "I might ask you the same thing. One could almost suspect you of fleeing my soiree."

"What? Don't be silly."

"Where are you off to, then?"

"Oh... just taking a little spin around the Cotswolds, then back in plenty of time."

"Very well. We shall accompany you."

"But... that is... oh drat! To be perfectly truthful, Aunt, an important meeting in New York makes it impossible for me to attend your soiree. I'm dreadfully sorry."

She gave a self-satisfied sniff and adjusted the train of her gown.

"Don't give it a thought."

"Really?"

"When I learned of your plans, I canceled my soiree. We are quite free to accompany you to New York."

Well, this was a blow to the midsection as you can imagine. I turned to Binky, who was innocently staring at the ceiling. "Did you make a general announcement at the club?"

"I only told Cheeseworth."

Cheeseworth was helping himself to the stuffed mushrooms. "And you know me. A sealed cwypt."

"All is explained," I sighed. I must say—that Jean Valjean fellow thought he had it bad with Javert, but if he'd had Aunt Hypatia on his tail it would have been a much shorter book.

"Well... make yourselves comfortable, everyone. Have you brought your luggage?"

Uncle Hugo had been staring around the cabin estimating the value of its contents. "We have... and sufficient packaged food for the duration."

"That really wasn't necessary, Uncle. You can't light a fire to heat anything, you know. Hydrogen, apparently."

"Impossible Mutton can be eaten cold if one scrapes off the congealed gravy. I rather prefer it."

I could no longer ignore the vigorous pantomime taking place between Euphonia and the palm tree, which had taken hold of her glove with an unbreakable grip.

"And you've brought Euphonia!"

My aunt gazed on her struggles benevolently. "I promised her dinner and I am a person of my word."

Euphonia took a breather from her exertions. "I'm sorry, could someone detach me from this plant?"

Binky jogged eagerly toward her. "Here, let me."

"Thank you."

"Not at all. Oh! Now it's got me as well."

The buttons of his jacket had been happily seized by the playful palm. Euphonia stamped a surprisingly large foot.

"Plants are always attacking me. I don't see why we're always trying to save them."

Binky was concentrating fiercely on his buttons. "Neither do I. Lot of work, plants. Always needing water and whatnot. Like babies, aren't they?"

"Exactly. Yet when I suggest that we replace them with artificial copies I get the most censorious looks."

"Well, I'm in favor."

He gave the plant a vigorous shake and gazed at it thoughtfully. "Do you know, I think it will be easier to remove my jacket and just leave it hanging. Like fruit."

"And I shall do the same with my glove. What fun!"

They proceeded to divest themselves of the articles in question. My aunt glared.

"Does this play have an intermission? One would like to sit down."

I indicated a nearby chaise. "Yes, do sit down."

Aunt Hypatia has always been partial to Cheeseworth, who brought his mushrooms and sat beside her.

"Hello, Cheeseworth. Coming to New York, are you?"

"Hoping to relive old memories. I spent some years there working as a shoe shine boy to earn money for cigarettes after my father cast me from the bosom of my family."

Aunt Hypatia shook her head. "An unfortunate time."

"He was not a tolerant man and my love of musical comedy was the final stwaw. He is in a coma now and our welationship has impwoved."

Again, our peace was shattered by a squeal of tires.

"I wonder who that could be?"

A car door slammed, the gangway thundered and the door of the dirigible was hurled open once again. Cubby Martinez, the officious Marshall of Twits, stood panting at the entryway.

"Stop this dirigible!"

"Cubby?"

"The same!"

"What on earth are you doing here?"

"Protecting the honor of my family."

Euphonia stepped forward and thumped Cubby on the shoulder. "Oh Cubby, go away."

My head swam. "Euphonia? You know this man?"

"He is my stepbrother."

"What?"

"And I'll thank you to unhand my sister, Chippington-Smythe."

"I'm nowhere near your sister, physically or spiritually."

"There is a name for men who spirit innocent young ladies out of the country for who knows what immoral purpose."

Binky raised a hand. "Is it Raoul?"

"Look here, Cubby—I know we have our differences but on this subject we are united. Take your sister and depart. I will not lift a finger to stop you."

Bentley was suddenly at my elbow. "Pardon me, Sir, I'm afraid that is no longer possible. We have begun our ascent."

"Have we?"

"It has been a smooth departure."

I ran to a window and goggled at the receding firmament. "Well, Cubby old man, it looks like you're coming to New York with us."

"What? Turn this blimp around at once."

Bentley shook his head gravely. "I'm afraid that is impossible, Sir. There is a brisk westward wind that makes returning impractical."

My aunt gave a contented grunt. "All has worked out in a satisfactory manner. Euphonia now has a family member to chaperone her and no one can say we have not observed the proprieties."

Cubby's eyes began to redden. "But who will enforce the club rules? The members will run riot."

I shook my head. "You've no one to blame but yourself, Cubby. If you didn't have such an infernal heavy hand there wouldn't be all this pent-up pressure to act out."

"Any physical damage to the club will be on your head, Chippington-Smythe!"

I sighed. "You really are a pustule."

Cook appeared, wiping her hands with a striped towel. "Dinner will be ready in five minutes."

Thank you, Cook."

"There's gazpacho, focaccia and leeks vinaigrette with walnuts."

My mouth began to water. "Yum!"

Aunt Hypatia was unmoved. "Just put out some of the packaged dinners we brought and a pair of scissors. We can serve ourselves. We must practice living in a classless society if we are going to America."

Cook gave my aunt a hard stare and pressed her lips together until they turned white. "Yes, Ma'am."

As the company disposed themselves, my aunt moved inexorably toward me, forcing me to hop around various potted plants and ottomans until I found myself trapped in a corner. It seemed there was no escape. Like a choir director holding open calls for the Christmas Fete, I would be forced to face the music.

"Well, young man, you have caused me a great deal of inconvenience. What do you have to say for yourself? And I may as well tell you that whatever you say I have already determined to disregard it."

"The truth is I couldn't stand another table full of prospective brides chewing and staring and simpering at me—especially the aptly named Miss Gumboot. It's more than flesh and blood can bear."

My aunt extracted a lace handkerchief from an invisible pocket and delicately blew her nose. "There is a simple solution."

"Which is?"

"Find an acceptable young lady and I shall no longer feel obliged to present you with the smorgasbord of femininity that you seem to detest so vigorously."

I spotted Judy heading our way and a light went on in the dusty attic just behind my forehead. "As it happens, Aunt, I have found just such a young lady."

She eyed me suspiciously. "Oh? I trust she is not in the theatrical profession. The family has been burned too many times by females of that ilk."

"Not at all. She's my head of Social Justice. A very intelligent young woman."

"I shall be the judge of that. I must assure myself that she is suitable. If not, Miss Gumboot remains within easy reach and can be proposed to with a minimum of preparation."

The unsuspecting Judy rolled up.

"Ah! Here she is! Judy, you remember my Aunt Hypatia?"

"Yes. Hello."

Judy presented a hand, which my aunt touched briefly with her fingertips.

"Your greeting is from the minimalist school. It reveals little. We must converse at greater length."

"You've met before you know, Aunt."

My aunt waved a hand. "When I encounter a person, I always assume that we have met before. It avoids much unpleasantness."

I turned to Judy. "I was just telling my aunt about us. You know... about us going for drinks... and the rest."

She looked at me oddly. "Oh. All right."

My aunt was staring at her through a small pair of glasses that she had produced from another pocket.

"You're quite a pretty thing. Your hips are rather narrow, but the babies in our family tend to be stunted."

Judy stared back at her. "Babies?"

"I am being premature... which is another characteristic of the family's offspring."

At that moment, thank heavens, Uncle Hugo called out from the dinner table, "Hypatia, would you prefer Chickeny Nuggets in a brown sauce or Implausible Ham in a yellow sauce?"

She bellowed back at him. "It makes little difference. They taste much the same." She turned to Judy. "Excuse me, my dear. My husband fancies himself a chef. If I do not intervene, he may attempt to improve my dinner by mixing the contents of various bags and adding quantities of salt to disastrous effect. I shall continue my interrogation at dinner."

She stomped off. "Stop what you are doing at once, Hugo, do you hear?"

Judy looked at me with her hands on her hips.

I smiled sheepishly. "Sorry about my aunt."

"What was all that about babies?"

I concentrated furiously. "I should have warned you—she's... eccentric. Never had children of her own and is obsessed with babies. Evaluates the fertility of every female she meets. Talks of nothing else. Just ignore her."

She glanced over at my aunt sympathetically. "Poor thing. Where are you sitting?"

I smiled winningly. "Next to you, of course. Save us a couple of seats."

"All right. Don't be too long."

"I caught Binky's eye and jerked my head in the general direction of a quiet corner. He looked at me uncomprehendingly.

"What are you doing?"

"Shh. Never mind. Come here!"

He strolled over. "What on earth is the matter?"

"I'm afraid something's come up and I can't give Judy the heave-ho just yet."

He stamped a hoof. "But you promised!"

"And I will honor that promise—after we return from America. For now, she is the only thing standing between me and the horrifying Miss Gumboot."

Binky looked over at the party in question and smiled. "Euphonia? I think she's charming."

I looked at him disbelievingly. "You really are the closest thing to a Bonobo."

"Of course she can't hold a candle to Judy. It's just that I appreciate her wit and good humor."

"Do you? Then do a chap a favor—use all of your animal magnetism to keep her off of me until I can kick her down the gangplank at the end of this adventure."

"What's in it for me?"

"Is friendship not enough?"

"No."

"Very well, what do you want?"

"I want that new tie you acquired from Borgen and Bots. The one with the palm tree on it."

"I love that tie!"

"Nevertheless."

I wriggled for a bit, but he had me by the ears and he knew it. "It's yours, you pirate."

Bentley wafted over. "Dinner, Sir."

"Look here, Bentley, there's been a change of plans. Until I am safely out of range of Miss Gumboot, I must maintain the ruse that Judy and I are engaged in a wild flirtation."

He fixed his optical sensors on me grimly. "It may make your ultimate aim of severing your connection with Miss Judy more complicated, Sir."

"It can't be helped. We must put out one fire at a time and Euphonia is a three-alarm flaming dumpster."

"I understand, Sir."

He paced away. Binky was eyeing me suspiciously. "It is only a ruse, isn't it? You're not trying to cut me out with Judy?"

"How can you say such a thing?"

He blushed with shame. "You're right. I'm acting like that Othello chap. Green-eyed muenster and all that.

"Monster!"

He looked injured. "What have I done now?"

I put a reassuring hand on his shoulder. "No. It's the green-eyed *monster*. Not muenster. Muenster was a cheese, I believe. Now come, they're waiting for us."

With a heart brimming with dread, I stalked toward the dinner table—a seething swamp populated with carnivorous predators in every direction... and gazpacho.

CHAPTER THREE

A Long Day's Journey to Manhattan

Dinner did not begin well. My aunt and her retinue sat at one end of the table, pouring turgid pools of neon-colored sauce from plastic packets onto their plates. As I approached the table, Euphonia waved at me gaily.

"Yoo-hoo, Cyril, sit here by me."

"I forbid it!"

Euphonia gave her brother a slap on the arm. "Shut up, Cubby."

Binky suavely inserted himself between them and slid into the vacant chair. "I'm afraid I must claim that seat for myself and reap the... plentiful bounty of your company in all its... autumnal splendor, Miss Gumboot."

She simpered at him. "Oh dear, that sounds gallant. Is it meant to be gallant?"

Binky frowned. "I believe so. I rather lost the thread about halfway through."

"I try never to utter a sentence of more than twelve words. It keeps me from losing my way quite so often." Uncle Hugo slid a plate over to her. She clapped her hands gaily. "Oh, I love implausible ham!"

Cheeseworth leaned over. "That was my review in the one foray into acting I attempted. The play was, 'Don't Just Stand There, Kill Something' and I was the lovesick gamekeeper. The Daily Snob called me 'an implausible ham.' I think I have the clipping about me somewhere."

He began rifling through pockets. I noticed that Cubby had refused the plate my uncle offered him.

"What will you have, Cubby? You're welcome to join us in sybaritic splendor as we revel in Cook's culinary genius."

"Nothing, thank you. Just a glass of water."

"Not hungry?"

"I will not dignify this kidnapping by eating the bread of my oppressors."

I sat back and regarded him with astonishment. "You know we'll be gone for days?"

"Nevertheless."

Binky shrugged. "You're made of sterner stuff than I, Cubby. I get woozy if I go more than two hours without a snack."

"And I suppose you're proud of that. All you elites are the same."

My uncle pointed a fork at Cubby. "Steady on, Sir."

"You've never known want. You've never gone a day without food."

I gazed at him in astonishment. "Have *you*?"

"I won't dignify that with a reply."

Euphonia looked up from her "ham". "Cubby was dreadfully poor as a child."

"That's enough, Euphonia!"

"His father was a scoundrel. Gambled everything away. It wasn't until our mother remarried my father that the family fortunes improved."

"I forbid you to say another word!"

Aunt Hypatia looked thoughtful. "I knew your father, Mr. Martinez. He led your poor mother a merry dance. I used to send her my old garments or she would have gone about looking like a scarecrow."

"This is excruciating! Please change the subject."

"It's nothing to be ashamed of," Binky gargled around a mouthful of leeks vinaigrette. "I've barely got two pennies to rub together."

Cubby sneered. "But you will never be thrown into the street. You have friends and relations who will always support you."

"Have you no friends?"

"I do not need or wish for friendship. I have my duty and that is enough. Now I insist that we speak no more of this."

As the host, the onus was on me to change the subject. "Let's turn our attention to this delightful dinner. *Bon appetit*, everyone."

Euphonia, who apparently didn't speak French, looked alarmed. "Are there bones in it? I hope I don't choke."

Binky winked at her coquettishly. "Would you like me to cut it into little pieces for you?"

"Would you? How chivalrous."

Binky went to work with the knife and fork, but his attention was focused on Miss Gumboot rather than the slippery slices of "ham," and a large chunk flew off the plate in Cubby's direction.

"Careful, you clod! I don't have a change of clothing."

"Slippery little devils," said Binky.

Euphonia smiled at him. "It's the sauce. It is oleaginous."

"What a spiffing word!"

"It is one of my favorites. I have far too few occasions to use it." She drew the word out languorously. "Oleaginous."

Binky reddened. "You are naughty, Miss Gumboot."

I nipped this flirtation in the bud. "Have you been to New York, Aunt?"

"Never. Travel is broadening, they say, and that is never a good thing."

"What about you, Uncle Hugo?"

"Heavens no. It is a savage place, by all accounts. We have business in America, but it is accomplished through the mail."

"I've heard New York is thrilling."

Aunt Hypatia shook her head grimly. "You prove my point. Being thrilled is cousin to being hysterical. They both involve adrenaline, which is the most uncouth of all the hormones." My aunt set down her fork and turned the full force of her regard on Judy. "Now, my dear, tell me about yourself. Who are your people?"

I could see Judy's hackles rising. "My... people?"

"What is your parentage? From whom do you derive? Are there any hereditary flaws in your gene pool or institutionalized madmen we should be aware of?"

"What?!"

"Aunt! Let's not give her the third degree!"

Euphonia turned to Binky. "I've always wondered what the first two degrees are?"

"By Jove, that's a thought. I have a degree in something from University. It's either for history or cricket. I can't remember which."

Cook brought a huge platter and set it down in front of Judy. She stood staring at Aunt Hypatia with her fists on her hips. Judy took one of her hands. "Well, as far as my parentage is concerned, my mother is currently serving us this delicious focaccia, which you seem determined not to try."

My aunt was unperturbed. "You mustn't take it personally, Cook. My digestive system is extremely delicate. So, your people are in service?"

Judy grew redder. "Is there anything wrong with that?"

"No, no. I think at least one person in a relationship should know how to light a fire or apply a tourniquet. We may not always be able to rely on civilization. How many children do you intend to produce?"

I gave Judy a significant glance. Her irritation changed at once to solicitude as she leaned toward my aunt.

"I'm sorry you were never able to have children of your own. Was it a medical problem?"

My aunt was taken aback. "Of course not. I am physically perfect in every respect."

"Then was it your husband?"

Hugo looked up from his plate. "I beg your pardon?"

"He too is, if not exceptional, then at least average in every way. It was the combination that proved toxic. My theory is that Hugo's sperm were so boring that my eggs simply went into hibernation."

My uncle threw down his fork. "This is hardly dinner table conversation."

"I have yet to find a subject that you find acceptable at table. Why masticating food should require such curated content I will never understand. Now, Jerry..."

"Judy."

"Indeed? I was sure it was Jerry."

"No."

"You could easily change it."

"I am fond of my name."

"Are you? Oh well. Back to the matter of children, as in, quantity of?"

"One or two, I suppose. I haven't given it a lot of thought."

"Two should be the minimum requirement. Siblings are the fiery crucible that smelts out the essence of our character. I had a brother and it was invaluable."

"Where is he now?"

"I have no idea. He stopped speaking altogether at the age of ten and began haunting public libraries. That was the last I heard of him."

"Poor thing."

"There are instances of one twin consuming the other in the womb. We were not twins but it was much the same thing."

Cheeseworth dabbed his lips with his napkin. "How I longed for a sibling. My father's member was lost in an incident involving a pwinting pwess and that was that. I was a lonely child, which I think explains my obsession with puppets."

Binky tore his gaze away from Euphonia and looked around the cabin. "I say, it's getting rather dark. One can barely discern where one's plate leaves off and the tablecloth begins. Couldn't we have some light?"

My uncle shook his head. "I'm afraid not. The nearness of the hydrogen makes lamps far too dangerous."

Euphonia gave a start. "Oh! I believe I've eaten my powder puff."

"Are you all right?"

She smiled at Binky. "Yes. Actually, it soaked up the sauce admirably."

Binky simpered. "The oleaginous sauce?"

She gave a little shriek and punched him in the arm. "La, Mr. Wickford-Davies, what a rake you are."

Cubby glared at Binky. "I trust you are not taking advantage of this darkness to play patty-cake with my sister."

Euphonia raised her fork. "Is there cake? I'll have a slice."

I threw up my hands. "Well, this is impossible. Darkness has come like a thief in the night. What on Earth shall we do now?"

My aunt huffed. "Whenever I find myself in an impossible situation I simply go to bed. That is the answer to most of life's conundrums."

"But how to find our beds? I can't see my hand in front of my face."

Bentley appeared at my elbow. "Pardon me, Sir. My sensors are unaffected by darkness. I shall guide you to your sleeping compartments one at a time."

"Excellent. While I'm waiting for my turn, just put a slice of focaccia in the old mitt, would you?"

"Of course, Sir."

Eventually, Bentley led me to my little sleeping cabin and in no time, I was snoring away and dreaming of pancakes.

I woke with the light streaming in and a moist mouthful of pillow. There was just time for a brush-up and a bite of a cold breakfast before we touched down and began unloading.

"This is the way to travel, eh, Binky?"

"According to the Captain we broke all records for an Atlantic crossing. Apparently, the wind was up our tails."

"I think that's called a tail wind, old mouse."

"I say, could I have a little word?"

"Of course, my lad. We are as brothers. Step this way."

We strolled to a pile of rusty old barrels. Binky cleared his throat. "The thing is... I don't know how much longer I can keep this up. Flirting with Miss Gumboot is exhausting and we didn't figure Cubby into the equation."

"You must not flag nor weaken. I need you to be a shield unto my right arm against the forces of Euphonia Gumboot for the weekend."

"All right, but one tie is not enough. I want a bottle of that cologne you drench yourself in."

"You mean 'Insouciance'? Fine. Done."

"And when you are ready to give Judy the heave-ho, I want to be nearby so that I can catch her on the short hop."

"You really are an excrescence and a plague."

"Wait until you fall in love. No power on earth can stay its course."

"My fondest wish is that you marry Judy and have plentiful offspring. That will be revenge enough for me."

"I knew you'd understand."

I looked around at the general decay. "I say, where are we? Rather dismal."

Bentley glided over as if he were on skates. "New Jersey, Sir. There is no closer airfield that can accommodate dirigibles of this size."

At that moment I noticed a rather disheveled looking fellow leaning against the car. He was trying to dislodge something from between his teeth with a toothpick and was eyeing the dirigible. He saw me looking at him and redoubled his efforts with the toothpick. A badge affixed to his greasy lapel suggested that he was the customs inspector.

"That your blimp?"

"It is."

"You can't leave it there, you know."

"I can hardly do anything else with it."

He shifted the toothpick. "I guess I could take care of it for you."

"Could you? That's awfully decent of you."

"Course it'll cost you."

"How much?"

He switched the toothpick to another gap in his teeth and wrinkled his forehead. "It's usually five hundred."

I turned to Bentley in shock. "Bentley?"

"I believe a bribe is customary, Sir."

"Is it a bribe?"

"I believe so."

"It seems like a lot."

The customs inspector sighed. "Course I could write you up a ticket. You could go down to the courthouse and pay a fine. Shouldn't take you more than eight or nine hours."

"Look here, my dear sir, I'm not accustomed to paying blackmail."

"Ain'tcha?"

"No, I am not."

He spat out the toothpick. "Welcome to Jersey."

Bentley stepped between us. "It's quite all right, Sir. I shall see to it. Why don't you make yourself comfortable in the automobile."

"All right. Get in, everyone. I'm dying for a proper wash up and some hot food."

We wedged ourselves into the automobile. As ill fortune would have it, I wound up next to Cubby. He looked around sourly. "Does anyone have a spare toothbrush? I came with nothing."

"We come into this world with nothing and depart with nothing," I chirped.

"But while we're here, a toothbrush is not an unreasonable request."

Bentley slid into the driver's seat. "I shall procure one when we reach the hotel, Sir."

I leaned away from Cubby. "Until then could you roll down a window, old sock? There's a distinct aroma of low tide."

"Laugh now, Chippington-Smythe. There shall come a day of reckoning."

The hotel was a grand old thing. We swept into the lobby only to be halted by an officious young person with a clipboard and pen.

"Excuse me, Sir, before you check in, I just have a few questions for you."

"Do you need to see my passport? Bentley has all that."

"No, Sir. This will only take a moment."

"Fire away."

She consulted her clipboard. "Green or blue?"

"Green or blue what?"

"Which is your favorite?"

"I suppose... green. No, blue!"

My aunt gave a grunt. "The correct answer should be gold, but apparently that is not an option."

The young lady made a little check on her clipboard. "Eight planets or nine?"

"I beg your pardon?"

"Scientists recently reclassified Pluto as a planetoid instead of a planet. Do you accept that there are only eight planets in our solar system or do you believe there are still nine?"

"I'm the last person to ask about science. Only last week Bentley had to explain to me how elastic works. Damned useful for keeping one's socks up, it turns out."

"Planets, Sir?"

"Well... eight, I suppose."

My aunt shook her head. "What does it matter how many there are? It is enough for a person of quality to know that planets exist. Counting them is the work of mathematicians or public accountants."

"The tomato: fruit or vegetable?"

Cheeseworth tapped his jeweled walking stick on the tile floor. "That's a twick question. Tomato is a paste, as everyone knows."

"This is becoming far too personal," huffed my aunt. "You Americans should learn that sharing one's innermost thoughts will drive away all but the most undesirable company."

Uncle Hugo could take no more. "What do these questions have to do with checking into this establishment?"

The young lady looked up from her clipboard. "Nothing, Sir."

I stared at her in amazement. "Do you not work for the hotel?"

"No, Sir."

My aunt gazed at her shrewdly. "Young lady, you have taken advantage of our credulity to winkle out our most intimate beliefs. I am impressed."

"Your input is invaluable. Social media could not exist without it."

"Well, really! Come on, everyone."

The desk clerk was vaguely reminiscent of the steam-powered servants that populated Twits. I suppose there was a generic type of automaton that was pumped out by the thousands all over the world. We did the necessary and I took the offered key.

"Could someone take the bags up to our room?"

The desk clerk looked at me solemnly. "We no longer provide that service, Sir."

"What? Why not?"

"The bell persons tried to unionize, and we were forced to eliminate them."

I stared at him helplessly. "How do we get all of this luggage upstairs?"

"Not to worry, Sir." He clanged a hand bell and focused his eyes into the middle distance. "This gentleman needs his bags taken to his room. The hotel takes no responsibility either legal or moral for any paid employment that might result from this situation."

A small mob of hungry-looking individuals suddenly appeared from the shadows.

"Carry your bags, Mister? Dollar a bag?"

Another ragged-looking fellow straightened the bit of string that stood in for a tie. "I'll do it for seventy-five cents a bag, Sir."

The first would-be porter gave him a shove. "You don't want him. Leper. Likely to lose a finger and come after you for medical bills."

"That's a lie! He's got fleas."

"I don't!"

As they argued, a third gentleman simply placed our bags on a wheeled cart and headed for the elevator. We quietly slipped away and followed him. As the doors slid closed the first two fellows were still arguing.

"Bit of a thicket, this dog-eat-dog economy."

The fellow with our bags sighed deeply. "It is, Sir. It is an affront to the dignity of man."

"You're very well spoken for a bellman."

"I used to be a teacher."

"What made you give it up?"

He looked down sadly. "I taught penmanship. When they banned cursive writing I could no longer find employment."

We arrived at my room. I opened the door and he tossed in the bags.

"This is your room. If there's anything you need, just go to the lobby and shout. Who's next?"

He wandered off with the rest of our party trailing behind him... all but Binky, who slipped into my room before I could close the door.

"Do you mind if I lounge about here for a while? I hate being alone in hotel rooms. I can't flush the loo because they've put that blue solution in it and I don't like to disturb it."

"Consider this your second home."

Bentley condensed out of thin air. "Yes, Bentley?"

"A gentleman is here to see you."

"Did he give his name?"

"He did not, Sir. He states that he is known popularly as the Social Media King."

"Wasn't the whole point of America to do away with Kings?"

"Perhaps the title is ironic, Sir."

"Yoiks! Irony is like a pink marshmallow. It promises delight but cloys after the first nibble. Show him in."

Bentley evaporated toward the door and soon returned with the gentleman in question. "The Social Media King, Sir."

Had I been one of those prognosticators who can pierce the veil of time and see into the future I would have done my best to stifle the fellow with a pillow at once, but alas, the flow of time carries us all inexorably toward the cataracts of our doom.

CHAPTER FOUR

The Pirate King

The King was a thin young man with strikingly long arms and fingers. His eyes maintained a fixed stare which was made more unnerving by a complete absence of blinking. I stuck out the old paw.

"Hallo. Cyril Chippington-Smythe. This is my boon companion, Cheswick Wickford-Davies, but everyone calls him Binky. Here for the conference, are you? I'm simply champing at the bit to wade into all that science and whatnot. Care for a drink?"

"I don't drink alcohol. Um... It slows your mental processes."

"Quite right. Nothing for me as well."

I slid my brandy and soda behind a nearby lamp.

"I hope you don't mind that I came to your room. Um... I wanted to talk to you privately."

Binky leaned toward the door. "Should I go?"

I seized him by the sleeve. "Certainly not. You are a trusted confidante."

The Social Media King eyed him dubiously. "Can he keep a secret?"

"Don't worry," I assured him, "whatever he remembers will be so garbled as to be unintelligible."

Binky gave a little bow. "Thank you very much."

I gestured to the seating area. "Let's park ourselves in these comfy-looking armchairs and have a good chin wag."

"If you don't mind, um, I haven't reached my daily step count, so I'll just..."

He began marching in place. Good manners seemed to dictate that we join him. We faced each other and jerked our knees up and down like wind-up tin soldiers.

Binky began to trip over his feet at once. "I don't think I'm doing it right. Is there a hop somewhere in the pattern?"

"It's just left, right, left, right, etcetera, old boot."

We settled into an easy rhythm and waited for the Social Media King, who I will refer to hereafter as the SMK, to begin.

"The thing is, I represent a group of individuals who prefer to remain anonymous."

Binky frowned. "Then how do you contact them?"

"They're not anonymous to me."

"They're not very good at it then, are they?"

The SMK shook his head and decided to ignore Binky, which showed some discernment on his part, I must say.

"This group I represent is pretty powerful. It shapes, um, public opinion on everything from fashion to politics."

I giggled nervously. "Goodness, it almost sounds like you're part of a secret cabal hiding in the shadows and pulling the strings while the world's governing bodies dance like puppets."

This seemed to alarm him. "There isn't any such cabal and if there were, like you said, um... it would be a secret."

I eyed him thoughtfully. "So if it existed, you would be forced to deny its existence."

"Right."

"Then your denial that it exists is proof that it does, in fact, exist!"

"It doesn't exist."

"So you're saying that it does exist."

Binky gave up marching and glared at us both. "Could you at least wink or waggle your eyebrows? I'm getting a headache."

"Um, has anyone approached you since you got here with a survey?"

"Yes. In the lobby."

"They work for me. I have an army of people that go everywhere, um, surveying the population about their opinions."

"To what end?"

"To find controversy. There are a huge number of issues that divide us."

"Just so. My club, 'Twits,' is divided between the 'Neat' and the 'With ice' factions that will never be reconciled."

"Right. So we've found out if you make people angry enough, they'll buy whatever you're selling."

I frowned at him. "It doesn't seem like that's improving anyone's life."

"Well, if by 'life' you mean a dull, gray slog where every day is just like the one before it: working, eating, sleeping and dying... then we give people excitement, a rush of adrenaline, um... passion!"

"When you put it like that..."

"People want to fight for a cause, even if it's petty. They want to believe in something, um, even if it's absurd."

Binky's eyes grew large. "It's like you're describing my whole life!"

"But what do you want with me?"

He slowed his jog to a walk. "We want to make you a partner."

Binky looked disgusted. "Him? A member of a cabal? Some fellows have all the luck. Secret handshake, I shouldn't wonder. Key chain with a mysterious medallion, one expects."

The SMK looked at me. "We have all of that and more. What about it?"

"Oh. Well, of course I can't say off the top of my head... complicated web of investments and all that. Why do you need a partner? You seem to be doing well."

"We're expanding into the overseas market. You have an army of hydrogen meter readers that go door to door and apparently your government has made it a crime to shut the door on them. They could carry my surveys with them on their rounds. I'd get my data and you'd make millions."

My mind began to buzz. "Do you know... I'll have to think it over for a bit, but it's damned exciting."

The squeaking of cart wheels announced the entrance of Cook, pushing a tiny trolley with a soup tureen and bowls. "Here we go. Cock-a-leekie soup with some lovely croutons."

Binky made a beeline for her. "Goodie!"

"Ah! Cook. Well, I suppose I'll have to stop marching if I'm going to eat hot soup. Self-preservation, you know."

The SMK ignored Cook completely and sped up to a jog again. "I'll keep going, if that's okay."

Cook smiled at him as if he were a benign lunatic. "Would your guest care for a wee bowl of soup?"

He glanced over. "Who makes it?"

She drew herself up indignantly. "I make it. Who else?"

"It's not from a factory?"

"You won't find anything from a factory in my kitchen."

He came jogging over. "Okay. I'll try it."

Cook ladled him out a bowl. He managed to get a spoonful into his mouth without slowing. "Um... that's... wow! That's good!"

I was accustomed to this reaction when people tasted Cook's food. I myself had once been rendered speechless by a cherry clafoutis, and on another occasion had to be revived after a particularly savory roasted cauliflower with sauce romesco. The SMK looked at me with newfound respect.

"You eat like this all the time?"

"I have canceled luxurious trips to exotic locales because Cook could not accompany me."

Cook smacked me on the arm. "You're laying it on with a trowel. Eat your soup and I'll bring you a nice treacle tart."

"My favorite!"

Cook squeaked away. There was a knock at the door, which flew open to reveal my aunt and Euphonia, who was dressed in an eccentric outfit that seemed to have been assembled at a military surplus store. "Is that what you're wearing to the conference, Euphonia?"

"I was told to avoid fashion at all costs."

She had succeeded admirably. I brought forth the SMK. "May I present the Social Media King. This is my Aunt Hypatia and Miss Euphonia Gumboot."

He continued shoveling soup into his cake hole. "Hello."

Euphonia made a staggering lurch. "Your highness."

"Um... you don't have to bow."

"To be truthful I didn't intend to bow. I lost my balance."

Binky smiled at her shyly. "Hallo, Euphonia."

"Hello... I'm sorry, I've forgotten your name."

"What?"

"I do remember your face."

Binky looked forlorn. "Binky. My name is Binky."

"Is it? How odd."

My aunt was examining the SMK approvingly. "Nephew, I am happy to see that you are associating with a rarefied class of people. Over which kingdom do you rule, Your Highness?"

"So... I'm not an actual king."

Her face fell. "Then you should not call yourself one. If people give themselves titles will you nill you, they will soon lose all meaning, and drawing up a seating chart for dinner will become impossible."

"Well, it's the only name I use. I have to protect my anonymity."

"Anonymity is greatly over-rated... and leads to very few invitations."

Euphonia had been staring vacantly about the room but this seemed to perk her up. "I was Anonymous once, but I missed having wine with dinner."

The SMK seemed to notice her for the first time. "That's good. You're funny."

"That's what my father always said. 'There's something funny about you, Euphonia.' He used to squint at me in the oddest way when he said it."

"Are you here for the conference too?"

"Oh no. I only came for dinner. There have been several other meals as well, fortunately. Dinner was quite some time ago and I am susceptible to hypoglycemia."

The SMK gave a barking laugh. "Is she for real?"

My aunt regarded Euphonia grimly. "She gives every indication of being real. The food must go somewhere."

Euphonia suddenly jerked her head to one side and gave a little hop. "Oh dear, my hair has gotten tangled in these parachute clips."

Aunt Hypatia took her arm. "Come into the other room with me, my dear. If I cannot untangle it, I shall find a pair of scissors. I have always thought that your hair expressed itself too freely. Excuse us for a moment."

She led Euphonia away. The SMK watched them go with a calculating look on his face then turned to me. "Um... I have the contracts in my room. Why don't I go and bring them back for you to take a look at?"

"Jolly good."

"I'll just be a minute."

He jogged out of the room, still holding the soup bowl. As the door closed behind him Binky turned to me.

"Are you going to join the cabal, you lucky brute?"

"I don't know. I say, Bentley?"

He had been there the whole time, of course, but had made himself invisible in that way he had.

"Sir?"

"Did you overhear our conversation?"

"Yes, Sir."

"What do you think of his proposal?"

Bentley's optical sensors vibrated for a moment and I heard a grinding sound from his cranium. "I believe he is correct in his assessment of your potential profits, Sir. It seems a lucrative venture."

"Wouldn't Uncle Hugo be agog?"

"He would indeed, Sir."

I didn't care about the money, of course—I rolled about in filthy lucre day and night. No, what excited me was the thought of doing it on my own. No Uncle Hugo or Board of Directors to make the decisions for me. I saw myself swaggering into the club and casually remarking, "Started a new business this week. Did it all on my own. No help from anyone. Bringing in a million a day. Anyone for tennis?" By Jove, it made the old blood rather sing in one's veins. I heard a strange, gurgling sound.

"Have you finished pouring your cock-a-leekie soup on the carpet, Sir?"

I snapped out of it to find Bentley looking at the floor sadly. "What? Damn! Forgot I was holding it."

"Quite understandable. I shall procure a mop."

Binky looked at his own bowl of soup. "Should I pour mine on the carpet as well? No, it's too tasty. I'm going to finish it."

The door flew open to admit Uncle Hugo and Cheeseworth. Cheeseworth was dressed in a dirty apron and wrinkled work pants.

"My old shoe shine uniform! I've kept it all these years as a memento and it still fits! I could go right back to work polishing boots."

"A brutal profession. You must have spent hours down on your knees."

"Still do, dear boy, still do."

My uncle had clearly attempted to go native. His torso strained to escape the flimsy T-shirt that confined it. "By Jove, these T-shirts rival anything Torquemada could have imagined."

Aunt Hypatia re-entered the room leading Euphonia, whose hair was noticeably shorter.

"Is that you whining, Hugo?"

"I was not whining."

Cheeseworth stared down at the rug. "This pool of soup on the carpet hints at a tale of violence and intwigue."

"Just clumsiness I'm afraid."

Bentley returned with a mop and bucket. "If you would be so good as to step to the left, I will clean it up in a trice."

"My left or your left?"

"Either would be thrilling, Sir."

Uncle Hugo fell into an armchair. "These Americans are a warlike tribe. The chambermaid asked me how many planets there are and when I said 'nine' she hurled a bar of soap at my head."

"Passions are running high," I agreed.

At that moment the SMK returned. He had changed for the conference and wore a polo shirt in a blue-green color I would describe as teal. He bore a thick sheaf of papers. He stopped upon seeing the crowd.

"Hello."

"May I present the Social Media King? King, this is my uncle, Hugo Dankworth and C. Langford-Cheeseworth."

He nodded at them. "Glad to meet you."

My uncle had jumped from his chair upon hearing the word "King."

"Are you here for the conference as well, Your Highness?"

My aunt shook her head. "'King' is more aspirational than actual, Hugo. I shall explain later."

I caught the King's eye and jerked my head toward a quiet corner. He and I crept away from the crowd.

"Let's keep our little business arrangement between us for the time being, shall we? Loose lips and all that," I murmured quietly.

"Sure, if that's what you want. Here's the contract."

He handed me a stack of papers. I set them on a nearby table. "I'll just set it here by the sofa until later."

He pulled out another sheet. "And here's the latest social media release. There's a bunch of posts in there about you and your friends."

I looked at him in surprise. "How can that be?"

"My people are everywhere, recording people's reactions to everything. We type up the results all day long and distribute them by hand."

I took the sheet of paper and scanned it. "'The well-known society boob Cyril Chippington-Smythe arrived in New York today dressed like a cross between Louis *Quatorz* and a circus clown.' I say! 'He was in the company of Miss Euphonia Gumboot, social influencer and heiress to the Gumboot fortune. Are wedding bells in the offing?' This does cross the line!"

He looked at me eagerly. "You can respond if you want. It would be on the street in less than an hour."

I sniffed. "No thank you. Such things are beneath me."

"Everyone thinks that at first. You'll catch on. It's fun."

My uncle began pulling at his clothes. "This T-shirt is driving me mad! Local customs be damned, I'm going to change! Don't wait for me, Hypatia."

"The thought never crossed my mind."

I rejoined the company. "But Uncle, won't you miss the presentations?"

The SMK was right behind me. "No one listens to those. It's just an excuse to socialize. It's kind of lonely, being a tycoon. Most of them will be in the ballroom getting hammered."

Euphonia perked up. "That sounds lovely. Let's go there immediately!"

My aunt seated herself. "In a moment. I refuse to be on time for Americans."

The SMK gave a little bow. "I'd be happy to escort Miss Gumboot downstairs."

"Goodie! Let's go."

I waved them toward the door. "We'll only be a few minutes. I have to finish applying sweat stains to my clothing."

"Don't worry about me. The King will keep me company."

As he and Euphonia opened the door, Judy entered, squeezing past them. "Oh! Excuse me."

The SMK nodded his head at her. "We were just leaving."

Euphonia put her head on one side and stared at Judy. "You look familiar."

"We rode over on the dirigible together."

"Did we? Such fun. Ta-ta. See you at the party."

Judy watched them go and shook her head. "What an odd woman she is."

"Hello Judy," I chirped. She looked my outfit over.

"You look very... proletariat."

"I am '*comme il faut*,' according to Bentley."

Binky's eyes bored into her like a weevil into a cotton ball. "Hallo, Judy."

"Hi, Binky, you've got treacle tart on your shirt."

He brushed ineffectually at his clothing. "Do I? Damn. You could have said something, Cyril."

"I have a lot on my plate right now, old man."

Judy's gaze was disturbingly proprietary. "Cyril, I've been thinking."

This did not bode well. "Have you? Double-edged sword—thinking."

"Despite your outgoing exterior you're really very shy, aren't you?"

My aunt looked thoughtful. "I have always suspected something more pathological. 'Shy' seems almost a virtue by comparison."

"Perhaps I am protective of my more intimate feelings. What is your point?"

"You need to let yourself go a little. We're only young once, you know. You don't want to wither on the vine."

My aunt nodded. "An apt metaphor. One should experience life while one is still bursting with juice like a ripe grape. The wrinkled raisin of maturity arrives all too soon."

"So, I'm going to take you in hand," Judy concluded.

They say at the last moment of life one sees the entire landscape of one's journey pass by the old peepers. The prospect of being "taken in hand" apparently tripped the projector and scenes from childhood rose up before me: Bentley spooning Pablum into my tiny maw; Bentley teaching me to tie a proper bow tie; Bentley telling me how babies come about. That same Bentley now broke into my reverie by clearing his throat.

"The conference is about to begin, Sir. You wouldn't want to be tardy."

My aunt rose to her feet. "Come, Judy my dear. I will regale you with tales of Cyril as a child. They will not reflect well on him, but you should know what you are getting."

There was a pounding of heels in the hallway and the door burst open to admit a panting Cubby Martinez. He stared around the room with wild eyes and took a threatening step in my direction. "Where is my sister?!"

"Steady, Cubby. What's the ruckus?"

He pointed an accusing finger in my face. "Her bag is gone and she left a note saying that she refuses to return home."

"What?"

My aunt shook her head disapprovingly. "Rash child! Her reputation was already teetering on a knife's edge."

Cubby came a step closer. Fasting had not improved his breath, I must say. "What have you done with her, Chippington-Smythe?"

"Me? Nothing."

My Uncle Hugo stood up. "She left here with the Social Media King a few moments ago. They were going to the ballroom."

"Come on! We'll help you find her!"

I headed for the door. Binky followed close behind me. "It's like a game of hide and seek."

This caused Cubby to erupt. "It's not a game! Euphonia can't be left by herself. She lacks a short-term memory."

I stared at him. "What? Is that why she didn't remember me just now?"

Binky's eyes were round. "Nor me? She forgot my name."

Cubby stamped a foot. "She's got to be found at once!"

My aunt drew herself erect. "Come, everyone! To the ballroom."

Uncle Hugo waved at her. "Go without me. I must change my shirt."

She looked at him indulgently. "Yes, Hugo. When I refer to 'everyone,' I seldom include you."

"To the elevator!" I cried.

We piled into the elevator and I mashed the button. The elevator did not share our sense of urgency and drifted lazily down through the various floors, stopping at random and opening its doors on empty hallways. The entire ride was accompanied by some sort of syrupy orchestral arrangement that might have been "April in Paris" or could as easily have been "Beethoven's Fifth." At long last we reached the ballroom level and rushed out to behold a seething mass of what were billed as "Titans of Industry." Most were dressed, like me, as if they had plans to paint their apartment later on. I turned to the group of hunters.

"Let's split up. Whoever spots them, give a yell."

We wove our way into the crowd like a pack of questing ferrets. I soon spied the wayward couple. They saw me at the same moment. The King grabbed Euphonia's hand and began pulling her in the opposite direction. So he was a party to her mad dash! I fought to reach them but the tide of humanity was too much for my sylphlike frame. I looked around me, saw a table covered with champagne glasses and swept them to the floor! Climbing gingerly onto the table I scanned the room. There they were, approaching the exit! Thinking quickly, I grabbed one of the remaining glasses and rapped on it loudly with a spoon. The noise abated somewhat.

"I say! Excuse me, ladies and gentlemen! May I have your attention please? There is an abduction in progress! That man there! In the blue polo shirt! Seize him!"

The crowd looked around in confusion. A gentleman near the SMK squinted at him and turned to shout at me.

"Who, this fellow? That's a green shirt."

His neighbor gave a disgusted grunt. "It is not. That's blue!"

"You're color blind. It's green."

This was getting us nowhere. I waved at them desperately. "All right then, teal! The man in the teal shirt!"

The second man put his hands on his hips and stared at me truculently. "Teal *is* blue."

"The hell it is! It's green!"

"Says who?"

"Says me!"

The rest of the crowd was starting to get interested.

"Sock him in the eye!"

"I'd like to see you try."

"Oh, you would, would you?"

I was practically wringing my hands. "Gentlemen and ladies, we are missing the point! The rotter is getting away!"

318 THE TWITS CHRONICLES: ANTHOLOGY #1

Alas, a punch was thrown and in an instant the room erupted into chaos. Screams of "Green!" and "Blue!" echoed amidst the stately columns. Champagne bottles arced lazily through the air. I saw my aunt fighting her way toward me with a terrifying singleness of purpose. Those in her way found themselves clubbed to the side by her capacious handbag. She waved urgently at me.

"Nephew! We must evacuate at once! The colonialists are revolting!"

In another part of the chamber a drunken reveler held Binky in a headlock while a shriveled nabob kicked him repeatedly in the derriere. Cheeseworth was struck in the midsection by a brutal slab of a man. He threw down his cane and delivered two sharp lefts and a right to the fellow's face, dropping him like a fallen tree... and as I watched helplessly Euphonia and the Social Media King calmly walked through the exit door and disappeared. Judy suddenly appeared next to me and held out a hand.

"Come on, Cyril. Let's get you out of here."

"Judy! They went that way!"

She nodded, grabbed my hand and hacked her way through the wall of human flesh. We flew out of the exit door and spotted the fugitives standing at the curb attempting to hail a cab.

"Halt! Not another step!"

The SMK looked at me nervously and held up a hand. "Okay, it's not what you think."

"It seldom is."

The exit door crashed open again and a discombobulated Cubby flew into our midst. He took in the situation at once and held out his perspiring hands to his stepsister. "Euphonia! How could you?"

"How could I what, Cubby?"

"How could you run off with this man? A virtual stranger."

"We're not running off. We're going to his office to sign a contract."

Cubby looked stunned. "A what?"

"The King has offered me a job."

"Doing what?"

Euphonia waved her hand gaily. "I'm to just say whatever comes into my head and someone will write it down for publication. He says it will drive people absolutely mad."

The SMK looked at her shyly. "She's phenomenal. No filter at all! Social media will love her!"

Cubby looked lost. "This can't really be what you want, Euphonia."

She looked at him kindly. "Yes, Cubby. You know I'm rather a joke back home. People snicker at me behind my back... I know they do. It's different in America. Here everyone lacks a short-term memory. I fit right in."

Cubby drew himself up. "I refuse. You do not have my permission."

"I do not need your permission. I am of age."

He slumped. "What if you are unhappy?"

"There is ample transportation between America and home, I believe. I shall simply buy a ticket."

Cubby looked at her helplessly. "Can this really be goodbye?"

"Yes. Goodbye Cubby."

I stepped forward. "Farewell, Euphonia."

She looked at me vaguely. "And who are you?"

"I'm Cyril. We've met."

"Oh, I don't think so."

Judy gave me a poke in the side. "Perhaps we shouldn't press the point."

I gave a little bow. "I hope, Euphonia, that being famous does not shatter the protective barrier between you and comprehension."

She paused for a moment. "What?"

"So far, so good."

A taxi pulled up, The King helped Euphonia into it and they sped off into the night. We stood and watched them disappear around a corner. Cubby spun toward me.

"This is your fault, Chippington-Smythe!"

"Mine? How?"

"You brought her to America."

"It was my aunt who brought her. It just happened to be my dirigible."

Cubby sneered. "That's right. You have a dirigible. I suppose that makes you better than me."

I sighed. "You really are exhausting."

Judy patted his arm. "Have you still not eaten anything, Cubby?"

"I have not."

"Maybe that's why you're cranky."

I had a sudden inspiration. "There was an admirable buffet in the ballroom which I had nothing to do with. Surely that wouldn't count as eating the bread of your abductors."

He looked torn, but there must have been a ravening animal in his vitals by now. "Well... I might have a small bite... only to fuel my struggle against oppression."

"That's the spirit. Let's load up a plate for you and head back to my room."

Judy smiled at me. "Yes, come dear."

And with that she wrapped her hand around my wrist like an iron shackle and calmly led me away.

We tumbled into my hotel room with a sense of relief. Bentley raised an eyebrow upon seeing Judy and myself hand in hand. Cubby retired to a corner and shoveled in the grub like it was his profession.

Suddenly the door was flung open and my aunt strode in. Her hair had escaped its carefully arranged coiffure and her gown was torn, but her glare was undiminished. She had wrapped a tablecloth around herself and resembled a Roman senator who had plans to poke some holes in Caesar after lunch. Binky slunk in behind her. Cheeseworth was practically dancing. He had a beauty of a shiner.

"What a donnybrook! One hasn't had so much fun in years! If I hadn't bwoken a nail I'd still be punching people in their widiculous faces! My word!"

"You're quite a pugilist, Cheeseworth," I said admiringly.

"Lightweight champion of my house three years wunning. When you pwesent yourself to the world as I do, you learn to defend yourself at an early age."

My aunt was attempting to recapture her stray hairs. "I knew coming to the frontier was ill-advised. Let us leave this awful place at once."

"I quite agree. Are you all right, Binky? That fellow gave you quite a kicking."

"Goodness yes. I was paddled so often as a child that I lost all feeling in my bottom by puberty. It's why I fall off of chairs so often."

"Bentley, do you want to go down to the lobby and shout for a bell person?"

"No need, Sir. I can carry the luggage myself."

"In that case, let's be off!"

At that moment Uncle Hugo, attired in his customary girdle and jodhpurs, stalked from the other room with his face red as a beet. In the hand waving over his head, I spied the Social Media King's contract.

"One moment, Sir!"

"Now Uncle..."

"Would you care to explain this? It looks very like a contract between the Social Media King and Smythe Corporation. What is the meaning of this?"

I looked around at everyone proudly. "Well... I meant it to be a surprise, but as a matter of fact I've pulled off a brilliant little piece of business. Did it all myself. No help from anyone. No need to thank me. You can congratulate me properly once we're safely airborne."

My aunt's hand darted to the emerald necklace around her neck. "We're ruined! Hugo, I refuse to sell my jewelry."

Cheeseworth stared at me gloomily. "Everything I possess is invested in Smythe Corporation stock! Without wealth I shall become ridiculous instead of amusingly eccentric."

They didn't seem to be appreciating my brilliant coup. "No, no! It's an incredible opportunity. You'll see."

Uncle Hugo raised a shaking finger. "I cannot in good conscience take another step without saying something to you, Sir."

There was a loud knocking at the door. "A moment, Uncle."

Bentley opened the door to reveal the bell person/former professor of cursive writing. He looked behind himself nervously.

"Listen, you all have to beat it! Someone in your party claimed there are nine planets and there's a mob of Eighters headed up here with tar and feathers to disagree with you."

"Quickly! Everyone! To the airfield!"

And that is how we left Manhattan: slinking out of a side door while a mob raced through the hotel, baying for our blood.

Chapter Five

Escape From New York

The Manhattan we drove through was a war zone. Gangs of citizens ran here and there chanting slogans like, "Eighters are Haters" and "Niners are Whiners." The occasional tomato landed on the windshield with a splat. It was with a huge sense of relief that we plunged into the tunnel below the Hudson.

New Jersey hadn't grown any cheerier. Our glittering dirigible hovered over its moorings.

We exited the car and headed for the boarding ramp, only to find our way blocked by the greasy customs inspector who had extorted us upon our arrival. The toothpick in his mouth was much the worse for wear.

"Welcome back. Good trip?"

"Tolerable. Now, my good man, if you and your grease stains would kindly take a step to the side we will be on our way."

He gazed off at the rubble piles that stretched into the distance. "Sure, but you got to pay the exit tax."

"Exit tax? How much is that?"

"Five hundred, just like before."

"Now look here..."

Bentley leaned in. "It is the custom, Sir."

The inspector carefully aimed and spat at an oil stain on the tarmac. The wind blew it wide of the mark. He sighed and shook his head. "Course you could pay it yourself at the courthouse. Should only take..."

"Fine! Pay the man, Bentley. Anything to get back in the air and away from this place!"

"New Jersey thanks you. Come again."

"Not likely. Not at these rates."

We piled into the cabin and dropped our things. The stevedores began to unmoor the blimp. I glared out the window at the customs inspector.

"I say, Binky, grab that paperweight, will you?"

He slid a large, ornamental paperweight off of the nearby desk. "Here you are."

I hefted it speculatively. "I'll bet you a tenner you can't knock the hat off that customs inspector."

Binky's eyes lit up. "It's a bet!"

I lowered the window and Binky took aim. He hurled the paperweight and we watched it conk the inspector just behind the ear. He went down with a satisfying thump and his hat rolled away into a ditch. Binky gave a little whoop.

"The hat's off. That's ten you owe me."

"It was worth it. Definitely."

The last rope was freed and we floated up into the blue. Safe at last! Cook began to lay out some snacks and there was a general air of unwinding. Judy seized my elbow in a grip that could crack a walnut.

"Why don't we go for those drinks when we land back home?"

"Why indeed?" I stammered.

She gazed at me possessively. "This has been quite a romantic adventure. Would you like to kiss me?"

My collar suddenly seemed to have shrunk. "Would I? Hmmm. Lot of people about."

"I don't mind."

To my consternation, her lips began to travel in my direction. I could see no way of evading them that would not lead to tears. Thankfully, my Uncle Hugo reared up on his hind legs again and Judy's lips were forced to retreat. My uncle cleared his throat to gain everyone's attention. "Sorry, but I was interrupted at the hotel and there are some things that must be said."

My aunt crossed her arms and glared at him. "Very well, say what you have to say and get it over with. You're like a revolutionary junta—always making declarations."

Uncle Hugo frowned. "As you know, my nephew has tried, on several occasions, to make decisions of a business nature

without my advice. In every instance this has led to disaster…"
I braced myself for what was coming. "…Until today! I have
now perused the contract and I am happy to announce that
he has struck an arrangement with the Social Media King that
will bring millions, if not billions in profits to the corporation
and therefore to the family. I would like to propose a toast. To
Cyril!"

Aunt Hypatia beamed at me. "My jewels are safe! Well done,
Nephew."

"Bwavo, Cywil!"

And with that, everyone raised a glass… to me! All except
Judy. She was frowning and biting her lower lip. Finally, there
was a lull in the general celebration and she cornered me by the
water dispenser.

"You're going into business with that man?"

"I am."

"But he's a monster! Do you know what he does?"

"I do."

"He creates division and hate. He preys on people's
insecurities."

I felt I had to speak up for my new partner. "As I understand
it, he's bringing excitement into their humdrum lives."

"And you're willing to be a party to it?"

"Absolutely."

She looked at me sadly and shook her head. "I am deeply
disappointed."

My ears perked up. "Are you?"

"I am. I must ask you to change your mind."

"But you heard Uncle Hugo—it's a damned fine arrangement."

"If you insist on entering into a partnership with that vile person, I can have nothing more to do with you."

"Really?"

"It is a matter of principle."

I struggled to keep a look of sad resignation on the old physiognomy. "Well, of course I'm dreadfully disappointed, but if that's how you feel then I shall respect your wishes."

She raised her chin bravely. "Thank you."

Judy moped over to an armchair and collapsed into it. Binky was on her at once like hot fudge on a sundae, leaping into the seat next to her with a look of deep empathy on his face and handing her a drink.

Cook was sidling toward me holding a tray of vegetable kabobs. "There's something I should tell you. Care for a kabob?"

"Absolutely. What is it, Cook?"

"It's onion, tomato and fennel."

"No, I mean what did you want to tell me?"

"That social media fellow tried to hire me away from you. Offered me a king's ransom."

This was appalling. I mean, I'd just stood up for the chap and here he was trying to shank me in the pancreas. "Did he? The pirate! He made off with Euphonia and now he's made an attempt on you. Got a taste for plunder, apparently."

"I thought you ought to know."

"But why didn't you go with him? You would have been rich."

"And become a slave of the oligarchs? I don't give a fig about money. I want to cook for people I care about."

A mist suddenly obscured the kabob gripped tightly in my mitt. I wiped the corner of my eye and took a nibble of fennel. Delicious! "Thank you, Cook. I'm extraordinarily moved. I hope I never give you reason to regret your faith in me."

She gave my arm a pat. "You won't. You've a good heart, dear."

"I'm dreadfully sorry if I've caused Judy any unhappiness."

"You and she were never right for each other. I've just been waiting for one of you to realize it. She'll be fine."

Cook trundled off to refill the platters. I noticed Cubby standing alone by a window, lost in thought.

"All right there, Cubby? I'm sure Euphonia is going to be happy in her new life."

"That's none of your business."

"I say, I was hoping there might be a thaw in our relationship after all we've been through."

He whirled to face me. "What have you been through? You're returning richer than you left. Some people have all the luck."

"Money isn't everything, you know."

"Don't condescend to me, Chippington-Smythe!"

"Not at all."

He drew himself up. "Nothing has changed between us. When you see me at the club, I'll thank you not to take liberties or behave as if we have any kind of understanding. The gulf between us has widened, if anything."

I sighed. "If that's the way you want it."

"It is."

"Very well. I shall treat you as the Marshall of Twits and nothing more. We shall be as strangers."

"Good!"

"Fine!"

He stalked away and snatched a large glass of water from the bar. Glaring at the platter of kabobs, he threw himself into a chair in the far corner of the cabin and hid his face behind a copy of Animatronic Horse and Hound.

Binky was weaving his way toward me with a sappy grin on his face. "She's letting me take her for drinks! Says anything's better than being alone just now."

"Sounds like you've reignited the embers of her passion, what? Well, happy endings all around. The beginnings of this odyssey were ill-omened, but it seems we have fought through with colors flying."

Binky grinned and adjusted the tie with the palm tree on it that hung around his neck. I would miss that tie.

"I'm going to the club when we land. Why not come with me?"

I shook my head solemnly. "Absolutely not! I am headed straight for bed and I'm not getting out of my pajamas until we run out of brandy."

Safe once more in my cozy little bedroom, I lolled about among the pillows and sipped a soothing cup of the old lapsang souchong. Bentley walked about picking up the various articles of clothing I had dropped.

"What joy. Why did I ever leave?"

"Indeed, Sir. It is pleasant to be home."

"Those Americans are a passionate people. Do you think they like fighting all the time?"

He stopped to consider. "Anger and resentment are commonly considered to be negative emotions."

"Why do they do it, then, do you suppose?"

"There are always those who will arouse the primitive instincts buried within the human race to amass power and wealth for themselves."

"I'm surprised they haven't attempted something of the sort here."

"Oh, they have, Sir."

I sat up and looked at him. "I don't recall ever being aware of it."

"No, Sir. I have rebuffed them."

"They've come to the door?"

"Yes, Sir. I sent them on their way and burned their periodicals as any competent valet would."

I leaned back and watched him thoughtfully. "Do you and the other servants communicate with one another, Bentley?"

"There is an informal network. We are all in agreement that we would be doing our employers a disservice if we allowed their baser emotions to be stirred in such a manner."

"Do you think I have those base emotions buried within me?"

He faced me and gave a little bow of the head. "No, Sir. You have a singular constitution."

"Thank you, Bentley. I say, that was rather lucky."

"What was, Sir?"

"That deal with the Social Media King putting the kibosh on my affair with Judy."

"Yes, I thought it might, Sir."

I sat up again and looked at him in astonishment. "Did you? Do you mean to say you planned it from the beginning?"

"We were seeking an egregious act that would induce her to reject you and this seemed to fit the bill."

"You said it was a lucrative venture."

"And so it is, Sir, but not really suitable."

"No?"

"No Sir. I'm afraid his sort of business is not the thing. It rouses the very passions you find so disturbing."

I frowned. "But how do I get out of it now?"

"Have you signed anything, Sir?"

"No, but I led him to believe that we were in business."

Bentley stood in absolute stillness for a moment. I listened to his gears grinding. Finally, he took a step toward the bed and gave a little cough.

"I should mention that the Social Media King queried me as to what emoluments would induce me to leave your employment and go to work for him."

I struggled to keep the panic out of my voice. "What?"

"I replied, of course, that no amount of money would suffice."

"Did you?"

"I did, Sir."

I stared at him, then struggled to my feet and rose to my full height in the center of the bed. "Bentley! Take a letter. To the right honorable Social Media King. Go soak your head! Sign it Cyril Chippington-Smythe and get it off in the next post."

"Thank you, Sir. I sent such a letter, couched in more diplomatic terms, before I brought your tea. Would you care for another cup?"

The End

If you enjoyed this book, please
take a moment to visit
Amazon or going to

https://www.amazon.com/dp/B0B1QWQKNL
and provide a short
review; every reader's voice is
extremely important for the life
of a book or series.

If you'd like advance notice on the next book's release head to:
WWW.TwitsChronicles.com
where you can sign up for my email list and where you can
ask Cyril and his friends a question which they may choose to
answer in a newsletter.
I hate spam as much as you do, so I will keep emails to a
minimum.

Afterword

Cyril, Bentley and The Usual Suspects will return in:

TWITS ON THE LOOSE

The next installment of the TWITS CHRONICLES. Read on
for a taste.

Great wealth is like an ill-tempered dog. One hopes for
a frolicsome companion and finds instead the teeth of

responsibility locked onto one's ankle. I had recently come of age and the weight of my family's fortune had transformed me from a witty and attractive boulevardier to a hollow shell who slumped over his brandy beweeping his outcast state. Playing cards even for astronomical sums brought no flush to my cheeks. What is money when there is an endless supply of it? Friends who had always slapped one on the back and shared a scandalous tale now grew silent at my approach or tried awkwardly to touch me for a tenner to pay the bar tab. Slowly all my acquaintance drifted away. All but my cousin, Cheswick Wickford-Davies (Binky to his friends). Years of sponging had left him with no sense of shame. Hence, he was immune to the corrupting influence of wealth.

It was a gloomy morning in April when my mechanical valet, Bentley, wafted into the parlor bearing a medicinal dose of something distilled by monks in the Pyrenees and the news that Binky was champing at the bit to see me.

"Show him in, Bentley. Mr. Wickford-Davies has the run of the keep at all times."

"Very good, Sir."

Bentley floated off in that way he has and returned with Binky moping behind him.

"Hallo, old sausage! Live free or die," chirped I, cheerily.

He looked at me blankly. "What?"

"That's the new thing. 'Live free or die.' I had it from Bentley this morning."

"Not 'Confusion to our enemies'?"

I flapped a flipper breezily. "No. That's old news."

He fell heavily into a chair and rubbed his face with his hands. "Why do these mottoes always feature death so prominently?"

"I suppose because thoughts of mortality cause one to reflect. These are national slogans, you know—not advertisements for soap flakes."

He looked up at me dryly. "May I point out that the ad for Sudso soap flakes mentions plague, pestilence and flesh-eating organisms in its jingle. I think rhyming 'hysteria' with 'bacteria' is awfully good." He subsided back into melancholia.

"Was there a reason you invaded the family domicile this morning?"

He ran his fingers through his hair and groaned. "I've come to the end, Cyril. Life is a hollow shell."

I had heard this sort of thing from him too many times to be very alarmed. "Bentley? Suggestions?"

Bentley gave a judicious little nod. "Perhaps an ounce of tequila and a serotonin reuptake inhibitor?"

"Good! On the double, before he sinks into an existential fugue. These things are contagious, you know."

"At once, Sir."

Bentley disapparated like a soap bubble and I examined the patient. "Out with it, old shoe. What's got you howling at the moon?"

He gave out with another shivering groan and stared at the ceiling. "There's this girl, you see..."

Well, that was all I needed to hear. This was more or less a weekly occurrence and my patience was threadbare. "Honestly, you'd fall in love with a shovel if there was nothing else handy."

He stared at me with bloodshot eyes. "She looks right through me."

"Myopic, is she? You're rather hard to miss. Beefy, what?"

This seemed to wound him. "I've never been so thin."

"Oh, absolutely. Nearly transparent."

"I'm too miserable to eat."

Bentley shimmered into view, holding a glass of tequila and a pill on a tray. Binky took them both and downed the pill gratefully.

"Will there be anything else, Sir?"

"Nothing, Bentley, thank you."

And he was gone, just like that. Bentley could have had a brilliant career as a magician, but of course fame means nothing to a steam-powered domestic.

"Drink your tequila like a good lad. Why does your lady love treat you so spuriously?"

He slumped and sipped his drink. "It's my own fault. I have no character to speak of and she's so... good. She's given away her entire fortune to assist the downtrodden... positively destitute now."

"She sounds gruesome, if you don't mind my saying so."

"You haven't met her. One is quite helpless before the torrent of her animal spirits. She attracts more followers every day."

"Really? Who's after her—detectives, creditors?"

"Spiritual followers. People who look to her for guidance."

"She doesn't sound like your usual poison, if I may say. You've always been drawn to girls who enjoy a good rugby match and that sort of thing."

Before I could inquire further, Bentley entered the room and it is some indication of his mental agitation that I saw him coming quite clearly from the top of the stairs. The look on his face was as close to horror as the materials it was constructed of would allow.

"I beg your pardon, Sir. Did you order a... TV?"

"Is it here already? That's fast work."

He looked at me as I'm sure Caesar looked at Brutus. "There were two persons at the front door. I sent them away."

What ho, this was a little high-handed! Bentley is normally as servile as one would wish a mechanical valet to be, but every now and then he takes the bit in his teeth. "Sent them away? By what right?"

He gazed at me for a moment and I heard his gears grinding away. "A TV is... unsuitable, Sir."

Bentley tosses out the word "unsuitable" the way prisoners hurl their slops during a prison riot, but a chap has to stand up for himself now and then if he is not to become a supernumerary in his own home.

"That's hardly up to you, is it? If I want a bally TV I'll have a bally TV. Who is the employer here, you or I?"

"You, Sir," he admitted... rather reluctantly, I thought.

"You run that couple down and bring them up here at once. That's an order."

There was a further grinding of gears. "Yes, Sir."

Bentley's accustomed pace is a dignified glide, but when the occasion calls for it, he has legs like pistons. Indeed, his legs are pistons. He was out the front door like a shot and in a few moments, I heard him climbing the stairs followed by a rather flashily dressed lady and gentleman carrying large cases. He gestured to them and all but sneered.

"Your TV, Sir."

The gentleman hefted his case and looked around. "Good morning, Sir. Where shall we set up?"

"I hadn't really thought about it."

The lady staggered a bit under the weight of her cases. "What room do you frequent most?"

I thought for a moment. "The bedroom, I suppose."

She frowned. "We can't recommend the bedroom, Sir. Too stimulating."

"Oh, then I suppose... here."

This seemed to cheer them up. "Very good. Just give us a minute."

There was a flurry of activity as they disposed of their cases by the wall and did some quick stretching exercises. Adjusting their clothing, they stepped to the center of the room and cleared their throats. The gentleman began. "All right Sir, here we go. I'm Smith."

"And I'm Jones."

"And we are..."

"Thought Vacation!"

"World got you down? Portents of death and decay ruining your fun?"

"Lean back and let us take you on a Thought Vacation!"

The lady had a little clown horn with a rubber bulb which she honked a couple of times.

Binky jiggled on his toes. "Oh, I say, What fun!"

"It is fun, Sir. What would you like to see?"

I stepped forth eagerly. "What are my choices?"

"Oh, anything. We can do comedy, drama, news and weather, sports, game shows—you name it."

Binky gave a little titter. "Where on earth did you find them?"

"Cheeseworth put me on to them. TV is the latest thing. What shall we watch?"

He thought for moment. "Comedy?"

"All right." I turned to the pair. "Comedy, then."

The gentleman stepped to a case and began to snap it open. "Very good. Let me just get out our custard pies and inflated pig's bladder."

"No, it's too much bother. What about some drama?"

Now the lady ran to another case. "Of course, Sir. Where did I put that pistol? Do you mind loud noises, Sir?"

This was more complicated than I had imagined. "What can you do without props?"

The gentleman thought for a moment. "Sports? We can do bare-fisted boxing, wrestling and the long jump and for an extra fee we can acquire a ping-pong table."

The lady clasped her hands together and looked at me imploringly. "Please, Sir, not boxing. My bruises haven't healed from our last engagement."

Smith turned and growled at her. "Don't whine. I've told you to protect the body."

I thought I'd better step in. "Just the news. That doesn't require props, does it?"

"No, Sir. News it is."

The gentleman stood center and cleared his throat. He stared off into the middle distance. "The standoff continues at the Vatican. The Pope still declares that she will not wear the traditional robes and mitre because, as she puts it, 'I wouldn't wear that outfit to a hootenanny.' The College of Cardinals is taking the position that if they can wear the robe and mitre in the heat of a Roman Summer then the Pope can do so as well and if she doesn't like it she can lump it. When reminded that the Pope is infallible, they replied that infallibility only applies to dogma and not fashion."

I turned to Binky. "What do you think, old boy?"

"In local news..."

I waved at the gentleman, who was plowing ahead. "I say, you can stop for a moment."

He looked at me with disappointment. "You should say, 'Off,' Sir."

"I see. There's a protocol."

"Yes, Sir. Off, on, faster, louder, funnier... that sort of thing."

"Very well... off."

The pair backed up and stood next to their cases. The lady raised her hand. "Before we sign off may we just say that Bunbury's Lotion gives your skin that melasma-free glow that the ladies adore."

The two entertainers lost all animation and stood on the carpet rather self-consciously. Smith gave a little cough. Binky looked at me nervously.

"Well now they're just staring at us."

I addressed the pair. "Do you mean that when you're 'Off' you just stand there all day doing nothing?"

Smith shrugged. "Ours is not an easy life."

"Can't you go for a walk?"

He looked sad. "Show business, Sir."

TWITS was originally produced and distributed by Dori Berinstein, Alan Seales and the Broadway Podcast Network - the premier digital storytelling destination for everyone, everywhere who loves theatre and the performing arts. BPN.fm/Twits.

About The Author

Born in Canton Ohio and raised in a box made out of ticky-tacky, Tom Alan Robbins spent his youth as a middle-aged character actor. He has appeared in nine Broadway shows, including *The Lion King* in which he created the role of Pumbaa. He recently received a Grammy nomination for the cast album of *Little Shop of Horrors*. He has maintained a parallel career as a writer, penning scripts for TV shows like *Coach* and writing plays, one of which (*Muse*) recently won the New Works of Merit Playwriting Competition.

The Twits Chronicles series is his first attempt at novel writing and it has been a pure joy. He hopes to keep creating adventures for Cyril and Bentley as long as there are readers who enjoy them.

Also By Tom Alan Robbins

THE TWITS CHRONICLES:

Twits in Love

Twits in Peril

Twits Abroad

Twits on the Loose

Twits on the Hunt

Twits to the Test

Twits on the Stump

38578414R00197